ACCIDENTS NEVER HAPPEN

Visit us at www.boldstrokesbooks.com

By the Author

Mesmerized

Accidents Never Happen

For Morgan,

ACCIDENTS
NEVER HAPPEN

Enjoy!

David-Matthew Barnes

by

~~David-Matthew Barnes~~

LIBERTY
— EDITION —

A Division of Bold Strokes Books

~~2011~~ 2012

THIS TRADE PAPERBACK ORIGINAL IS PUBLISHED BY
BOLD STROKES BOOKS, INC.
P.O. BOX 249
VALLEY FALLS, NY 12185

FIRST EDITION: JULY 2011

CREDITS
EDITOR: GREG HERREN
PRODUCTION DESIGN: STACIA SEAMAN
COVER DESIGN BY SHERI (GRAPHICARTIST2020@HOTMAIL.COM)

Acknowledgments

Many people helped bring *Accidents Never Happen* to print. To them, I offer my deepest gratitude:

To Len Barot and Greg Herren, for believing in this novel, and for giving it such a terrific home. The ten-year wait was well worth it.

To my wonderful Bold Strokes Books family: Cindy Cresap, Connie Ward, Kim Baldwin, Lori Anderson, Ruth Sternglantz, Sandy Lowe, Sheri, and Stacia Seaman. And to my fellow BSB authors, particularly Anne Laughlin, Carsen Taite, Clifford Henderson, D. Jackson Leigh, J.M. Redmann, Lisa Girolami, Lee Lynch, Lynda Sandoval, Nell Stark, Rebecca S. Buck, and Rebekah Weatherspoon.

To Linda Daniel, for her tremendous input and encouragement.

To these incredible organizations for their support of my work: the Amelia Island Book Festival, the Atlanta Queer Literary Festival, Capital Public Radio, the Decatur Book Festival, Giovanni's Room, the Lambda Literary Foundation, Now Voyager Bookstore and Gallery, Outwrite Bookstore and Coffeehouse, and the Saints and Sinners Literary Festival.

To my students at Southern Crescent Technical College, who teach me more on a daily basis than I could ever dream of teaching them.

To my wonderful colleagues for putting up with me, particularly Alexis Jackson, Arthur Hammond, Ashley Calhoun Stout, Brad Jester, Dr. Dawn Hodges, Gail Daniel, Jamie Hughes, Janis Phillips, Jean Cash, Jennifer Brooks, Jennifer Edwards, Kate Williams, Kelly Batchelder, Leila Wells Rogers, Liz Hawkins Jester, Lynn Futral, Mary Ann Whitehurst, Michael Cook, Olivia Andrews-Beard, Paul Scott, Rebecca Johnson, Shellie Morgan, Sherry Brooks, Sloan Passmore, Steven Marks, Teresa Brooks, and Trevor Alexander.

For their never-ending support and words of encouragement: Aaron Martinez, Andrea Patten, Anita Kelly, Bethany Hidden-Cauley, Billie

Parish, Bryan Northup, Carmel Comendador, Christian Thomas, Christine Svendsen, Collin Kelley, Cyndi Lopez, Dale Smith, Danielle Downs, Dawn Hartman Towle, Debbie Hartman Otto, Debra Garnes, Dellina Moreno, Elaine Mulligan, Elena Corral, Elizabeth Whitney, Elizabeth Yokas, Erin C. Murphy, Fay Jacobs, Frankie Hernandez, Franklin Abbott, Gilbert Villalpando, Haldi Kranich, Janet Milstein, Jessica Lopez Murray, Jessica Moreno, Jessica Moyer, Jill McMahon, Jodi Blue, Joey Jones, Joseph Ramos, Karen Gomez Vega, Karen Head, Kathleen Bradean, Kelly Kinghorn Hurtado, Kelly Norris Delafield, Kelly Wilson Lopez, Kel Munger, Kimberly Faye Greenberg, Lety Cruz, Linda Velasco Wread, Linnea Lindh, Logan Hindle, Loretta Sylvestre, Maria Canela-Fisher, Marilyn Montague, Melanie Faith, Melanie Reynolds, Melita Ann Sagar, Michele Karlsberg, Michelle Boman Harris, Mindy Morgan, Nea Herriott, Nick A. Moreno, Nita Manley, Patricia Abbott-Dinsmore, Raquel Short, Rena Mason, Robin Roberts, Robyn Colburn, Ruby Kane, Ruby Sketchley, Sabra Rahel, Selena Ambush, Sheryl Hoover, Stacy Scranton, Stefani Deoul, Susan Madden, Tara Henry, Therease Logan, Todd Wylie, Trisha Mendez, Trish DeBaun, and Vanessa Menendez.

To my parents, Samuel Barnes, Jr., and Nancy Nickle, and my brothers, Jamin, Jason, Andy, and Jaren, for letting me be the writer in the family.

To the loving memory of my grandfather, Samuel Barnes, and my grandparents, Clifford and Dorothy Nickle.

To Edward C. Ortiz, for the wonderful life and love we share.

To God, for everything. Without You, I'm nothing.

To the beautiful city of Chicago. And the always-inspiring people who live there.

Dedication

For Elizabeth Ellen Warren
Who taught me to dream bigger, laugh louder,
and make magic.

*Let them see that the important thing
is not the object of love,
but the emotion itself.*

—Gore Vidal

ALBERT

Albert was like a car accident that couldn't be avoided. He was a boxer, constantly tortured by an impulse to destroy something. He walked with an angry gait, tense shoulders, tight jaw. He moved with his head bent to the wind, dodging the pockets of dusk October air that pummeled his numb ears. He was heading south to a fifth-floor gym on Belmont, just blocks from the icy mouth of Lake Michigan. He had a tempestuous look in his dark eyes—fiery, even— determined to prove a point or take on a triple dare. He rounded a corner, nearly clipping the edge of a brick building.

Albert rammed into a stranger's left shoulder. The hit was hard; it would have been heard had the train not muted the sound. At the moment of contact, the "L" train above them slammed on its brakes. The metallic scream reverberated against the sides of the skyscrapers before exploding into an echo of a thousand warnings. A shower of blue and orange sparks rained down from the wooden tracks and kissed the sidewalk.

The stranger stumbled back, instinctually reaching out to empty air, grasping for something to break his fall. Albert's quick hands moved on impulse. He held the stranger just above the elbow, steadying him.

They stood in front of a 7-Eleven. Evening commuters streamed back and forth in a dizzying display of neckties, briefcases, leather shoes, and paper cups of coffee spilling splashes of milky brown on hands, sleeves, concrete. Fast-forward city motion circled and swirled around the two men, who were standing completely still, as if the collision had momentarily suspended them.

The connection between Albert and the stranger was immediate and severe. Energy ignited; it was fierce and electric. Their eyes locked, and they couldn't look away.

❖

Albert was a Puerto Rican with a bad attitude and delicious lips. He was intimidating, even in a soft blue and wheat brown flannel jacket, black sweatpants, and a pair of athletic shoes threatening to break open at the soles with another step. A red and black duffel bag was slung over his shoulder.

The stranger was gangly and tender, with refined grace and a tempting naïveté. Girlish, even.

At once, Albert was fascinated by the stranger's vulnerability. He seemed like the sensitive sissy type, constantly waiting for someone to tell him what to do and feel. His boyish innocence allayed the swell of the rage that soaked Albert's blood like century-old tequila. The timid way the tall kid lowered his pale eyes to the ground, to the frays in the laces of his scuffed Adidas, before lifting his gaze up again with flushed cheeks, caused an arousing conflict in Albert. He wasn't sure if the stranger was perfect for an ass kicking, or a new disciple capable of unflinching hero worship.

And one thing Albert needed was to be worshipped.

Albert gave him a playful wink and asked, "You all right, kid?"

"That scared me," the stranger admitted in a voice just as gentle as Albert had imagined it would be. The kid looked down again, shivering beneath his hooded sweatshirt, blinking the frosty air. "I wasn't watching where I was going."

Albert's hand moved up to his own face, caressed his chin and dark goatee, nervous and apologetic as if forgiving himself for something. It seemed like the stranger was waiting for him to speak again. "It's a good thing I was here to catch you. Must got a lot on your mind."

The kid answered with a slight shrug, "I haven't slept in a couple of days."

"You a party animal?" Albert asked, grinning.

The stranger responded, "No, but I did something I shouldn't have. I guess it took longer than I expected." His expression widened a little. He leaned in. "Your eye. It's black." He stepped back, cautious. "Did I do that to you?"

Albert laughed a little. "How could you?" he asked. "No offense, but you don't look like no fighter."

The kid's eyebrows shot up. "Are *you* a fighter?"

Albert's words rang like a round two bell. "Yeah. Amateur boxer. Cruiserweight."

The stranger's eyes filled with a deep admiration, subconscious lust shifting the expression on his young face from smile to desire. His tone changed. His words sounded more secretive, hushed; an awkward attempt at flirting. Perhaps he was scared the conversation would end too soon. "You should have someone look at that."

Albert stared at the stranger, felt his jawbone throb. *What the fuck is this kid doing to me?* Albert couldn't define or deny the incredible sense of want slinking through his body and shaking the corners of his soul. He hadn't felt this much passion in years. Not even on his wedding day.

It seemed evident the kid was gay. Yet Albert was intrigued by him because of the alluring sweetness he sensed in him. The way the kid looked at him, with an enamored fondness, gave Albert a buzz, making him feel like the vigilante he always imagined he would be. And the kid didn't come off like he was looking for sex. He seemed lonely, even desperate, for a friend.

Albert had often pretended to have a definitive disdain for gay men. Said that he hated them, calling them fags and cocksuckers whenever they popped up on television, swearing he'd punch one in the face without a second thought if they came on to him, and telling his buddy Jackson once over shots of Stoli at a strip bar that he considered them weak and ridiculous.

They were freaks of nature.

But the truth was Albert was curious, and had been since the day of his father's funeral. Only fifteen, he'd needed a place to cry. He found refuge in the basement laundry room of the apartment building where he'd grown up in Humboldt Park. He tucked his tears away when his grief was interrupted by a basket-carrying neighbor boy who brushed against Albert in an attempt to squeeze by the narrow space between them and the machines. The sensation scared him, caused Albert to race back upstairs. He'd barricaded himself in the bathroom and beat off to a fantasy he hadn't allowed himself to have since.

Albert returned the questions lingering in the stranger's eyes with the same invitation in his voice. "You hungry, kid? I'm starvin', myself."

The kid's eyes shone hot with anticipation. "I'd like that," he answered with a small nod. Thick strands of his toast brown hair fell across his sea green eyes as if he were playing half a game of peek-a-boo.

"C'mon." Albert moved and the kid followed. Albert knew that he would.

The two men walked in silence, shoulder to shoulder. At the next corner they waited for the light to change. Albert saw their reflection in the dirty passenger window of an idling cab.

They were an odd pair. The giraffe-like stranger stood next to short, stocky Albert. Albert's gaze was locked on the image in the finger-smudged glass but the kid's eyes were turned toward Albert, studying his profile. He stared at Albert, almost as if he were a present about to be opened on Christmas morning.

The kid's nose was too thin and large, marring what would've been only an average face. He wasn't what most people would consider attractive. He was simple, the type of guy who was overlooked. His apparent weakness made him a likely target for ridicule and domination.

Albert looked at his own reflection. He was equally unattractive. His hair—dark and unruly—had started to recede near the edges of his temples. His nose had been busted twice. Neither time was a result of a fight in the ring, as most people supposed. It was his wife's wrath that broke it. His bent nose brought attention to his face, because it looked like it belonged to somebody else. He had a thick scar above his right brow; a souvenir from a neighborhood fight when he was twelve. His front teeth were crooked—they bent in toward each other—and he had a slight overbite. His features had a roughness to them, adding to his street-smart persona. Yet, his lips betrayed his image—they always looked like they were begging to be kissed.

The light changed and they stepped off the curb in unison.

I'm old enough to be this kid's father, Albert thought. And it was true. Albert had turned thirty-nine on his last birthday. The stranger looked eighteen, maybe twenty at the oldest.

Albert led the kid to a coffee shop on Belmont Avenue. They were seated in a booth in the front window. The kid stared through the open slats of dusty miniblinds to the world outside. Strangers passed by, intent on their destinations. The neon pink and green OPEN sign was buzzing and flickering, as if the lights were aware of the lives merging inside.

"I don't usually eat dinner this early," the kid said.

"Yeah, me neither," Albert agreed.

After ordering a club sandwich and a vanilla Coke with no ice, the stranger nervously toyed with a straw wrapper, stealing occasional glances at Albert. Albert sat back with his arm draped over the top of the red upholstered booth, waiting for his basket of onion rings and a bottle of mustard. He took a couple of gulps of tongue-burning black coffee, cleared his throat, and looked at the boy.

"Why so nervous, kid?"

His bottom lip quivered. "I'm not."

"Since I almost knocked ya out, I figure the least I can do is buy you dinner."

The kid flashed a sudden smile. "It's nice of you, thanks."

Albert's jaw tightened. "I'm not usually this nice," he warned.

The boy looked up, expressionless. "No?"

"No. I don't like people."

The kid's eyes fell again as he concentrated on twisting the straw wrapper around his index finger so tight the tip began to turn purple. "I don't either," he said. Albert wondered if this was the first time that the kid had admitted his dislike for people. "That might surprise you since you probably think I'm some dumb kid, but I think most people are motherfucking assholes." The boy laughed a little, amused by his own thoughts.

Albert leaned in, caught off guard. The kid was unpredictable. Albert liked that.

A lot.

"Oh yeah?" he urged. "Tell me more."

The kid's voice dropped to a whisper. "What do you want to know?"

"I don't care. I just like hearing ya talk," Albert replied, also in a whisper.

He blushed a little. "Really?"

"Yeah. Tell me who ya hate the most."

The kid chewed on the right corner of his bottom lip before answering, "The obvious choice is my mother."

Albert finished his cup of coffee and signaled to a lazy waitress for a refill. "Why do you hate your mom? What'd she do to ya?" he asked.

The boy shrugged. "She embarrassed me, I guess."

"What's so bad about that?"

The edges of the kid's pale colored eyes dimmed from the inside out with a sense of remorse. "She died."

"You're embarrassed because she's *dead*?"

The kid shook his head, looked out the window. Maybe he was trying to find someone he knew in the passing crowd of the evening rush. "My mother drove them off a cliff. My father was with her."

A lick of fear touched the center of Albert's spine and shot a round of tension into his posture. "On purpose?" he asked. "She did it on purpose?"

"No," the kid said, maybe too casually. "I guess the brakes failed."

An element of truth danced in the heavy air between them, like an invisible string pulled from the sudden tears the kid was trying to keep from falling. In that moment, Albert suspected what the kid had done. And it scared him. But it thrilled him, too.

"Did you hate your dad, too?" he asked.

The boy shook his head. "No. It wasn't his fault." He leaned forward and his voice dropped again. "He wasn't supposed to be in the car."

Albert breathed. "Where'd it happen?"

"In Maine. Where I'm from...Portland." He said it like the place was hell.

"Damn, when did this go down?"

A few tears won the battle and spilled down the sides of the kid's face. "Last night," he said.

The waitress appeared with a coffee pot. She splashed more into Albert's cup with a sigh before sauntering off again. "That's rough," Albert said.

The kid looked Albert in the eye. "No, it wasn't."

"How come you say that?"

"It was so quick. How fast she went. Right through the barricade. Down to the rocks and water. Then...*smash*."

"Wait—you were *there*?"

The kid nodded. His eyes continued to flash with a sad fire. "Even though I hated her, I really didn't want it to happen."

Albert was at a loss for words. He simply said, "Oh, yeah?"

"Yeah," the boy said. "My sister will probably go next. She's been through...a lot...a lot of crazy shit."

Albert nodded. "I got a wife that I wish would drive off a cliff."

The kid pulled back a little, leaned against the back of the booth. "You're married?"

"Is that such a shocker? You think an ugly fucker like me can't get a wife?"

The boy grinned. "Anybody can. Everybody's lonely."

"Her name's Bonnie and she's a lowlife with a mean mouth."

The kid shook his head, flustered. "I didn't mean it."

"Didn't mean what?"

"To act so surprised when you said you were married."

Albert sipped his coffee and said, "It's a'ight."

"No...it's just..." His voice trailed off.

"Spit it out, kid."

His attention went to the straw wrapper around his finger. He avoided Albert's eyes when he spoke. "Well, I don't think you're ugly."

Albert looked toward the pie case where the waitress leaned. "You don't?"

The boy's voice sounded choked. "No."

Albert smiled. "Are ya fucking blind in one eye or both?"

"You're not ugly."

Albert wrapped his thick fingers through the handle of the coffee cup, and contemplated smashing it against the waitress's skull. He loved to hit things, destroy them. It made him feel alive. He struggled constantly with the impulse to strike out, kill. "That's good of you to say."

"I feel embarrassed."

Albert smiled. "Because of your folks being...killed? You shouldn't. I've heard of some crazy situations before. Been in a few of them myself."

"That's not what I meant," the kid said. "I don't know your name. What you do."

"My name's Albert. And I already told you, I'm a boxer."

"Albert," the kid repeated. His voice caused the head of Albert's cock to throb a little and Albert didn't know why. Under the table he smashed his rising dick down with the base of his palm. He pressed hard against the front of his black sweatpants like he was shoving a bad dog away from the table, to keep it from begging.

"Yeah," he said, feeling his face infuse with heat. "I'm Albert."

The kid smiled and said, "I'm Joey." He unraveled the straw wrapper from his finger, allowing the blood to return to the tip. "I like your bruises."

The waitress arrived and half dropped their plates in front of them, spilling a couple of onion rings on the table.

"Hey. Ya forgot my mustard," Albert said. She gave him a sour look and sighed loudly, fetching one from behind the counter. Albert snatched the bottle from her, giving her a look that shooed her away.

The anticipation of the unknown made Albert high with a mind-racing thrill he feared was revealed in his eyes and the ridiculous smile he hoped didn't betray him. Albert dipped each onion ring in a puddle of mustard and licked his greasy fingers clean. He watched as Joey took furtive bites of his club sandwich and delicate sips of his vanilla Coke. He dabbed at each corner of his mouth with a napkin after every bite, as if the crumbs around his lips were pieces of evidence that he didn't want to leave behind.

❖

An hour and ten minutes had passed since they first collided beneath the train tracks. They stood outside of the coffee shop on Belmont, unsure of what to do with their nervous hands. Joey shivered from the cold and Albert felt the impulse to offer his jacket or put an arm around him to warm him up. He did neither. He felt the black handle of the red duffel bag slipping down his shoulder. He pulled the bag up again and slid his hands into the pockets of his flannel jacket.

Joey's teeth chattered when he asked, "What were you doing before we ran into each other?"

Albert shrugged. "I just got off work. I was going up to the gym for a workout."

"To box?"

"No. I'm training right now. No more fights for a few weeks."

"Wow," Joey said. "I'd love to see you box sometime."

Albert nodded. "Yeah…maybe."

"Are you going there now?"

"Don't know." Albert breathed deep. "What 'bout you?"

Joey pulled an envelope out of his back pocket. It was smashed a little and the handwriting on it was messy. He held it out as if it were an offering of some type to Albert. "I have to find a mailbox."

"Got a bill to pay?"

Joey shook his head, put the envelope away. "No. A letter home. To my sister."

"I thought you didn't like her."

"I don't. I mean, I do. Sometimes. The letter will answer her questions…I hope."

"There's a post office not far from here," Albert said with a quick jerk of his head.

Joey nodded. "I was trying to find it when I met you. I guess I got lost."

They both grinned like lifelong friends who shared a deep secret.

Albert stepped forward. He spoke and his breath fell onto Joey's mouth. He licked his lips. "I could take you there if ya want."

"You would do that?" Joey asked. "What about the gym? I could go with you. Watch you train."

Albert shook his head. There was no way he could explain a kid like Joey to the guys at the gym. They'd eat him up alive. They could spot a sissy from a mile away. "No. That place ain't good for you."

"I bet you're an amazing fighter."

The kid made Albert smile again even though he didn't want to. Albert nodded and even blushed a little. "Yeah…I am."

Joey started to turn away. "Well…it was nice meeting you."

What the fuck? Where's this kid think he's going? "Hey," Albert said. "What are ya doin'? You leavin'?"

Joey took another step farther away. "I'm sorry. You're angry."

Albert looked deep into Joey's eyes. "Maybe I wanna take you to the post office," he said, almost shouting to be heard over the sound of a city bus passing by.

Joey didn't look away. "I don't want to bother you. You've been nice to me."

Albert was firm. "I already told you—I'm not usually this nice."

Joey's mouth trembled a little when he moved close to Albert. "I liked having dinner with you."

"Then why do you wanna leave?"

"You need to train."

Albert leaned in. "How do you know what I need?"

They both fell silent, inhaled the warm mists exhaled from each other's mouth. Albert felt his lungs aching from the cold and uncertainty. He felt a gnawing frustration turning into a desire to smash something. He glanced at the lamp post on the corner, taking in the chipped black paint. The knuckle bone of his right index finger twitched. If Joey left, he knew he would hit the post as hard as he could.

"Kid, I'm messed up," he said suddenly, surprising them both.

Joey smiled. He raised a hand and reached toward Albert on instinct, to touch him. Quick, Joey pulled his hand back, lowered it. "No, you're not."

"Yeah. Yeah, I'm fucked up. And I don't know what we're doing here."

Joey looked away, across the street to a cell phone store. He bit his lip, looked nervous. "We can walk away. You go one way and I'll go—"

"No," Albert insisted. "No, that ain't happening, kid."

Joey shook off a sharp shiver. "I'm not sure what you want from me, Albert."

Albert faced the lamp post, ready to strike. He was surprised to feel tears burning the edges of both eyes. "Why do you hafta be so nice to me?"

Joey's voice sounded thick with concern. "Nobody's nice to you?"

Albert put his knuckles under his chin and popped his neck to the right. His bones made a crunching sound and his shoulders relaxed a little. "Not since when I was a kid, ya know."

"Maybe that's it." Joey moved closer to Albert. "Nobody's been nice to me in a long time either."

"No?"

Joey shook his head. "No."

"I dare someone to fuck with you now."

The boy's face bloomed into a grin. "Why? What are you going to do?"

"I'll take 'em out."

Joey lowered his tone, as if his words were meant only for himself. "I wish you would."

Albert said, "Dare me."

Joey shrugged and backed away from Albert, as if the moment were too intense. "Why do you look so—?"

Albert's eyebrow shot up; the one with the scar in the shape of a half moon above it. "So *what*?"

"You seem upset," Joey said.

"I just—I don't want ya to—"

"Go on. Say it."

"I ain't a fag or nothin'."

"Okay."

"You just…you need to know that, a'ight."

Joey shrugged. "You said you were married."

"Yeah, but she don't love me."

Joey looked into Albert's eyes. "She should."

"I'm glad she don't."

They started to walk. Albert lowered his voice, worried that some of the people in suits and ties would hear him. "You a queer, Joey? I mean, you can tell me if ya are, ya know."

"Does it really matter?" Joey asked.

They crossed the street. The post office was a few yards away.

"It's cold, Albert." Their eyes met as they shifted and elbowed through the crowd heading the other way. "What do you want to do?"

Albert cracked his knuckles, switched his duffel bag to the opposite shoulder. "I don't know. Hang out. Spend some time together."

"Why?"

Albert's smile vanished. "Who the fuck knows? Maybe I think you're an okay guy."

"That sounds sweet."

"I told you I ain't—"

"Maybe you just need a friend, Albert."

"Don't have lots of those. Had some back in the day, but I punched most of 'em out."

They started walking again. "Are you planning to hit me?"

"No…No, I wouldn't do that to you, Joey."

"You could kick my ass without even trying very hard."

"Yeah, I wouldn't hit ya, though." Albert looked at him and said, "It seems to me like you've been hit before."

Joey stopped outside of the crowded post office. "You know something," he said, gripping the edge of the envelope and holding it over the hungry blue metal mouth of a mailbox, "I started hitting back last night."

Albert seemed impressed. "Oh, yeah?"

"Yeah," Joey said. "And I'm not so sure if I can stop." Joey glanced down at the thin crust of beach sand that still licked the sides of his shoes. "I took the first plane home today," he said. "And I'll probably get caught for what happened."

Albert's jaw tightened. "Not if I can help it," he said.

Joey seemed liberated once the letter was out of his possession. His eyes flashed with a contagious excitement when he turned back to Albert and asked, "What do you want to do, now? The city belongs to you and me."

Albert smiled and breathed. "I know someplace warm we can go. We gotta walk, though. My van's in the garage 'til tomorrow mornin'."

They crossed another street, walking beneath the train tracks cutting through the city like a symmetrical forest, with a backdrop of wooden walls plastered with posters that announced the upcoming release of a CD by a female rap star.

"Where to, then?"

"Canada," Albert said.

Joey stopped in his footsteps. "Are you serious?"

"You'd go wit' me?"

Joey grinned. "I would."

"Shit, I wish I had the money."

Joey reached for his wallet in his back pocket. "I have thirty dollars to my name."

"Then you a helluva lot richer than me. I spent all my money on dinner."

"Why Canada?"

"First place that popped in my head, ya know."

"Is that true?"

Albert looked away, smiling again. It seemed like Joey already knew him better than anybody else. "No…" Albert suddenly seemed shy. "I've always wanted to see the gardens. They're in a place called Vancouver."

"I know where it is."

"Oh yeah?"

"On the other side of the continent."

"I like gardens."

"Why do you look so embarrassed?"

Albert looked away. "You think it's dumb?" he asked.

Joey shot him a look. "Are we talking vegetable gardens or flowers?"

Albert's smile faded. "I like flowers, a'ight."

"More than boxing?"

Albert shook his head. "No, man, it's different."

"You're lucky," Joey said. "I haven't found anything to like yet."

Albert's smile returned. "Yeah, well, you're still young."

"So it gets better than this?"

Albert shrugged. "That depends."

"On how well you fight?"

"No," Albert said. He suddenly stopped. Joey did the same. "Everything depends on who you're with."

"Then I'm out of luck," Joey said. "I'm not with anybody." He pulled his hands out of the front pockets of his sweatshirt and blew into his palms. On impulse, Albert reached out and grabbed both of Joey's hands. He pulled them toward him, holding them right beneath his face. His head bent forward a little, and he breathed onto Joey's skin. Joey winced, as if he had been burned. Albert didn't let go. He tightened his grip on Joey's hands, pulling on them so Joey had no choice but to step closer.

"You're wrong, kid," Albert said. "You're wit' me now."

JOEY

Joey was twelve the first time he caught his sister smoking pot. Lily was in the basement straddling the washing machine with the precision of a pro bull rider. One of her white slip-on sandals had fallen off of her foot and was lying on the cement floor. The other one was hanging to the tip of her big toe for dear life. She struggled with a cheap yellow lighter, a fiend for a flame. Her calloused thumb slid over the metal wheel that usually sparked beneath her touch. A rolled joint was caught between her lips. She wiped her palm on the front of her cut-off shorts and tried again. Finally, the lighter spit up a tiny flicker, illuminating the half grin on Lily's face. She brought the fire to the tip of the paper and breathed deep. Her eyes closed as relief enveloped her. A spaghetti thin strap of her pink tank top slid down her right shoulder, but she didn't seem to notice or care. Lily exhaled a silver cloud of smoke that spun up in slow drifting circles to the wooden beams in the low ceiling. The washing machine suddenly jerked into spin cycle. Lily seemed surprised, but quickly surrendered to the newly discovered sensation. Lily's legs vibrated for a few seconds before she let out a giggle meant only for her ears.

The third to the last step of the stairs betrayed Joey's stealth approach. The old wood made a mouse-like squeal, causing Joey to freeze. Maybe if he was still enough, his older sister wouldn't see him.

But she did.

She turned toward the stairs with whiplash speed. "What the fuck are you doing down here?"

Joey's words came out broken. "I'm sorry. I didn't mean to. Don't tell Mom." He pointed to a blue circle on his T-shirt.

"You stained *another* shirt?"

"It dropped. It melted."

"You're a goddamned retard." Lily took a heavy drag on her joint. She held the pot in her lungs for a few moments before streaming it out of her mouth in a thick, gray line. Lately, she had been obsessed with crimping her bottle blond hair. She often resembled a victim of an accident involving electrocution. Today was no exception. Her eyes were also frightening, circled and smudged with black eyeliner in a botched attempt to look retro. Lily sniffed, wiped her nose with the back of her hand. "Last time I ever let you eat a Popsicle."

A new thought hit Joey and it stumbled out of his mouth. "I'm not the retard," he said. "*You* are." He took a step back, up to the fourth stair.

"Fuck you," she spat.

"You *are*." Lily looked at him with wide eyes, caught off guard by his insistence. "Look at your eye," he continued. "It's crooked."

Lily threw the lighter at him. It smacked against his ankle with a sting. He ran down the last four steps and kicked it across the floor as his sister exploded with rage. "It's amblyopia, you asshole!" she shrieked.

Joey grinned and asked, "Is *that* why you're smoking pot?"

"None of your fucking business." She stubbed the joint out on the gray cinderblock wall. Expertly, she licked two fingertips and squeezed the end of the joint, snuffing out the last bit of smoke. She tucked it into a hip pocket in her shorts.

Joey decided to use a different tactic. "Cooper says you have a lazy eye."

Lily shot up an eyebrow. "Cooper really said that?" Joey nodded, sat down on the stairs. "When?"

"Yesterday, when he came over to mow the lawn."

Lily looked to the floor. Maybe she was expecting to find her heart there. The sadness in her voice was heavy. "But I was born this way."

"Exactly," Joey said. "Then that makes you retarded."

Lily shook her head as her anger seemed to slip into an avalanche of regret. "It's Mom's fault because she's an idiot. I have no idea why Dad married her. He's too good for her."

Joey started to leave. On the stairs, he turned back. "You're ugly."

Lily leaned back on the machine, pressing the middle of her back against the round knobs that controlled the temperature of the water and the cycle of the wash. She spread her legs a little more and the inside of her ankles rattled against the white metal. Her other sandal slid off and hit the floor. Lily threw her head back as the first wave of pleasure swept over her body and said, "Like I fucking care."

Joey went back upstairs to the kitchen and closed the basement door. He listened for a moment with his ear pressed against the wood. He could hear his sister moan. The sound was muffled by the violent whir of the machine.

❖

In the following week, Lily became addicted to the washing machine. She found any excuse to use it. She carted down baskets full of clothes, curtains, tablecloths, pillow covers, sheets, towels, bath rugs, place mats, and pot holders. She spent hours down in the basement, appearing occasionally to refill her sports bottle with water and ice cubes, like she was taking a quick break from an aerobic workout. She snuck a cigarette or two on the back porch while their mother was at the grocery store, or picking up donuts for the Thursday night Bible study group she hosted in their living room. But back Lily would always go, her sandals thumping on each step as she disappeared down the wooden staircase.

Each time Lily emerged from her pleasure dungeon, her cheeks were flushed. Her bottom lip trembled when she spoke and her hair looked more fried than usual. It was like Lily was permanently vibrated. She'd become the dazed little sister of the Bride of Frankenstein. She didn't speak to anyone specifically, but threw out phrases like "We need more Tide" or "Can we use a different fabric softener? The smell of the blue stuff makes me sick" to anyone who was in the kitchen.

Joey started keeping a close eye on his mother's reactions to Lily's bizarre new fascination with the laundry. Joey figured it wouldn't be long before his mother caught on to Lily's new, preferred form of masturbation.

A routine began. A scenario played out for three nights in a row, duplicated almost word for word and motion for motion each time.

Joey sat at the kitchen table, pencil in hand, bent over his math homework. His mother stood at the sink, silent and grim, her long, mud brown hair pulled back into a severe ponytail. Lily popped up for a thirty-second dash to the refrigerator door for filtered water and crushed ice. "Mom," she said, "if you need anything special washed tonight, you just let me know. I'm starting a delicate cycle next."

Miranda stared at her daughter like she didn't recognize her—as if some alien had invaded Lily's body and taken over her personality. His mother's expression almost made Joey laugh. Years ago, Miranda had shaved off her eyebrows. Now two thick straight lines lay across the tops of her eyes, drawn with a black marker. The fake eyebrows gave her a constant expression of sternness, maybe contemplating some new form of punishment. Coupled with her slicked-back ponytail that caused the skin around her eyes to tighten, Miranda looked permanently pissed off.

"I don't need anything washed," she said, looking at the top of Lily's head, perhaps searching for a transmitter device of some kind.

❖

Joey knew from an early age his mother was not an affectionate woman. There was a cold streak running down her spine that seemed to freeze her blood and paralyze the maternal instinct Joey and Lily had every right to think she should possess. She would smile at them only in the presence of others—especially the neighborhood mothers. Alone, Miranda appeared to forget her children existed. She didn't acknowledge their achievements—not even when Lily brought home straight A's for the first and only time in seventh grade. She didn't attend Joey's soccer games or Lily's dance recitals. She didn't bake, sing, craft, mend, or decorate. Rarely did she laugh, joke, hum, or blush. She did what little was required of her. She spent most evenings and weekends sitting in a brown leather recliner in a corner of the living room. Beneath the pale yellow light of a standing lamp with a moveable arm she positioned with the precision of a dentist, she worked diligently to all hours of the night on her needlepoint. She wore a pair of round reading glasses too small for her broad, square face and an expression of intense concentration, as if her task was both exhausting and detailed.

Like she was building a bomb.

Joey was thankful his mother was not a violent woman. Although he suspected she was capable of backhanding him without hesitation. She was physically intimidating—she stood two inches taller than her husband—but she never struck her children. Instead, she ignored them. When they were younger, Joey and Lily would cling to her legs and beg to be held. They would reach for her with sticky fingers until hot tears slid from the edges of their eyes. She snapped at them, hoping they would learn to obey. She implored them to be like Sparky, the next door neighbor's show champion schnauzer who was so obedient for his owner. As they grew older, Lily and Joey learned to seek comfort elsewhere. They knew their mother was incapable of loving them. Yet Lily and Joey never spoke about it.

Joey was surprised when Miranda became a successful real estate agent two years ago. But that was before he realized she could turn niceness on and off like the kitchen faucet. From the backseat of the family car, he had witnessed his mother in action, in the prime of one of her many fine afternoon performances. A young house-hunting couple asked to meet his mother at an available property. Joey listened to their chatter as they stood on the front lawn, on the other side of the white picket fence. They fawned over his mother, saying they found her delightful and amusing. The wife had even said, "Your children are lucky to have you as a mother." In return, Joey's mother convinced them the American dream was possible. In order to sell the house, she charmed them with humorous tales of a family life that didn't exist. She bragged about mother-daughter pie baking contests at church, volunteering to chaperone Joey's class on a field trip to the aquarium, family camping trips that included fireside songs and roasted marshmallows, romantic getaways with her husband of seventeen years, preparing his favorite meal of Yankee pot roast after he had come home from a long day at the office (even though he was a house painter) and day-long shopping trips with her mother-in-law (even though she'd died four years earlier by falling off her roof while trying to rescue her cat, who was stuck in a vent).

If there was one thing Joey admired about his mother, it was her ability to fool people. He wished he could wear an invisible disguise like she did; the way she was able to put on a friendly face the minute the family ventured out into public. In the grocery store. At the post office. At bake sales. She would smile, wave, her eyes shining bright with an internal love she would rather bestow on a stranger than her own family. And just as quickly, she could tuck that personality away into a dark corner of her Arctic soul. What surprised Joey and Lily even more than their mother's bizarre duality was how their father never seemed to notice the drastic opposites his wife demonstrated. If he did, he never mentioned it to anyone. In fact, he never said much of anything. He usually looked half-asleep, communicating mostly with nods and shrugs.

❖

On the fourth night after Lily had started her sexual affair with the Maytag top loader in the basement, their mother put an end to the relationship. Lily had been downstairs for nearly two hours, since the dinner dishes had been cleared. Miranda sat in her chair, needlepoint in hand, stitching a design of purple and pink flowers. Without a word of explanation, she put the thread and needle down, and walked to the basement door in the kitchen. Joey glanced up from his homework and waited with lip-licking anticipation as his mother stood at the door. The linoleum floor beneath Joey's socked feet buzzed and hummed from the washing machine below. His mother opened the door and slipped into the darkness. She reached for the silver chain hanging from the bare bulb at the top of the staircase. The garish light clicked on and illuminated the basement, revealing the truth about Lily's habit. She screamed in protest and embarrassment, and called their mother a bitch. Joey strained to hear his mother's words but couldn't make out what she was saying. Her tone of voice sounded controlled and instructive. Seconds later the washing machine stopped. The kitchen windows quit vibrating and the floor became still. The house itself seemed to shrink as Lily's heated passion slipped away. Her joy disintegrated.

Joey knew his sister would never be the same again.

Miranda appeared seconds later. She stood like an intruder in the doorway of the basement. Her mannish shoulders blocked most of the light behind her and for that moment she looked like a monster, the big bad wolf. She had something in her hand but Joey couldn't figure out what it was until she stepped closer. It was then he saw Lily. She stood behind her mother with knotted, crimped hair and red, swollen eyes smeared with black. The front of her denim skirt was accidentally tucked inside her underwear. She followed her mother into the kitchen.

Joey tried not to laugh at the sight of his sister's pink and white polka-dotted panties. Then he noticed her thighs, and the sight of them made his breath stop in his throat. They were red and raw, chafed—like she had scraped them with rocks, or metal.

Miranda raised the object in her hand. Joey swallowed the lump of fear that suddenly shot up from his lungs. He recognized the gray T-shirt, the blue raspberry Popsicle stain. "*This* is how you treat the clothes I buy you," she said to her son. Miranda then looked at her daughter, at her half-raised skirt and the dumbstruck expression on her face, her bad eye wandering helplessly toward the refrigerator. "Pull your goddamn skirt down," she sneered. "You look like a whore." Lily blushed and quickly fixed her skirt. She shot a death stare at Joey, and flipped him off once Miranda had turned her back.

Miranda took center stage in the kitchen, positioning herself at an equal distance between her children. She held the T-shirt in both hands. With a single motion, she ripped the T-shirt in half. She moved to the silver metal garbage can underneath the sink. She placed the two strips of material into the trash, wiped her hands clean from imaginary dirt, and turned back to Lily and Joey. "Both of you make me *sick*," she said. Lily and Joey remained silent and still. They knew what she'd said was true. They'd known it for as long as they could remember. But at last, she had admitted it.

Miranda moved toward the open archway leading to the living room, where she would spend the rest of the night needlepointing furiously. She stopped for a moment as another thought struck her. "From now on Joey will do the wash," she said. "No exceptions." Miranda left the room.

An aching silence filled the kitchen, interrupted only by the occasional tick of the clock on the stove when the second hand got stuck on the number twelve before jumping forward to the two. Lily stood motionless, breathing deep—breathing *hatred*. Joey tried to turn his attention back to his homework. The math problems seemed like a jumbled mess of black. They were blurred and they started moving in a slow, shivering wave. It was then Joey realized he was crying. His sister moved toward him and her hip accidentally banged against the table. The sudden jolt caused Joey's pencil to roll off and fall to the floor. He reached down to pick it up, his palm grazing over the cool linoleum before his fingers grasped it. Pain suddenly shot up his arm when Lily covered his hand with her white sandal, smashing it against the tile like a bug she wanted dead. "You're a fucking crybaby," she said, standing over him. She waited for nearly half a minute until she released her brother's hand. She moved across the kitchen to the back door.

Joey pulled his hand close to him. The moment made him feel awkward. It seemed like someone should be comforting him, getting him ice, reprimanding his sister. But no one appeared to make sure any of these things occurred. Joey put his hand in his lap where it throbbed with a blinding pain. He glanced down at his skin and realized his sister's sandal had left a shoe print across his knuckles.

"You're a dumb fuck," she said, her hand on the silver doorknob. "If anyone gives a shit, I'm going to find Cooper."

Lily slid out of the house and stumbled into the orange buzzing glow of a back porch light. Her presence lingered in the dim kitchen. It drifted up through the pale yellow curtains hanging across the small window in the center of the back door. It crept across the wallpaper, prancing over the sun-faded pattern of blue cornflowers. It twisted around the glass containers of flour, sugar, salt, and oatmeal sitting on the countertop that always smelled like lemon and ammonia. It rattled the door of the pantry like a minor aftershock.

Joey sat motionless for a moment. His eyes darted back and forth between his aching hand and the math problems on the pages of his textbook. He listened for a moment, and was temporarily comforted by the gentle, slow rhythm of his father's snoring. Nightly, Joey's father drifted off on the sofa within minutes of the dinner dishes being cleared. The TV roared like a lion. The audio of a reality television show bounced off the walls in the living room, but Joey's father slept on. Joey imagined his father was most likely sleeping on his side with an old olive green throw pillow tucked under his ear.

To be sure, Joey stood up and inched close to the archway. He peered into the living room without leaving the kitchen. His father was asleep in the position he had predicted, in his gray sweats and favorite New England Patriots football jersey. His dark hair, thick and full, was speckled with bits of Bahama blue paint, the color of the house he was currently working on. Joey smiled at his father, even though he was fast asleep.

From where Joey stood, he could not see his mother. Her seat of choice was in the corner of the room, against the wall dividing the living room and the kitchen. But her shadow loomed on the living room wall in front of him. He watched her movements for a moment. She worked with diligence, her needlepoint project apparently requiring the skill of a surgeon—or a wicked witch preparing some kind of poison to take down some younger, prettier, happier princess.

For some reason, the shadow scared Joey. It seemed sinister. He backed away from it, and the living room. He welcomed the coolness of the kitchen floor against his bare feet. He turned and almost collided with the open basement door.

The basement beckoned to Joey. It looked like a mouth waiting to devour him whole; a secret passageway to an underground world. The light from the hanging bulb urged him on, promising comfort and refuge. He crossed the doorway, standing at the top of the wooden staircase. He pulled the door to the basement closed. The silence that wrapped around him was frightening, yet thick with relief. He took his first step; then another, and another. The third to the last step creaked beneath his feet.

He walked across the concrete floor and stood in front of the washing machine. The source of his sister's secret pleasure seemed to smile and wink at him as rays of silver moonlight streamed in through a tiny window near the ceiling, bouncing off the white metal. Joey reached for the machine with the hand that didn't hurt. He ran his palm across the shiny cool. He wrote his invisible initials on the lid of the washer. He tapped out a soft rhythm on the machine like some easy-going drummer in a mellow band.

He looked down. At his feet was a hot pink laundry basket. His sister's cut-off shorts sat on top of a pile of clothes reeking with her cheap impostor perfume. He reached down and picked up the fringed denim shorts. On instinct, Joey reached into the hip pocket—where he discovered a half-joint. He grinned, muttering a few evil words about Lily.

He scanned the basement for a lighter or a book of matches. Finally, he discovered the same temperamental yellow lighter he'd kicked across the basement floor only days ago—before Lily's obsession with the washing machine, before his mother had confessed the sight of him made her sick.

He kicked the laundry basket and it somersaulted out of his way. He sat down on the floor, the coldness stinging the back of his legs for a second. He shifted in his shorts until he was comfortable. His hand still ached from Lily's sibling rage, so he didn't use it. He left it limp in his lap, useless. Joey lifted the joint up to his mouth, slid it between his lips. The taste of it was sweet and smoky and made his lips tingle a little. He raised the lighter. It took a couple of tries, but finally...*fire*. He brought the flame to the tip of the singed paper and breathed in deeply. Joey felt his lungs expand and swell with hot, thick, sticky smoke. It felt as if the smoke had drifted up through his throat, to dance behind his eyes before it warmed the back of his skull.

This is awesome.

Joey grinned as the comfort arrived, and his sister, mother, and the basement all floated away.

When he exhaled, he spoke aloud. His words were slow, dragging out the syllables. They seemed to bounce off the concrete floor and lift up to the wooden beams—where they threatened to rip a hole in the ceiling, crawl up to the living room and slice the backs of his mother's ankles. *That* would get her attention.

"Fuck...you...*all*," he said. Joey coughed, wiped his mouth with the sleeve of his T-shirt, and took another drag. Within seconds he found himself craving a blue raspberry Popsicle. Only this time, he wouldn't care if it melted.

ALBERT

When they left the post office, Albert took Joey to his favorite place to escape the cold—a hideaway in the form of a used book store on a side street near the Belmont train stop. It was a cave of a place: windowless, overheated, wooden floors creaking with every step. The walls were lined from floor to ceiling with books, most of them paperbacks. The low ceiling was a metal maze of installation tubes, wooden beams, and air-conditioning vents. Strands of tiny white lights were wrapped around the square posts straining to hold the decaying place up.

Albert and Joey stumbled in from the sidewalk, away from a sudden burst of snow flurries falling like tiny angels over Chicago. A string of bells jingled as the front door closed behind them. Their faces were flushed. Blood filled their cheeks as they fought to shake off the sudden drop in temperature. The cold had seeped into their bones and refused to let go.

They were greeted by the fifty-something owner of the place. Shelley was a broad woman. Her hips and ass spread over the width of a wooden stool she was perched on, behind the main counter. She was hunched over the cash register, protecting it, burying it beneath the heavy heave of her massive breasts. She wore a loose-fitting floral-printed house dress, emblazoned with a bold lavender and scarlet pattern. A decadent purple hat was strategically placed on her head and tilted at a perfect diagonal. It looked like something that should have been worn to church, or worn by a gun moll in the 1940s. A wilted daffodil was pinned to the thick brim, close to her ear. Her hair was a mass of badly permed tight curls, spotted dull brown and gray. She had the tip of a pipe in her mouth. She puffed, coughed, spat out a wisp of smoke, fanning the air with a hand adorned with long candy apple red fingernails. The entire store was saturated with the sweet stench of tobacco.

"Ya got something warm to drink, Shelley?" Albert asked.

"That depends," she answered. Her words were flat, like her voice had been bulldozed smooth, ready for concrete to be poured over it. "What did you bring me?"

Albert shook his head, rubbed his palms together, and blew hot breath into his cupped hands. "I'm not working today."

Shelley shook her head. "Fresh flowers, you dirty bastard. That's all I ask for."

"Yeah, yeah, yeah. I'll bring you some tomorrow, toad face."

Her eyes went to Joey. "Who's this?"

Albert cleared his throat, and cracked his knuckles. "He's with me."

Shelley's eyes danced back and forth between the two men. She narrowed in on Joey, and Albert wondered if she had the ability to read the kid's mind. "I see that," she said, looking him over from head to toe. Shelley pulled the pipe away from her mouth. She pointed its once ivory tip at Joey. "What do you read?"

Joey stepped forward furtively. His voice seemed small, absorbed by the spines of paperbacks surrounding him from every angle of the overcrowded room. Albert suspected the kid was overwhelmed, not just by Shelley and her abrasive manner, but also by the way the book store felt like it expanded in every direction possible. It was never-ending. Joey looked like Dorothy from *The Wizard of Oz* the first time she met the great wizard. He was certain the kid's knees were shaking. "Do you have any books on architecture?" he asked.

Shelley gave him an odd look, raising one eyebrow. "*Architecture?*" she repeated. "What do you know about architecture?"

Joey cleared his throat before speaking. "I'm studying to become one. An architect, I mean."

Her eyes narrowed even more. She squinted, searching for something microscopic on his body. "You're in school?"

"I'm a sophomore in college." Joey lifted up his brown paper bag of purchases from the drug store. "I like to build things."

"Hmmm." She took a puff from her pipe. "You don't say."

Albert stepped into Shelley's line of vision, interrupting her inquisition. He stood in front of Joey, spurred by the instinctual need to protect. "We just came by to warm up a lil'," he said. "It's pretty rough out there, Shelley."

A swirl of smoke seeped out of her mouth. "Why do you think I never leave this place?"

Joey's voice suddenly filled the room, louder and braver than Albert had thought possible. "Never?" he asked. He stepped out from behind Albert, moving closer to the counter.

Shelley raised her head a little bit and gave Joey a half nod of approval. She locked eyes with him, mildly impressed he was making it a point to prove he wasn't intimidated by her. Albert felt flustered, and this irritated him.

"What's the point?" she asked Joey. "Anything I need, I can have delivered. Most of my family members don't do nothing but irritate me, so why should I get on a plane or a bus to visit them? This is where I belong." Her eyes moved back and forth between Albert and Joey again. Albert wondered if she was trying to pass along a secret message to him. He repeated her words in his head, quickly tried to decode them, dissect them for hidden meaning, innuendo, a double entendre. *This is where I belong.* Shelley's words untangled in Albert's mind and their meaning became as clear as the hot pink letters in the title of a romance novel in Albert's peripheral vision.

Albert glanced over at Joey, at the beauty and temptation of him. He swallowed, accepted Shelley's silent blessing of him and Joey—and whatever they were becoming to each other.

Joey asked, "Are all of these books yours?"

Shelley didn't smile back, but her eyes softened and her steady grip on her pipe lessened as the hand holding it relaxed. There was a slight change in her tone, but Joey didn't know her well enough to realize this was as friendly as Shelley could be. It was as if a hidden laugh—not so much as a laugh as it was a chuckle—darted from behind her words and circled around the sentence, floating in the air between them like an invisible hug. "I own the store, don't I?"

Albert felt a connection between Joey and Shelley. He wasn't sure what to make of it, or why it made him feel strange. It was like too many worlds were colliding in one day. He slapped his hands together to make a sound. Their eyes moved to him, acknowledging his demand for attention. "Ya got something back there to kill the cold in my bones?" he asked Shelley.

SHELLEY

Shelley brought the tip of the pipe to her lips, breathing in. It was what she loved about Albert the most: his ability to command a room with his intense energy, the powerful hostility and rage oozing from his pores like a pheromone. He was so uncomfortable in his own skin that he could detonate at any moment and beat the shit out of everyone in the room. His hurricane could annihilate anything in its path, if it were ever to be unleashed. She reached for her leather pouch of tobacco, grabbed a pinch and packed her pipe with it, and said to Albert, "I'm all outta gin, you dirty bastard, so will you settle for some oolong tea?"

"Shit," he said, with a strange smile revealing his crooked front teeth, the slight overbite that made his mouth like that of a teenager in desperate need of braces. The focus was back on Albert, which is where he liked it. "I can't pronounce it but I love to drink it."

Joey's shoulders rose. Shelley started to admire him, even though he bore a striking resemblance to her dead son. "I'll take some tea," he decided.

"Yeah," Shelley said to Joey, her eyes growing heavy. Albert had finally met his future. "I figured you would." She struck a match and inhaled the tobacco, careful to blow out the flame before her fingers were burned.

ALBERT

Moments later, Albert and Joey were sitting in dusty loveseats opposite each other. Between them a wooden trunk served as a makeshift table. They were surrounded by open antique curio cabinets and china hutches spilling books out onto the bare floor. Shelley delivered a tray containing a cracked porcelain pot of lukewarm tea and mismatched cups and saucers. Albert poured the tea and offered Joey a cup.

"I've never had tea before," Joey admitted. The kid reached down and tied his Adidas before taking the cup and saucer from Albert. He placed them down on the splintered surface of the old trunk, next to the bag of items he had purchased from the pharmacy just minutes before they had arrived.

"I drink it all the time," Albert confessed.

"Flowers and tea," Joey said.

"You making fun of me, kid?"

Joey shook his head. "No…you just don't seem the type," he said. "Why do you bring Shelley flowers?"

"Because it's my job."

"You own a flower shop?"

"No…but maybe someday," Albert replied. "An old friend of mine named Francine hired me as a delivery driver. I help her out, ya know."

Joey slid his fingers through the handle of his pink and blue cup. "How long have you been a delivery driver, Albert?"

Albert swallowed and spoke. "Over twenty years now."

"You never thought of doing anything else?"

Albert leaned back in his chair. He felt small in it, like he was shrinking, as if the cushions were devouring him whole. He dug his fingernails into the ripped arms, holding on for dear life, and asked Joey, "Why do you wanna be an architect?"

Instinctively, Joey reached into the bag. He pulled out a glue stick and a box of tongue depressors. "I don't know...I just like to build stuff." Joey went to work with the masterful skill of an artist. He connected tongue depressors with quick swipes of glue. Within moments the skeleton frame of a house emerged.

Albert watched Joey's hands, amazed. He said, "I've always wanted to be a boxer."

The four walls were already up. Joey started on the roof. "How long have you been boxing?"

"Only a year," said Albert. "My wife didn't like the idea."

"She was worried you would get hurt?"

Albert shook his head. "No. She was worried about the cost. She doesn't let me spend much. Then again, I don't make much."

"Maybe you could go to school."

"What, *college*?"

"Yeah," said Joey.

"No way. I never even finished high school."

"You dropped out?"

Albert's hands curled into semi-closed fists. "My dad died. I had to take care of my mom."

"How old were you?"

Albert drained his cup and reached for the porcelain pot to pour himself some more tea. "Fifteen," he answered.

"How old are you now?"

"How old do ya think I am?"

"Thirty, maybe."

"Yeah—close enough."

"How did your dad die?"

The cup in Albert's hand froze midair, inches from his mouth. "He drowned."

"An accident?"

"No," Albert said, "I don't believe in accidents."

"Do you think it was fate?"

"My dad dying in Lake Michigan?"

"Yeah…and you and me."

Albert shrugged. "Who knows why shit happens the way it does?"

Joey snapped a few tongue depressors into smaller pieces and started building a chimney. "I think there's a reason for everything. Like…the only college that accepted me was in Chicago. If I hadn't gone home to Maine yesterday, I wouldn't have missed all of my classes today. I wouldn't have been looking for a mailbox. I wouldn't have found *you*."

Albert grinned, wondering what Joey would build next since the house was almost done. "You make me sound like something you were missing."

"Maybe."

"What's it like in Maine?"

"You've never been there?"

"I've never been anywhere…except we went to New York once to visit my cousin. It was right after my dad died."

"I have nothing against Maine, but if I never go back there again…"

They fell silent. Albert glanced around at the books. A few covers caught his eye, held his attention for a moment. He watched Joey put finishing touches on his design.

Albert's gaze shifted, resting on Joey. He looked at the boy's hands, his forearms, the rolled-up sleeves of the oversized sweatshirt, the two beads of sweat forming just above his lip, the fingertips layered with traces of glue. Joey's passion for building was frightening. He resembled a madman, a wire-haired scientist bent over a secret formula in an underground lab. But his intensity was also seductive. The way he blocked out the world around him, slipping inside the corner of a universe where only his imagination ruled—it made Albert want to sneak off to this utopian place with him, to land smack dab in the middle of Joey's fantasy world of wooden houses. Albert knew he would be safe there.

He wasn't sure if what he was feeling was an attraction for Joey. Albert just knew that he liked being with him.

As he watched Joey work, Albert felt the impulse to touch him. He wanted the kid to be as devoted to him as he was to his tongue depressors and glue.

Albert said, "My wife thinks I'm cheating on her."

Joey's hands stopped. He looked up. "Are you?"

"No...but she gets real jealous of Francine." Albert silently scolded himself for bringing up Francine again, for saying her name a second time.

Joey wiped his sticky hands on the thighs of his jeans. "Is she pretty?"

"My wife?"

"No. Francine."

Albert looked away as if he could see a younger version of Francine, standing in a dim corner of the store. "She used to be."

"You've known her a long time?"

"We're from the same neighborhood. She used to be beautiful."

Joey reached for his tea cup. It was empty. "What happened to her?"

"She got her heart broken and I guess she ain't ever been the same since."

"May I have some more tea?"

"It's good stuff, huh?" Albert poured the last few drops into Joey's cup.

"It's got a nice taste. Makes me feel good inside."

"I figured we needed to warm up."

Joey finished his tea in two gulps. "You probably have to go home soon," he said. He wiped his mouth with a sleeve. "For dinner. To your wife."

The thought of home caused Albert's elation to fade. "Bonnie doesn't cook dinner no more," he said. "I usually just heat up a can of soup. Clam chowder. A coupla pieces of bread. Have a few beers. Call it a night."

"What do you do on the weekends?"

"Spend most of my time at the gym. Or help out Shelley."

Joey leaned forward and his knees pressed against the side of the trunk. "Albert, do you have a lot of friends?"

Albert felt the back of his neck stiffen. "What do I need friends for?"

"I only have one friend. Her name is Molly. But she lives in Portland."

"I had a friend for a while. His name was Jackson. He liked to go to strip clubs a lot."

"What happened to him?" Joey asked.

"He moved to St. Louis. Got married."

"Have you had a lot of women?"

Albert grinned. "What, you mean sex?"

"Sex. Love."

"No…not really."

Joey's arms moved to his sides. He braced his palms against the edge of his chair. His fingertips curled against the sagging fabric. He looked at Albert and playfully asked, "You don't like sex?"

Albert blushed a little, and it surprised them both. "Yeah, of course I do. Just…me and Bonnie…we haven't had sex in a few years."

Joey crossed his ankles. "I've never had sex."

"Never?"

"Once. Almost."

"What happened?"

"My mother caught us."

"How old were you?"

"Fifteen. My sister was crazy about the guy," Joey said. "It destroyed her."

"You make it sound like a good thing."

Joey smiled. "No…I feel bad about it now. But, at the time…"

Albert shook his head. "Joey, I've never met someone who had it out for their family as much as you do."

Joey stood up. He carefully picked up the house he had just built. "You didn't know my mother," he said. "If you had, you'd understand everything."

Albert reached up and touched Joey's arm. He left his hand there. It covered the kid's skin. It was an impulse, and the spontaneity ignited a hot buzz of lust that rolled through Albert. "You're happy she's gone," Albert said, looking up.

Joey stared down at him and whispered, "You don't know the half of it."

Albert's gaze lowered to the front pockets of Joey's sweatshirt, to the front of Joey's jeans. How could he explain how badly he wanted to be as close to Joey as physically possible? He couldn't understand it himself, couldn't find a name for the pang he felt in the center of his heart. He wanted nothing more than for Joey to reach out with both arms, and pull Albert to him. He wanted to be told that everything would be okay. He wanted to feel that euphoric belief that anything was possible—a feeling that had sunk to the bottom of Lake Michigan along with the drowned body of his father when he was fifteen. Albert had given up then.

On everything.

Albert long ago accepted the fact that life was a merciless joke, particularly cruel to those who dared to dream. His own dream, for as long as he could remember, included the roar of an adoring crowd chanting his name religiously as he battered an opponent in the ring. Joey made him feel, somehow, like this wasn't just possible—but it was Albert's destiny.

He was surprised when Joey walked toward the front of the store.

"Where are you going?" Albert asked. He sounded afraid.

Joey offered a reassuring grin. "Since you didn't bring her any flowers today, maybe Shelley will settle for a house."

Albert swallowed his fear as he watched Joey move away with the wooden house balanced in his delicate hands.

JOEY

I was an accident," Joey explained a few hours later. "My mother wasn't supposed to have me."

They were sitting on the edge of Joey's bed, shoulder to shoulder. Albert raised an eyebrow. Joey fought the impulse to reach up and touch his crescent-shaped scar. "Oh yeah?" Albert asked.

"Yeah," Joey said. "She was almost forty when I was born."

After successfully sneaking Albert in to his third-story dorm room (a feat including an illegal ride in a freight elevator and Albert almost punching out a nosy resident advisor named Buddy), they were now sitting on a thin twin mattress. They shared a paper cup of instant cocoa Joey had purchased from a vending machine at the end of the hall. The powdery liquid coated Joey's teeth and burned his throat. He sat at the head of the bed, ankles crossed, near the only window in the room. It looked out over Sheffield Avenue. Fresh flakes of snow tapped against the glass like hungry ghosts. Across the street shone the familiar glare of a Blockbuster Video store. Neon spilled through the window, soaking everything in an artificial glow that resembled pale candlelight. The asthmatic radiator creaked and hissed below the windowsill and swelled the walls of the room. Joey felt trapped inside of a steam iron.

Joey's dorm room was tiny, cramped, and smelled of dirty socks and cheap, spicy cologne. The room duplicated itself: each side housed a twin bed, a dresser, and a desk. But the two sides of the room couldn't be more different. Joey's was neat, tidy. His roommate was a slob.

In the opposite corner of the room from where they sat, a small television with a homemade antenna comprised of a wire coat hanger and aluminum foil was housed on a stack of blue milk crates.

The wall next to Joey's bed was decorated with a poster-sized black-and-white photograph of a woman and a man. They stood at the bottom of the Eiffel Tower, only seconds away from what appeared to be their first kiss. The wall on his roommate's side of the room was covered with posters of professional skateboarders with names like Tony Hawk, Shaun White, and Chris Cole. There was a wall calendar featuring a half-naked Pamela Anderson as the model for the month of October. Two strategically placed pumpkins covered her outrageous boobs.

They sat in silence for what felt like an eternity. It was the first time they were alone. Finally, they did not have to be concerned with strangers who glanced at them with uncertainty, silently trying to define how these two men knew each other and why. No longer were they battling with the distractions of the city—the flash of the traffic, the buzz of the train, the rumble of pedestrians. Here, Joey knew they could be themselves, explore one another if they chose to; try to determine why they both felt so compelled to be in the other's company.

Albert unzipped his flannel jacket. The sound seemed unusually loud, magnified. He grinned a little and it was contagious, so Joey grinned, too. He peeled off the coat and Joey felt his breath stick in his throat. Albert wore a white tank top that revealed his solid arms, his cocoa-colored skin, and a tattoo on the back of his shoulder that read *Love is a Battlefield* in blue-black ink. His dark chest hair peeked out over the low neckline. His nipples seemed strained, pushing against the white ribbed cotton shirt, begging to be bitten.

Albert kicked off his shoes. The black sneakers fell with soft thuds to the floor next to where his duffel bag rested like a sleeping cat. Albert stretched, cracked his knuckles, and let out a half sigh, half yawn. "Wow," he said. "I feel like I'm at home."

This made Joey happy, because he never wanted Albert to leave.

Joey's stare remained on Albert's skin. "Your house looks like this?"

Albert kept smiling. "No, I mean…comfortable. You know, chilled out."

"Oh. That's good. I want you to be comfortable here…with me."

Albert cleared his throat. "Where's your roommate?"

"He's a dishwasher at some hole in the wall. He works the graveyard shift and sleeps through most of his classes."

Albert asked, "So…you and me…we're alone?"

Joey looked out the window. "He won't be back until the morning."

Albert's eyes moved to the calendar, to Pamela. Joey wondered if Albert found her attractive. Did the sight of Pamela Anderson give him a hard-on? Was he searching for proof that he still liked women? Albert's gaze shifted to Joey's mouth. He stole glances at Joey's lips when he got the chance. Was he imagining what they'd feel like on his body? "Looks like you and he don't got much in common," he said.

"I don't have much in common with anybody," Joey answered quickly. He licked his lips, passing the cup of hot chocolate to Albert.

Except for the miniature wooden houses, there was little evidence to suggest someone lived and slept on Joey's side of the dorm room. The houses were important to Joey; they were everywhere. He had built at least twenty of them. A handful of glue sticks stood like miniature statues on the windowsill.

Albert seemed fascinated by the houses. He kept looking at them, and Joey felt awkward and self-conscious.

"You got a lotta little houses, man."

Joey smiled, nervous. "Do you like them?"

"Sure." Albert relaxed, shifting farther back on the bed and leaning against the concrete wall. Joey waited for a second, and did the same. "But why do you make 'em?"

Joey shrugged, kicking off his Adidas. "When I was twelve, I started walking around my neighborhood when things got bad at home. It was a nice neighborhood. Beautiful front lawns. Big front windows. We didn't live far from the ocean. But the ocean is never far away no matter where you live in Maine."

Joey took a breath and continued. "I would walk around for hours, even when it was dark. It seemed like the whole world was eating dinner without me. I wanted to be with a family—any family. I wanted to be with the dads that would laugh and the moms who would say things like, 'Eat your green beans, dear. They're good for you.' I would sit on the sidewalk or the curb outside of a pretty house as the sun went down. I would pretend I lived there. I imagined what life was like inside."

Albert stared off into the distance, as if he were visualizing Joey's memory. "So you started to build your own little houses?" he asked.

Joey grinned. "Only because I got into trouble a lot."

"You don't seem like the type to get into much trouble, kid."

"I really love blue raspberry Popsicles. You ever have one?"

"Nah, I don't like sweet stuff too much."

"I can eat boxes of them."

"A whole box? But you're so skinny."

"When I was a child, the rule was that I could eat one as long as I didn't make a mess. But sometimes—especially during the summer—they would melt faster than I could eat them." Joey stopped for a moment and finished with, "I would get punished."

Albert's eyebrow shot up again. "You got hit?"

"No...she never hit me...she put me in the basement for a while."

Albert looked like he wanted to kick someone's ass. "For how long?"

"A day or two," Joey answered. "Sometimes longer. One day while I was down there, I pulled out my stash of Popsicle sticks. I'd hidden them so my mom wouldn't know I was eating so many. My dad had a little work station in the corner. I found some carpenter's glue in a drawer and so I started to build a house—a better house than the one I lived in."

"So you could pretend you lived there, right?"

"Yeah. Or sometimes, I would pretend that my mother lived inside of it. And I would burn the house to the ground in a fire pit we had in the backyard."

Albert shook his head. "Man, you really hated her, didn't ya?"

Joey's body tensed. "No...I never hated her. I just wanted her to be somebody else's mother."

Albert asked cautiously, "So...her death...it was an accident... right?"

Joey shook his head and his eyes moved to the window, to the snow dancing in the neon glow. "Accidents never happen," he said. "You said it yourself earlier—at the book store."

"What about *you*, then?" Albert asked. "You said *you* were an accident."

"I was. I *am*. So that means I never happened."

Albert banged his head against the wall a couple of times lightly, joking but frustrated. "That sounds like fancy school talk to me."

Joey laughed. "I'm not fancy."

"Well, good. 'Cuz I ain't either."

"They gave me a scholarship to come to this place." He looked around the dorm room and then to the window, where the skyline stood, jagged against the dark night in the distance. His eyes closed a little as the word slid from his lips, "Chicago."

Albert beamed. "Your parents must've been proud of you."

Joey's half smile faded. "My father was."

"He died, too?"

Joey looked away, flinched. "He wasn't supposed to be in the car, remember?"

Albert waited for a second and then asked, "Did she do it on purpose?"

"The cliff?"

Albert nodded.

Joey answered, "No."

"How then?"

Joey shrugged. "It was an old car. The brakes failed. Besides, she was a shitty driver."

"Oh, yeah?" Albert nodded. "Maybe that's what happened. Maybe her foot slipped and she hit the gas 'stead of the brakes."

"Maybe." Joey became aware of how close they were sitting together. His head was pressed against the wall behind them. His face was turned sideways; he could see Albert's profile. In the light, Albert's features seemed softer, romantic. The silhouettes of snowflakes drifted down Albert's cheek. He looked like a leading man in an old Spanish movie; the type of hero who would rescue the heroine and ride off with her into the sunset on a white horse by the end of the film. He was breathtaking.

Joey felt the sudden urge to touch Albert, to curl up next to him. Instead, he remained still. He glanced down to the bed. His right hand was just inches from Albert's left. Their fingers leaned toward one another's with subtle longing to touch. Joey lifted his eyes and stared into Albert's. Joey inhaled and felt a slight ache, a tiny tremor somewhere in his heart. He knew he wanted Albert. He had known it since they'd first met. Joey just didn't know if it was possible.

Joey had fantasized about being touched by rough, calloused hands. He secretly pined over the guy he shared the dorm room with; watched him sleep and studied the curves of his thick penis through a peach-colored bath towel always hanging like a dare from his hip bones.

Albert didn't turn away. He held Joey's stare, as if silently challenging him to take the moment a step further. Sitting next to Albert made Joey feel he was capable of building the perfect house. Already, in his mind, he was designing it. He would include a terrace so Albert could look down at a garden.

Joey thought about his sister and what her reaction would be once she got his letter. Lily would read it while sitting at the kitchen table. She wouldn't cry. She would be angry. She'd break something. He hoped she wouldn't hurt herself, even do herself in. Finally finish off the damage that had been done to her, mostly by Cooper McGill and his dirty friends.

Joey would be alone if Lily stepped over the edge. He already missed his father, but Joey knew in time his memory would fade. He would travel through life the way he was meant to, the way it was safest: alone.

Unless Albert decided to take the journey with him. But it was only a slim chance Albert would stick around. He was simply curious about being with another man.

And once that curiosity was fed, Albert would be long gone, back to his bitter wife and boxing rounds.

ALBERT

Albert's mind swam with the events of the day: meeting under the train tracks, the dinner at the coffee shop, the post office, the book store. The time spent with Joey felt sped up, like someone was playing a cruel joke on them, robbing them occasionally of minutes and seconds when they didn't have an eye on a clock or a watch.

Albert had been conflicted since he had met Joey. Part of him wanted to stand up and leave, insist to Joey that he liked women. He loved tits and ass and pussy and especially ladies with long legs. He wasn't a queer and had no plans to become one.

Yet there was a part of him that wanted to devour Joey. He had flashes of imagined instances when he grabbed Joey, bent the kid over, and banged the hell out of him, hard. He would hold him after, real tender-like, and tell him that no one—and he meant *no one*—would ever hurt Joey again.

Finally, Joey spoke. "There's probably going to be a funeral."

"There is," Albert said. "When you were in the bathroom earlier your sister called." He pointed to an answering machine on the dorm room floor. A digital red number one blinked back up at them. "She left you a message. Said the funeral is Saturday."

Joey's eyes were still on the machine when he asked, "Did she sound upset?"

"Nah, man. She didn't sound broken up about it."

"That's because she's not. She hated our mother. I mean, *really* hated her."

Albert swallowed and spoke. "So...who did it?"

Joey looked him in the eye. "What do you mean?"

Albert held his stare. "The brakes," he said. "Who cut 'em? You or your sister?"

Joey's mouth moved, slipped down into an expression revealing his inner feeling of guilt. "Are you kidding?" he said. "My sister could never do anything like that."

Albert brought his knees up, toward his chest, placed his elbows on them. His toes curled inside of his white socks, digging into the faded quilt that they were sitting on. "What about *you*?" he asked.

Joey was quiet for a moment before answering with, "What do you think?"

Albert took a long look at Joey, trying to imagine him killing someone, his own mother. "I think I've known you less than a day, man, so…uh…it's hard to say," he decided.

"Is that so? I was under the impression you had me all figured out."

"Nah, man, I don't."

Joey sat up a little. "Is that why you're here?"

Albert looked confused. "I'm here 'cuz you invited me over."

"Why did you say yes? We've spent the whole day together. You're not sick of me yet?"

Albert smiled. "No."

"No?"

"What—you don't believe me?"

"Tell me the truth."

That sounded like a dare to Albert, and he never backed down from one. "I will if you will."

Joey crossed his ankles again. "Fair enough."

Albert took a deep breath. His words were rushed, nervous. His mouth felt dry. "I'm here because I like you. I feel like you and me… we just…well, we know each other…it's like this connection…I can't explain it…I figure you're probably a queer and either you won't say it or you just ain't never messed around with a guy before. Maybe you're thinkin' you want to do that with me. But I don't think I can. Even though I like you. I don't mean I like you like a man likes a woman, I mean…you and me…we're really messed up…in the head and shit like that…so I figure I like being with ya…'cuz now I don't feel so messed up. You make me feel…happy…and I ain't ever felt like that…like something good is gonna happen to me…ya know?"

A moment passed before Joey spoke. "Are you scared of me?"

Albert's jaw tightened. "I ain't scared o' nothin'."

Joey reached out. His hand landed on Albert's thigh. It was the first time they had touched since they were at the book store. "Nothing?"

Albert looked down at Joey's hand, at his half-bitten nails and gnawed cuticles. "I told you—"

Albert felt Joey's fingers tense against his black sweatpants. "You're not a queer. You have a wife. I know."

"You're mad at me?"

Joey pulled his hand away. "No."

"Yeah, you are."

"Maybe."

Albert shook his head. "I don't understand it myself. It don't make sense to me, Joey."

Joey's eyes returned to the window. "Maybe it's not supposed to."

"Nah. It has to for me. If it don't make sense, I don't want nothin' to do with it."

Joey closed his eyes as if he were carefully choosing his words, seeing them written out in his mind before he said them. "I see so much in you, Albert."

Albert gave him a strange look. "What are ya sayin'?"

Joey reached up and touched the tattoo on Albert's shoulder. He traced the letters in the word "love." Albert shuddered a little, but if Joey noticed, he didn't let it show. He said, "I would if I could."

"I know you're having thoughts—"

Joey chose to say the word in a whisper. "Thoughts?"

"About me and you. About me and you doing stuff. *Queer* stuff."

Joey folded his arms across his chest. "Is that so bad?"

Albert felt his body weaken, as if someone or something had stripped the rage out of his soul. "I don't know."

On impulse, Joey leaned over and kissed Albert's cheek. It surprised them both that Albert didn't pull away. Instead, he closed his eyes for a moment. He opened them again and Joey was startled, concerned that Albert might actually cry.

"Whatcha do that for?" Albert asked.

"Because," Joey said, "I think you're beautiful."

Albert blushed a little, looked down at the quilt, at the paisley pattern of red and gold. "But I'm not."

Joey reached for Albert, lifted his face up by his chin. He looked him deep in the eyes and asked, "Who told you that?"

Albert sniffed. "Bonnie."

"Then she must not love you, Albert."

The words stumbled out of Albert's mouth, and they hung in the air. "Could you?"

Joey folded his hands, placing them in his lap like a child sitting in a classroom waiting for story time. He nodded a little. "I think maybe I can."

Albert exhaled, ran a hand through his hair, and wiped his palm on the front of his sweats. "Wow," he said. "That's some serious shit, Joey."

Joey's mouth slid into a half grin when he asked, "What about now? Are you scared?"

The expression on his face answered all of the unanswered questions in the room, but Albert spoke anyway. "Ya don't scare me, kid."

"Are you sure?" Joey asked.

Albert knew that the question had many meanings.

Albert nodded. He leaned into their first kiss, the moment, the absolute point of no return. Their eyes closed in unison and their breath became one. Their mouths met and they were hungry. They tasted of chocolate and snow, of an unspoken promise.

Albert pulled away first. He was shaking. "I'm nervous," he admitted. He glanced down to his sweatpants and hoped Joey hadn't noticed how hard he was, that their kiss had made his cock throb. He thought about it for a second: about pulling the waistband of his sweats down and guiding Joey's mouth to his dick.

"Why are you nervous?" Joey said with a grin. "It's just me."

"I don't think...I'm not ready to..."

Joey put a finger to Albert's lips. "Shhhhhh."

"I don't know what I'm doing," Albert said. "This is freakin' me out, kid."

"Do you want to go home?" asked Joey.

Albert shook his head. "No," he said. "I don't."

Joey lay down on the small bed. He gestured to Albert to do the same. "We don't have to do anything," Joey decided aloud. He pressed his back against the wall to give Albert enough room to curl up on the edge of the twin mattress.

Albert hesitated for a moment, and lay down next to Joey. He looked up at the ceiling and exhaled deeply. "I'm sorry. I can't, Joey. Not yet."

Joey rolled over on his side to face Albert, to look at the boxer's profile, his black eye. "That's not important to me."

Albert flashed an anxious smile. "No?"

"I'm just happy you're here," Joey said. He waited a second before putting an arm around Albert. His hand rested on Albert's stomach. The thin cotton of Albert's tank top separated Joey's fingertips from Albert's skin.

"That feels nice," Albert said.

❖

The dream was intense. It was always the same.

But it had been a few years since it had returned to torture Albert at night.

In the dream, he wasn't fifteen. He was younger, maybe seven.

He was standing on the wooden walkway at Diversey Harbor next to the thirty-five-foot power boat docked in slip D-55. Albert knew that's where he would find *him*.

The night air was cold—even though it was August—and it smelled like rusted iron. The harbor was dark, except for the occasional random patch of moonlight. The dock felt deserted, soulless.

Albert glanced down and noticed his feet were bare. He saw the blood in the water. It was as thick as syrup, splashing against the pale sides of the boat. How could the blood already be there? *I haven't killed anyone yet.*

The bottle was already in his hand when the dream began. In real life, he'd picked the bottle up from the corner of the boat where it had rolled onto a faded patch of cobalt blue marine carpet. It was an empty Corona bottle with a rim of foam still oozing from the glass lip. It made the perfect weapon. In the dream, the bottle felt much heavier.

Albert floated onto the boat with ease as if an imaginary hand was lifting him up from the dock and carrying him through the air. Once he was on board, the crime he had come to commit was already done. There was blood bubbling and squishing between his toes. The man lying face down on the boat was bleeding so much it scared Albert. He started to cry. His tears felt hot against his face. He wiped them away with the back of his hand.

It was then he realized he was still holding the bottle. But the bottle shifted shape. It metamorphosed in Albert's grip and became a giant bouquet of white carnations, nearly a hundred of them. The flowers felt so heavy Albert had to use both hands to hold them. But soon, they began to drop down to the blood-soaked fiberglass floor of the boat.

There was a voice. It was calling to Albert, saying his name. He turned toward the sound. Some of the stems flew out of his hands, propelling the flowers into the water. They floated and bobbed on the surface of the lake before spawning out and away from the boat like discarded remnants from a water parade.

"Albert..." the voice started to wail. "What have you done?"

Albert turned away from the voice and looked behind him to the Chicago skyline. The sight of it squeezed the breath in his throat. The lights and the buildings looked majestic. They promised love and opportunity. They made him feel alive. He swallowed his tears and tossed the remaining flowers overboard.

He turned back to the desperate voice that kept calling his name.

"Daddy," Albert said. But there was no response.

The boat began to rock as it was momentarily whipped by the temper tantrum of a summer wind that had found itself trapped in the harbor. Albert steadied himself, afraid he might fall.

"Albert?" the voice said. Albert felt a warm hand on his face. He opened his eyes, but it was dark. "You okay?" It was a soft voice. A boy's voice. It wasn't Bonnie's.

"What?" Albert asked.

"I think you were having a nightmare."

Albert craned his neck, turned his face toward the window offering the only source of illumination. Light from the city, the moon, and the video store across the street. *The dorm room*, he remembered.

"Joey?" he said. There was a frantic edge in his voice he hoped Joey hadn't heard.

"It's all right," the boy said. "I'm here."

Albert moved closer to Joey, until their bodies touched. "I did something bad," he whispered.

"Who hasn't?" Joey asked. Albert was certain there was a smile on his face.

"I was fifteen when it happened." Albert closed his eyes as they felt too heavy to keep open. Sleep was coming back and fast. "It wasn't my fault."

"Sleep now," Joey said. "You can tell me in the morning."

❖

When Albert woke again, he knew where he was. The dorm room was becoming familiar to him. It was a new haven.

His arm was draped over Joey, who was asleep beside him and breathing deep. They were curled up together like a rope. Both of them were facing the wall next to the bed. Joey's back was pressed against Albert's chest. Albert held on to him tightly, worried Joey would fly away. Albert inhaled the faint coconut scent in Joey's hair.

Albert's eyes widened and his heart thumped. He heard movement behind him, near the door of the dorm room. Someone else was in the room with them. *The roommate.*

Albert froze for a few seconds, unsure what to do. He pretended to be asleep and hid his face beneath a pillow. He was worried the roommate might recognize him. Yeah, he was just some college kid, but what if the guy worked out at the gym? What if Albert had delivered flowers to him before? What if...

"Hey...Joey." The voice was next to their bed, talking in a loud whisper. It woke Joey, who didn't pull away from Albert. He didn't panic. The roommate's voice was mellow and subdued. Maybe he was high. "Sorry to wake you, dude, but can I borrow your meal card? Mine doesn't have any cash left on it and I'm starving."

Joey moved. He sat up. "Um...yeah...it's in the pocket of my cargo shorts."

The voice moved away from the bed. "Thanks, man. I'll pay you back."

"Don't worry about it."

The roommate's tone dropped to a lower whisper. "Hey...I didn't know you had company. Sorry about that."

Joey put a hand on Albert's shoulder, his tattoo, and Albert wondered if Joey was claiming him. "We didn't have anywhere else to go," he said.

"Don't worry about it, dude. No big deal." The roommate moved across the room, to the door. "I'll catch you later."

Seconds later the dorm door clicked closed and the roommate was gone.

Joey lay back down. He lifted the pillow away from Albert's face, and they were eye to eye. Neither spoke—they just stared until Joey reached out and touched Albert's face, his fingertip trailing across Albert's lips.

Albert half grinned, and shuddered.

Joey's hand moved up to Albert's black eye, touching it with tenderness.

Albert sat up then. He looked to the window, to the city coming alive for the day. "I have to go get my van," he said. "I'm sure Francine needs me. This week is going to be busy. This Saturday is Sweetest Day."

Joey also sat up. He tried to hide the layer of disappointment in his voice, but it was heavy. "Yeah, sure. You probably have lots to do."

Albert turned to him. "I want you to go with me."

Joey climbed off of the bed and sat in a chair that faced the window. He picked up some of the glue sticks on the sill and moved them into a zigzag formation. "To work?"

"Yeah," Albert said. "We can talk and stuff while I make deliveries."

Joey nodded. "I could help you. But...what is Sweetest Day?"

"It's sort of like Valentine's Day...you're supposed to give someone flowers and candy and shit like that...it's a big fucking deal in Chicago."

"Flowers and candy," Joey repeated.

Albert leaned toward Joey. He reached out and covered Joey's hand with his. Joey looked down at the fading bruises on Albert's knuckles. "I want to know you," Albert said, and knew it sounded more like a command than a sentiment.

Joey smiled. "That sounds kind of deep."

Albert pulled his hand away. "You makin' fun of me, kid?"

Joey's face paled. Fear flashed in his eyes. "Oh shit," he said.

Albert followed Joey's gaze down to the street below. A police car had arrived and parked in front of the main entrance of the dorm. Joey turned to Albert, panic spreading across his face. "Do you think they're here for me?"

"I don't know what you did, Joey," Albert said. "But I don't want you to get caught."

Joey stood up with a new sense of charged energy. He paced for a few seconds and then said, "We need a plan." He reached underneath the bed, pulling out a navy green duffel bag.

"You make it sound like you have one."

Joey reached for his glue sticks and tossed them in the bag. "I always do."

"I can't figure you out, kid."

"You'll have plenty of time on the way."

"On the way?" Albert said. "Where are we going?"

"To the gardens, Albert. To Vancouver."

"What?"

"Help me pack. We can take the freight elevator and avoid the cops."

"I'll do it," Albert decided. He reached for his favorite of the wooden houses. It was small and cozy. If it had been real, it was just large enough for the two of them to live in. He handed the house to Joey. "I'll go with you," he said.

Joey leaned down. "Let's do it," he whispered. "Let's leave together."

Albert arched up and met Joey's lips. Their mouths melted as the morning sun slid over Chicago. The snow on the sidewalks dissolved to slush.

The lust and trepidation Albert felt in his heart turned to love.

ALBERT

Albert was fifteen the night Francine first tried to kiss him. He didn't want to, but there she was, with cool moonlight in her long dark curls. Her eyes were blue, and when she looked at Albert, they seemed to shine with a wicked lust for all things daring and forbidden.

The night air was humid and heavy. It wrapped around them, squeezing hot lust from their lungs. School had ended for the summer earlier that day. Liberation clung to the backs of their throats and coated their taste buds with an unquenchable hunger for reckless fun.

The teenagers stared at each other with intrigue. Francine was movie-star beautiful and knew it. She was both envied and adored. Albert was considered one of the sexiest guys in the neighborhood. Rumor had it they were hot for each other and it was only a matter of time until these two supernovas would merge. Their collective power had the potential to become legendary in Humboldt Park.

Francine was leaned up against her cherry red Mustang, a recent birthday gift from her wealthy tycoon father who owned half the condos in San Juan, Puerto Rico. She wore a denim skirt that was too short and a thin-sleeved white top that made her copper skin glow with the promise of a wild summer affair. Her heart-shaped face and delicate nose were doll-like. She blinked a few times, bit her bottom lip, and stared at Albert with intense longing. She shifted and moved toward the curb where Albert stood. Her hips fell forward, so her body pressed slightly against his.

Albert felt a beer buzz deep in his veins. At Francine's suggestion, they'd slipped out of the kegger they'd been at. They were in a residential neighborhood, a few blocks from the whir of Division Street where riots had raged long ago in June of 1966. That was the same year the first Puerto Rican Parade shook the city of Chicago. Their parents had told them the story so many times, Albert and Francine could have been there.

"What's on your mind?" Albert asked, frightened by the longing on Francine's face, but numbed by the beer. He swayed a little, tipping forward toward the car, and regained his footing on the concrete edge of the curb.

The hot girl slipped her fingers through two belt loops of Albert's faded jeans and pulled him closer to her. Her eyes closed and a soft moan escaped her lips.

Francine always smelled like gardenias. It was a scent that had drawn Albert to her months ago in the hallway at school. He had sniffed her out like a dog, and arrived at her locker in a daze. She was a year older than Albert and very experienced with men.

Well, at least according to the many boys who boasted to have nailed her at least once.

"I want you to want me," she whispered, a play on the title of the song playing on the car radio. The music floated out to them from the half-rolled windows.

Albert shook his head. "I can't want you, Francine."

She put a hand on his chest, surprised by how firm his body was. He seemed weaker because he was shorter than most boys. "Why not?" she asked him with a pout. "We're from the same neighborhood, Papi."

"Don't matter."

"Of course it does."

"Nah, I can't. I gotta help out my dad this summer at the harbor."

Francine grabbed a handful of his T-shirt and pulled him toward her. They fell back toward the hood of the car.

Francine raised her hips up to meet his. She ground herself against him, and they both shuddered. "No one knows you like I do, Albert," she whispered in his ear.

He pulled away from her and returned to his post on the curb. Francine remained half-sprawled across the car, a jilted look on her face. "It won't work," he said. "I'm not giving in to you tonight."

"Then why'd you come out here with me?"

He grinned. "I like the way you smell."

"Oh yeah?" She stood up and joined him on the sidewalk. She slid two arms around his neck. "I'll let you smell me all over, Albert."

He swallowed. "All right."

"And I won't say a word to anyone," said Francine. "Everyone thinks you're a saint. I know you like it that way."

Francine was turning him on. Albert felt a heat for her he'd never experienced before. It was throbbing and intense. "Okay," he said.

She reached for his hands and placed them on her hips. "But I don't care if they find out what we do," she said. "No one really likes me." She looked up at him with her blue eyes. "Except for you."

Albert held her stare. "I don't wanna do nothin', Francine, unless things are serious between me and you."

His words had sunk deep inside her. The look on her face shifted. A sense of sorrow filled her eyes, dimming the wild lust. "How can you be serious with a girl like me?" she asked. "I don't deserve you, Albert." For a moment, he thought she might cry. He was relieved when she didn't. That would have been too much for him to handle.

"What do ya want from me?" he said.

She blinked away the tears that had swum into her eyes. "I just want some company," she said, with a weak attempt at a smile. Her emotions had clearly taken hold of her. The tears sprung up again and threatened to spill down her cheeks. She looked Albert in the eyes and placed her palms against his chest as if drawing strength from him to steady herself. "This place scares me sometimes."

Albert placed a hand over both of hers. "You don't seem like the kinda girl who scares easy."

A single tear broke free and she wiped it away quickly. "You'd be surprised," she told him.

"Hey," he said, "I get scared, too."

She smiled then. "I don't believe you."

He put his hands on the sides of her face gently. "What, you think guys can't get scared?"

Her fingers wrapped around his wrists. "I wouldn't tell anybody about this if I were you."

"I know my secrets are safe with you," he said. He leaned forward and kissed her forehead softly.

Francine closed her eyes and tightened her grip on Albert, like she never wanted the moment to end.

❖

Francine drove Albert around the city that night. They cruised by the edge of the lake, which held the reflection of the half-moon on its glassy surface. They sped past the harbors and yacht clubs and the rocking boats. They shot by Navy Pier and the monstrous Ferris wheel that was moving too slow to suit their exhilarated mood. They zoomed around corners and turns and held on tight to the fantasies that race-tracked around their hearts. They were silent, muted by a permanent shared grin on their faces. It was a manic high that had reached inside of them and injected a liquid-like charge, leaving them longing for an escape in their imagined getaway car.

The city had never looked so beautiful to Albert. The sight of it—and the hot rush of the August air blowing in his face as they leapt onto the Dan Ryan Expressway—made him feel invincible. He licked his lips and nodded his head in rhythm with the Latin freestyle classic booming from the car speakers. He tried to get a handle on the million ideas that were flooding his brain at once. Each one slid into a next. He wanted to get better grades. He wanted to go to college. He wanted to get a good job, make a lot of money. He wanted to make his parents proud, especially his father. He wanted to be a champion boxer. All of this seemed possible, because it was pulsing in the lights of the cars, the city, and the billboards. It seemed like the world knew Albert was destined for greatness and was revealing his future to him, for the first time. For Albert, it was overwhelming. He was filled with the sense that the best was yet to come.

Francine drove them to a row of warehouses on a dark street. She parked the car next to a brick wall splattered with sloppy graffiti. Immediately, she pulled her skirt up a little higher toward her waist. She reached across the car for Albert's hand. She guided it toward her lap. His fingertips trembled with anticipation as she slid two of them inside of her. She moaned low and loud as her hips and body began to buck against his hand. He thrust deeper into her as a rhythm was established between them. The inside of her thighs began to shake. She gripped the steering wheel and tilted her head back. Her breath quickened and she begged Albert not to stop. He complied and moved his fingers in and out of her faster with an urgency that seemed to only make her moan more. Moments later, she collapsed into a limp heap of bare skin and heavy panting. She said something but her words were tough to hear. Albert pulled his hand away from her and settled back in the passenger seat.

"It's your turn now," Francine said. Her hand darted in the dark and dove to the zipper of Albert's jeans before he could protest. She reached inside and pulled his cock out of his boxers. It throbbed against Francine's soft touch and when she started to move her hand up and down, Albert felt ecstasy invade his body for the first time in his life.

"Oh...fuck," he heard himself say as an orgasm ripped through his muscles.

"Wow," Francine marveled as he shot on the dashboard, the window, the silver door handle, his stomach.

Albert's breathing was sharp and shallow. His eyes grew heavy and half closed. He tilted his head and looked sideways at Francine, who was busy digging in her purse for tissue.

"You made a mess," she said with a grin.

Albert's eyes were glazed with afterglow when he said, "I'll never do it again."

❖

The following afternoon, Albert had a conversation with his father.

Paco stood over the bathroom sink with a shaving razor in one hand. He reached out and wiped a circular spot clean of steam on the mirror so that he could see himself. A white towel hung from his hips. His body was tall, muscular, and smooth and it glistened with drops of shower water. At nearly forty years old, he was as agile and as good looking as he had been at Albert's age. He was the subject of many fantasies by the mostly married women who lived in their six-story brick apartment building. But Albert knew that his father couldn't care less about the flirtatious looks and blatant innuendo thrown at him each day.

Although he loved his wife, everyone knew that Paco's heart only belonged to one woman: Julia de Burgos. She was one of the most famous poets of Puerto Rico. Even though she had died in the 1950s, Paco considered her to be his personal saint and spoke of her almost incessantly like she was a relative who lived with them. He recited her poem "El Rio Grande de Loiza" daily like it was a prayer that protected his family.

Paco turned to the open doorway of the bathroom where his son stood, leaning with a shoulder pressed against the wooden frame and his arms folded against his chest.

Paco tossed him a smile. "I hear Sergio's girl has a thing for you."

Albert blushed. "Who told you that?"

"I overheard your mother on one of her *maratón* phone calls. That woman would die without a phone." Paco turned the razor blade toward the lather of cream on his face.

Albert shook his head. "I think Francine and me are just gonna be friends."

"You sure about that, *m'ijo*? I've seen that *chica bonita*. Man, if I was your age—"

"I mean, I like her," Albert said. "She's pretty."

Paco laughed a little. "*Pretty*? That's like saying Julia is just a poet. She's a *diosa*. Both of them."

"I've known Francine forever."

"Yeah, well, that's not a bad girl to know."

Albert jumped on his father's words. "Because she's got a lot of money?"

"It's not a bad thing to have in this life, *m'ijo*."

Albert shoved his hands into the pockets of his jeans. "Her dad rips off poor people in San Juan so he can buy more condos."

"He's a smart man."

"He's a crook."

Paco rinsed the blade off in the sink and continued to shave. "Well, he's got a nice boat. I should know. I have to clean it once a week."

Albert looked away, at a steam faded pattern in the rose-colored wallpaper. "I don't know what's going on with Francine."

"What do you mean? Is she pregnant?"

"No. I don't know. If she is, I had nothin' to do with it," said Albert. "I think she's got problems."

Paco smiled. "They all do. Women. They're crazy and the sooner you know that—"

Albert looked down to the pale pink tile on the bathroom floor. "Sometimes I feel like I'm crazy, too," he said, wanting to say much more.

Paco shook his head. "Nah. You're just fifteen."

Albert shrugged and shifted his weight from one foot to the other. "What if I'm different than everybody?"

Paco smiled at his son. "You are. That's what makes you special. You're smarter than these *tontos* that put all their money and time in their cars. They think it's gonna get them by."

"I think about crazy stuff sometimes," Albert said. "That's all."

Paco lowered his voice to a whisper. "If you decide to do something with her—"

"I'm not sure if I want to."

"I can buy some protection for you if you need it."

"Don't bother. Tío Juanito gave me some."

Paco grinned. "That's because your Tío Juanito doesn't need any for himself."

Albert fought back his laughter. "Don't make fun of him, Dad. He's your brother-in-law."

Paco's sweet smile seemed to evaporate. His tone shifted to a serious one. "I never doubted it once," he said. "Marrying your mother."

Albert tried to dismiss the weight of his father's words. "Well, I'm not marrying Francine. I don't wanna marry anybody unless it's serious between us."

Paco reached over and ran a quick, rough hand through Albert's shaggy hair. "I have no regrets, boy," he said. "That's important for a man to be able to say."

Albert looked his father in the eye. "I never thought you had any."

Paco nodded in agreement. "I love your mother very much."

Albert felt a tiny flicker of panic boot kick the pit of his stomach. It was a strange feeling, a fear that something very bad was going to happen. "I know that," he said.

The smile returned to Paco's face and it immediately lightened the mood in the damp room. "Well, you might remind her of that once in a while. Especially when I'm not around."

"Neither one of us will be around much this summer."

Paco took a deep breath before he spoke. "I'm sorry you gotta help me out with cleaning the boats," he said. "You'll get used to working through the night."

Albert passed his father a hand towel to wipe his clean-shaven face with. "It will give me an excuse to sleep all day," he said. "Besides, I need some time to figure things out in my head."

"I can't figure out what you could possibly be worried about, *m'ijo*." It sounded like a question, so Albert just shrugged in response. "You know me and your mother love you more than anything," Paco said. "But I'm gonna love you helluva lot more if you become a boxer."

Albert's mouth pulled back to reveal a crooked-tooth grin. "I will."

"Just make sure you take care of your *padre* when you do." Paco struck a few random poses, flexing his muscles. "I'm not gonna be this good looking forever, ya know."

Albert smiled and said, *"De tal palo tal astilla."* It was a common expression that Paco loved almost as much as Julia's poetry. It meant "like father, like son."

The boats knocked against the wooden edges of the dock like a hundred hands rapping on the doors of strangers, hoping to be invited in and asked to stay awhile. The sound and the rhythm of the boats as they tilted and swayed in the water kept Albert awake. He was four hours into an all-night shift. It was his second night on the job and he was already regretting his decision to commit for the summer. The worst part was not being able to work with his father. They had been assigned to opposite ends of the harbor.

A black guy named Jackson, who was a couple of years older than Albert, instructed him on how to scour and scrub the boats. Jackson was tall and lean and lugged the heavy cleaning equipment around with him with ease. He laughed too much and his dimples made him seem almost pretty, but he was proud of his summer job as he worked side by side with Albert. "Someone's gotta clean these boats for these mothafuckers. It might as well be us," he told Albert more than once.

Jackson liked to talk to pass the time. He told Albert his father had split on his family five years ago. Jackson had been supporting his mother and younger brother and sister since. He spoke about his childhood spent in Memphis and how the move to Chicago had been forced on him. By the second hour of meeting each other, Jackson confided in Albert that he had never had sex with a girl but wanted to, desperately. After this admission, girls—both imagined and real—populated at least every other sentence slipping out of Jackson's hungry mouth.

Although Jackson chatted too much, Albert was happy to have a friend. "I gotta tell you," he said to Jackson. "I've never hung out with a black guy before. But you're pretty cool."

"Yeah, well don't expect me to learn Spanish just because you and me got stuck working together," Jackson said with a dimpled smile. "I heard you Puerto Ricans got bad-ass tempers, so I'll be real careful not to piss you off."

"Yeah, I might cut you if you do," Albert said with a wink.

"Your dad get you this job?"

"He put in a good word for me."

"Paco's a real cool guy."

Albert nodded. "He's a good dad."

"You're lucky."

Albert grinned. "I know."

"Your dad talks about you all the time. He says you're gonna be a boxer."

"I will be one day."

"No," Jackson said, "you look too small to be a fighter."

"Hey, I might surprise you."

"You know what would really surprise me? If we found a fine-ass girl on one of these boats. She could be asleep. Then we show up. And she's real horny. And she lets us take turns on her."

Albert laughed. "Then you fucking woke up."

"Damn, this job would be worth it then."

"Why do we have to clean the boats at night?"

"Because them rich fuckers don't want anybody to see us doing their work for him. You ever see 'em out here during the day? They hang around and look busy, posin' and shit with a hose and a bucket and a scrub brush actin' like they've been at it for hours."

They climbed on board a twenty-five-foot Sun Tracker.

"I guess if they got the money," Albert said. He followed Jackson's lead and started to scrub the floor of the boot with a hand brush.

"I don't know how much they're paying you, but I got two other jobs on the side."

"Oh yeah? Doing what?"

"I work at a bakery."

"What do you do there?"

"I bake stuff, you dumb ass," Jackson said.

"What, like cookies?"

"Yeah, and muffins and loaves of bread, and sometimes they let me make a cake."

Albert smiled. "You like it, don'tcha?"

"Why you say that?"

"I can tell by the look on your face," Albert said and then sang, "You like to bake."

"If you tell anybody about it, I'll kick your ass."

"Who am I going to tell? There ain't nobody workin' here but me and you."

"No, they got us spread out all over these harbors." Jackson tossed a bucket of water toward their feet to rinse the soapy cleanser from the fiberglass. "We work the whole night through and nobody knows we exist."

Albert reached down to roll up the cuffs of his jeans. "Well, we do," he said.

"Yeah, you got that right."

"What's the other one?" Albert asked. Jackson stared at him blankly. "You said you had two other jobs."

"Dishwasher. At a seafood restaurant over on Grand Avenue."

"Don't you ever get tired of cleaning stuff? Boats. Dishes. Cake pans and shit."

Jackson pulled the bucket across the surface of the lake water to refill. "What else am I gonna do?"

"You said you'll be eighteen next month. You could join the military."

"My mother would kill me before I left for boot camp. She don't like the government very much. She thinks Angela Davis should have been president."

"Who?"

Jackson smiled and his dimples radiated in the moonlight. "Yeah," he said, "you're definitely Puerto Rican."

They worked another hour before Albert remembered the grocery bag of food his mother had sent with him. A *pastille* wrapped up in aluminum foil. Some *arroz con pollo* in Tupperware. A thick slice of flan in a paper cup. Food cooked in their tiny kitchen in between her hundred phone calls to her circle of friends who all relied on her for the best gossip. He would have to eat the meal cold, but it would be worth it.

"I gotta go find my dad," Albert told Jackson the third time his empty stomach growled.

"If you find a lonely woman on the way, send her to me. I got the cock to keep her company."

Albert wiped his hands on the front of his jeans. "If I find one, I might keep her for myself."

"Fair enough."

Albert jumped off the boat they were cleaning and landed on the dock with cat-like grace. "I left a bag of food in my dad's truck."

"Feel like sharin'?"

"Sure," he said over his shoulder as he walked away. "I'll be right back."

Albert felt like he was tiptoeing through a minefield of ghosts as he made his way to the opposite end of the harbor, where the larger boats were moored. The white flicker from the occasional overhead light did nothing more than toss misshaped shadows onto the sides of boats. At quick glance, it was easy to mistake one of those shadows for a hand reaching up from the dark water, or even a face emerging for air. Albert shivered a little and chided himself for being scared. No one could hurt him here. If anything, he could run fast. He'd swim if he had to.

On sight Albert recognized the fifty-foot power boat that belonged to Francine's father, Sergio. Like its owner, the boat was oversized, and it seemed desperate to dwarf the others around it.

Albert felt fear punch the inside of his lungs. He wasn't alone in the harbor. And he was certain the voice he heard was not his father's.

It was the low, muffled sound that convinced Albert to climb aboard. It wasn't words being spoken—it was a cry. Like someone needed help. The urgency sent a chill through Albert, and he broke out into a cold sweat.

He mounted the chrome ladder and stepped onto the boat. His chest tightened at the sight of skin—at the fat ass that greeted him. It was hairy and pale and it was thrusting against something or someone on the floor of the boat. Albert's immediate response was to leave the boat, embarrassed that he might interrupt Sergio's secret date with a mistress. And Albert almost did leave. He turned away from the bald spot on the back of Sergio's skull and planned to hop back to the dock. But it was Francine who stopped him.

"Albert!" she cried out with fear and fury that rode the edge of her voice and bellowed out of the boat. It bounced in violent ripples on the surface of the water around them.

Albert turned back. It was then that he realized Francine was pinned beneath her father. He had stumbled upon the truth that Francine had kept hidden from everyone, even him. His knees weakened. He bent down and placed both trembling palms against his caps. He gagged with disgust, from the magnitude of the moment. Sweat swam down the middle of his back and stuck between the bottom of his spine and the waistband of his jeans. Albert knew he had to do something. He was compelled to.

Francine let out a second sharp cry and struggled beneath the heaving lift and fall of her father as he rammed in and out of her. She searched for Albert's eyes in the shred of moonlight that shone on the upswing of the boat's rhythm. The water was becoming angry.

Albert moved on instinct. He heard the beer bottle. It rolled and hit the door to the galley. He picked it up, wrapping his hand around the word "Corona," fingers around the thick neck. It felt like someone else had picked the bottle up and handed it to him. Then it was raised, up against the summer's star-dashed sky. There wasn't enough time to breathe, to stop, to think. The bottle was brought down in the heat of a rage Albert had not known he was capable of feeling. The bottle did not break. It thudded only once against Sergio's bald spot. The middle-aged man went still for a moment, before collapsing on his daughter.

She covered her mouth to stop herself from screaming.

Then Sergio began to convulse. He jerked and writhed like

a hooked fish that hoped to be saved or put out of his misery fast. Francine pushed her father off. She scrambled across the floor of the boat, moving like a spider toward Albert's legs.

Francine searched for Albert's eyes in the darkness. "Hit him again," she said, an odd calmness in her voice.

Albert shook his head as the convulsing started to slow, as the swollen, fat fish started to die. He gurgled and choked on his saliva, made a mournful moaning sound twice.

"Albert," a voice said from behind them. They turned. Paco stood with one foot on the top rung of the silver ladder and the other in midair as he searched for a place to land it on the floor of the boat. "What have you done?"

Albert could see his father standing in front of the city skyline, as if the majestic backdrop had been put there just to make Paco loom with an angelic glow. "Dad?" he said to the image.

Paco moved across the boat. He struggled to lift Sergio up into his arms. "Help me!" Paco shouted to his son. But Albert stood motionless, dazed. The bottle slipped from his fingers and hit the floor.

In the second that Francine climbed to her feet, Paco fell. It happened so fast that neither she nor Albert had realized what had happened. Perhaps it was a surge in the water. Maybe it was the volatile spirit of Sergio as his soul slipped away. Whatever it was, the boat rocked like it had crested a single, massive wave. Paco fell backward. He had reached out with a panicked hand. He grasped for the back of Sergio's shirt as the dead body slipped from Paco's arms.

Albert watched in horror as his father flew backward and overboard, head first. The flesh of his bare feet shone like wet bone in the moonlight and the garish flicker of the dockside lamp as they lifted up and followed the rest of his body into the water. Albert rushed to the edge of the boat. He tripped and fell over Sergio. He crushed the man's hand with his foot as he stood up and peered into the water.

"Dad!" Albert heard himself scream. Behind him, Francine began to sob.

Albert ripped his T-shirt off and dove into the water. The cold liquid threw his body into overdrive, jolted his senses with an electric-like shock. He swam to the bottom of the harbor, opened his eyes, and was greeted by an endless liquid stream of blackness. He kicked his way back to the surface and sucked in the humid air.

Francine leaned down over the edge of the boat. "Albert," she said.

Albert spat in the water. "I can't find him," he said.

"Oh God," Francine said, looking into the water. "There's blood. He's hurt."

"Get me a light. Get me something. I can't see down here!"

Francine raced around the boat and hunted for something to light the surface of the water. She returned seconds later. "It's too late," she said to Albert. She reached down to him and offered a hand.

"God damn it, get me a light, Francine!"

Her mouth trembled as she spoke. "Albert, he's already gone."

He took her hand reluctantly and lifted himself up and over the edge of the boat. Francine lifted a finger and pointed toward the lock in the distance, toward the horizon. It was there that Paco was floating face down, drifting like buoyant wood toward the rest of Lake Michigan.

Albert staggered as he nearly passed out. Francine steadied him and touched his face with her hands.

"We have to go," she told him. "We can't be found here, Albert."

He shook his head. "We didn't do nothin' wrong," he said. "He was hurting you."

"I know. I know. But they'll put us away. You hit my father with that bottle."

"My dad—"

"Go back to work," Francine instructed. "Whatever you do, act like nothing happened."

"I can't fucking do that."

"You don't have a choice," she said. "Do you hear me?"

Albert wiped his eyes with the back of his hand. "I can't lose my dad," he said. Emotion burned his throat and eyes.

Francine placed a palm against Albert's heart. "It's okay," she told him. "We have each other."

❖

Albert swore he would not cry. Not just during the funeral service, but ever again. Not in his whole life. He held on to his mother as she begged God for mercy and for Him to take her. As the priest read from the Bible and Albert listened to his mother's agonized wishes to be dead so that she could be with her husband again, he knew he would never forgive himself for what happened on that boat. He stared at the casket, at the circle of sad faces that looked like painted frowns on porcelain puppets. He remained stoic, unaffected. He had to be the brave son, the protector and provider.

Francine was also at Paco's funeral. She stood on the other side of the closed casket, speaking silently with Albert. She was dressed in black and her eyes spilled tears onto the white flowers she was holding in her hand. Already, she seemed older. It was as if she had aged ten years or more in less than a week. Her face seemed hollow and her skin had paled. She also wore a permanent expression of nonchalance, as if nothing fazed her—not even the death of her own father.

The police had ruled the whole thing as an accident. They suspected Sergio had gotten drunk, slipped and hit his head on the door to the galley. They concluded that Paco—who was being depicted as a hero—found Sergio unconscious and tried to revive him and in doing so slipped overboard. They discovered evidence Paco had hit his head on the dock and most likely bled to death within a matter of minutes—if not seconds—in the water.

Ruling Sergio's death an accidental one was beneficial to the Chicago Police Department. In his will, Sergio left a considerable sum to their Annuity and Benefit Fund. It was Sergio's guarantee that after his death, his family would never be bothered should any of his unscrupulous business practices be discovered or questioned. It was also an unspoken rule that when and if Sergio was found dead, the police were to make certain there was never a mention of a mistress or a prostitute if either were found with him. They had no idea his last moment of pleasure had been against the will of his own daughter. She herself would become a very wealthy woman at the age of eighteen per her father's will. She had already spoken of plans to open a business of some kind.

Selling flowers, maybe.

Francine had been the clever one that night. She had fished out a handful of Coronas from the galley and poured them down her dead father's throat. She repositioned his body to make it appear as if he had slipped. She went to Paco's truck and retrieved Albert's bag of leftovers. She returned to the boat with the food and with Paco's scrub brush she found on the dock. She propped the brush up near the section of the boat where Paco had fallen over. She handed Albert the food and sent him back to the opposite side of the harbor, to rejoin Jackson and finish his night of work until the police came for him at dawn, with the sad news his father was gone.

❖

The already-cramped apartment was overflowing with neighbors and family members offering awkward words of sympathy. Albert bolted and found solace in the basement laundry room. He sat in a sliver of a space between the side of a washing machine and the stucco wall. His dress shoes were scuffed with mud from the graveyard, and the seam in the cuff of his pants was unraveling. His belt felt too tight—the gold buckle was gouging his stomach. He shifted on the floor and the buckle became less annoying.

Albert sat there for what felt like an hour. He thought about school. He thought about Francine. He thought about his father.

He replayed the moments on the boat over again, mentally rewinding it like a scene in a movie he could continue to dissect. He wanted to pinpoint the exact second fate had taken over, when the night had gone to hell and his life changed forever.

He silently repeated the words to the beloved poem by Julia de Burgos. It made him ache for his father so much that tears choked him and dripped from his chin. *Fuck, I wasn't gonna cry.*

The sound of footsteps on the concrete floor forced Albert to swallow his grief. He wiped his eyes, loosened his tie. He took a deep breath and shook Julia's haunting words away from his mind.

Albert recognized the boy with the baby blue laundry basket from school. He was the same age as Albert, but looked older. He was tall, tan, and had sun-bleached blond hair. He wore a pair of cut-off shorts that seemed too short and tight, and a ribbed tank top that stuck to his torso like a second layer of skin. He shuffled into the laundry room in a pair of rubber flip-flops, slapping against the floor with a sarcastic flair. He placed his basket of clothes and bottle of liquid detergent on the lid of a top loading washing machine, only a few feet away from the corner Albert had slid himself into.

The boy looked at Albert and asked with a sneer, "Jesus…who died?"

Albert turned to the boy and said, "My father did. In a boating accident in Diversey Harbor."

"Oh shit," he said, his eyes widening. "That was your *dad*?"

Albert looked the boy in the eye. "Yeah. That was him."

The boy turned back toward his basket of clothes but stopped. "Wait. Which one was he? The rich one or..."

Albert shot him a look. "What do you think? Look where I live, man."

"Sorry. I had no idea. I just thought you were dressed weird."

Albert almost laughed. It was the first time he had smiled in almost a week. "You think *I'm* dressed weird? No offense, but look at what you've got on."

The boy put a hand on his hip. "Um...*hello*...it's summer." A lot of people at school said the boy was gay. He was effeminate and spoke openly about wild trysts with older men. He had no friends that Albert knew of and was one of a few white guys in a sea of Puerto Ricans. It was surprising to Albert the boy had survived living in Humboldt Park.

"Don't remind me," Albert said. "Worst summer of my life."

"Hey, do you know how to work this machine?"

Albert stood up. His head spun a little—a reminder that he hadn't eaten anything in two or three days. He put a hand against the wall until the dizziness passed. He walked over to the boy and stood next to him. They both looked down at the washing. "You've never washed clothes before?"

"No," the boy said in a soft voice that tickled the back of Albert's ear. "My mom usually does it for me."

"Is she mad at you or somethin'?"

"No. She took a leap of faith."

"What does that mean?" Albert asked.

"She quit her job at the bank and decided to open up her own business."

"Oh yeah? What kinda business?"

"A used book store." The boy laughed. "I don't get it. Who's going to buy a bunch of old books when they can get them for free at the library?"

Albert shrugged. "Maybe she wants a new life."

The boy shook his head. "No such luck. She's real fat now. She used to be skinny until my dad left us. But she porked out and lost her mind."

Albert couldn't help but be amused by the boy's blatant, catty humor. "Here," he said, putting the basket of clothes onto another machine. He raised the lid and reached for the metal knob. "Let me help you."

The boy shifted and stood behind Albert, like he was afraid the machine might detonate. Albert leaned closer to the machine to keep their bodies from touching. The space between the wall and machine was really only wide enough for one person to be in. But Albert felt he understood the boy's reasoning for standing where he was. The front of his crotch brushed against Albert's ass. Albert knew he should have moved. He should have prevented the moment from happening in the first place, just like the horrible night on the boat. Now there were two moments he could never take back. Two moments that would change his life.

Instead of moving out of the way, Albert pressed back and welcomed the soft head of the boy's cock against the back pocket of his dress pants. He could feel the boy's dick swelling inside of his frayed jean shorts. The boy exhaled a few short bursts of warm air on the back of Albert's neck. The sudden slink of desire that inched its way through Albert's body took him by complete surprise. The hard-on that started raging inside his pants throbbed with an intense ache to be touched. It was a desperation that felt animalistic to Albert, as if it were devouring him.

"I gotta go," he said. He pushed off the washing machine with both hands, as if he were propelling himself through a body of water.

"I hope I see you around," the boy called after him, but Albert was already halfway up the first flight of stairs.

Inside the apartment, he moved through the maze of half-drunk faces that all wanted to look him in the eye and tell him how much they would miss his father. They were like road blocks with heads floating in and out of his line of vision, trying to collectively keep him from being alone. He ignored them and repeated "Excuse me" over and over again so he wouldn't appear ill-mannered. He elbowed and slid his way through the apartment and to the end of the hallway, where he locked himself in the bathroom.

The walls felt like they were struggling to breathe through the blanket of humidity that hung outside of the apartment building. Albert pressed his cheek against the cool-to-the-touch wallpaper. He closed his eyes and succumbed to the erotic images go-go dancing in his mind. The laundry basket boy with his long, tan legs and come-and-get-me eyes was performing a hot routine, just for Albert, a male variation of a lap dance. In his imagination, Albert was back in the laundry room with the boy. He shoved him forward, chest to the machine, pulled the boy's shorts down, fondled his ass, rubbed his rigid cock against him until he moaned.

Albert didn't realize he was touching himself until the first wave of an intense orgasm caused him to shudder and arch. He moved toward the sink quickly, afraid that he was going to come. A few hot drops hit the pink tiled floor and a soft gasp tumbled out from between his lips. In his mind, he was thrusting deep into the basement boy with the blond hair, pounding his ass with a mixture of spite and lust.

As the last ring of pleasure slipped from Albert's body, he glanced up to the mirror above the sink. It felt like his heart stopped for just a fraction of a second. In that moment, Albert swore he could see his father's reflection in the glass, standing behind Albert. The words his father mouthed became audible and crashed around Albert's mind.

"De tal palo tal astilla," Paco said as his son's body hit the bathroom floor with a gentle thud of sound, just like the one a heart makes the second it's been broken.

ALBERT

The police arrived at Joey's dorm room on Thursday morning. They knocked and Joey answered after hiding his duffel bag he'd been packing. There wasn't time for a quick getaway in the freight elevator—the police were too fast. But they weren't there to arrest him. They were bringing him some very sad information.

Joey reacted to the news his parents were dead with so much believability that Albert felt choked up at the sight of the tears splashing down Joey's cheeks. Joey coughed and sobbed and begged to be spared of the gory details of their fatal drive. He paled when they mentioned the car had exploded on impact and there was no way anyone could survive such a crash. There would be no investigation because there was no suspicion of foul play. It was just an accident and, as the female officer with the long braid and freckles said, "Accidents happen all the time." Her partner—an Italian guy with a cleft in his chin—agreed and said, "Everything happens for a reason, even if we don't understand why it's happening to us."

"I think they believed me," Joey said, after the police left.

"Hell," Albert said, "even *I* believed you, and I think I know the truth."

"I hope my sister doesn't open her big mouth."

"What do we do now?"

"We make a plan. If we do this right, we never have to come back."

"Wow," Albert said with a nod and a smile. "I like that."

Joey glanced at the alarm clock on the nightstand. "Shit, I'm late for class."

"You have to go to school today?"

"Don't you think I should?" Joey asked.

"But your folks just died. Don't you get a day off for somethin' like that?"

Joey tilted his head. "That's a good point."

"So, what about this plan of yours?"

"I'll tell you all about it later."

"Later?"

"I want you to pick me up this afternoon."

"I thought we would spend the day together."

A hollow sadness filled Joey's eyes. "I don't want you to get sick of me, Albert. You've already been so nice."

"Don't get used it," Albert said with a sniff. "I'm not usually very nice to people. Especially when I'm in the ring with 'em."

Joey winked and smiled. "Am I a new opponent?"

"No. I was kinda hoping you'd be in the crowd someday cheering me on."

Joey reached for his backpack full of books. "When's your next fight?" he asked.

Albert zipped up his coat and reached for his wallet. "Every day of my life, kid."

❖

Albert hit the streets in search of food and an explanation. He welcomed the few minutes of solitude to clear his head. Although nothing sexual occurred between them the night before, Albert knew it was just a matter of time before the desire he felt for this skinny college kid would take over reason and elevate the intensity between them. Albert wondered if he could actually go through with it: sex with another man.

His eyes darted around the store at the men standing nearby. One guy with a pot belly was trying to pour himself a cup of coffee without much luck. He spilled most of it on his boots and the floor. Another guy was reading the label on a box of allergy medicine. Sure, he was an okay-looking guy, but Albert didn't feel any lust for him. Albert didn't feel the need to suck the guy's dick or jerk him off. And he certainly didn't want to fuck him. Maybe Joey was the only man he could consider being intimate with. Maybe there was something about Joey he liked that had nothing to do with the fact Joey was a guy.

It was the cashier who rang up his items that made Albert fear he really was gay. The guy was tall and built and had dark hair. There was a tattoo on the inside of his wrist like a hieroglyphic symbol from a cave wall somewhere in Egypt. He looked to be in his late twenties and had an inviting smile.

"Find everything you need?" he asked Albert.

"Yeah," Albert said with a nod, not sure if the cashier winked at him or not. The two men held each other's stare for a moment too long and Albert knew he could have the guy if he wanted.

As he handed over the cash Joey had given to him, Albert forced himself to think about women. He loved their breasts and hips and thighs. He flirted with women. He knew a few that he wanted to sleep with even.

But then the memory of the incident in the laundry room flickered in the back of his brain, a light bulb that refused to die. That had been twenty-four years ago. Certainly if Albert was truly gay he would have acted on his impulses long before Joey had entered his life. *Wouldn't I have done somethin' about this sooner?* Or maybe part of his soul had been put to sleep. And Joey was the prince with the magic kiss who would jolt him back to life.

❖

For a living, Albert drove a rust-colored delivery van with the word "Francine's" painted on the side of it in lemon yellow. The job of delivering flowers suited him, as Albert considered himself a loner. He preferred his own company to those who felt inclined to question his authority or second-guess his dream of becoming a professional boxer. People like his wife.

Albert waited eagerly that afternoon for Joey to finish a shift working at the school library. He was parked outside of the old building. The van was like his own private boxing ring, his own place to perform one-man shows. Each day, he dreamt of roaring crowds chanting his name with deafening devotion. At stoplights he practiced a few punches. Right. Left. Left. Right. He imagined the final round in a tight match when his opponent was ahead and Albert unleashed on the guy in such a fit of fury, the crowd rose to their feet and pandemonium erupted. "Al-bert!...Al-bert!...Al-bert!" they stomped and screamed. In Albert's daydreams, he was always the winner.

Albert listened to the radio when the antenna wasn't acting up. He sang along with songs that fueled his ire. He drummed his thick fingers on the black steering wheel, occasionally smacking the top of the cracked dashboard to emphasize the pounding energy of rock 'n' roll, particularly the music of Pat Benatar, his favorite singer. Some days Albert was lucky enough to catch a boxing match on an AM channel. He hung on the commentators' every word.

Except for Francine and the occasional chatty receptionist he delivered a bouquet to, Albert had little interaction with anyone. Days could go by before he'd have a conversation consisting of more than a casual greeting. He never realized how lonely he was.

Until he met Joey.

Joey single-handedly restored the faith in himself Albert felt had been stolen. For that, Albert was more than grateful, he was in love. The feeling consumed him to the point of distraction. He found himself counting down the minutes until they'd leave Chicago. They planned to leave for Vancouver on Sunday morning. In the meantime, they would exist as if life were normal—like they were living just another day.

Until Joey was sitting next to him in the ripped-up passenger seat and they were driving through the damp city, Albert feared he'd continue to feel a strange sense of sorrow that plagued him since they temporarily said good-bye that morning. It was the first time in his life that it bothered him to be alone.

At the sight of Joey emerging from the library, his spirits boosted, rocketing to the sparkling tips of the city skyline and showering down with the warm October rain. The snow had melted and dripped down into storm drains. The slight increase in the temperature promised that they'd be spared of the wrath of a Chicago winter for at least a few more days. The forecast for Sweetest Day was sunshine with a high in the upper 60s.

"I think I missed you," Albert said when Joey climbed into the van.

Joey ran a hand through his rain-soaked hair, smiled in the soft patches of the setting sunlight, and said, "I guess that means you're happy to see me."

"I want to take you somewhere," Albert said, driving away from the university. "A place where we can watch the sun set."

Joey shut the air-conditioning vent that was coughing cold air in his direction. "Should I be scared?" he asked.

Albert kept his eyes on the road ahead. "Do I scare you?"

Rain dripped from Joey's chin. "More than anything."

Albert drove Joey to the Lurie Garden in Millennium Park. Aside from Shelley's book store and the gym, the garden was his favorite place to be. Albert was nervous—he'd never taken someone there before. It was a private sanctuary for him. He was hoping Joey would love the two-and-a-half-acre garden as much as he did.

The park buffered the looming city from the edge of the lake shore. It was a place shimmering with romance and promises. Couples strolled by, hand in hand or arm in arm. Mothers pushed babies in strollers. Men shuffled around with binoculars. Tourists created mini seas of flashes with their digital cameras. Joggers zoomed by, oblivious to everything but the music in their headphones.

Albert and Joey entered the garden just as the sun was starting to set. Albert felt his chest tighten. The first sight of the place always took his breath away.

"This is incredible," Joey said. They stood shoulder to shoulder.

"You've never been here before?"

Joey shook his head. "I never knew this existed."

"I found it a few years ago," Albert said. "Bonnie and me had a bad fight so I bounced and drove 'round for a while. I came to Millennium Park because of all the fuss the city made about this place a while back. I wanted to see it for myself, ya know."

"I've never seen something so beautiful."

Albert waited a moment before he spoke. "You're the first person I've brought here," he said.

"I am?" Joey asked. "Wait…is this like a date for us or something?"

Albert folded his arms across his chest. "Why you say that?"

Joey shrugged. "Just wondering."

Albert put his hands in the pockets of his flannel jacket. "I figured since we're going to Vancouver to see the gardens, this would be good practice for us."

Joey smiled. "So, it *is* a date."

"A'ight," Albert looked away as his cheeks blushed a little. "If you want it to be."

"I do," Joey said. "Is that okay, Albert?"

Albert looked away. "I don't think I have a choice about all of this, ya know."

"You *do*."

"No. I told you yesterday when we first met, I'm real fucked up."

"But that's why I like you. I'm fucked up, too."

"No. No, you're okay."

"No, I'm not, Albert," Joey said. "I let it happen…my mother…I helped cut the brake line in her car and watched her nose-dive off a cliff. I did *nothing* to stop it from happening. I'm kind of hoping that when my sister gets that letter from me today that she does the right thing and turns me in. I'm flunking out of college because I don't give a shit about anything anymore except building my stupid houses out of sticks and glue. I know you think I'm some dumb kid who just wants to be with you, but I'm telling you, Albert—I'm a bad person."

"Well, I've done some fucked-up shit, too."

"You've never even cheated on your wife. How awful can you be?" Joey said.

"My father died because of me."

Joey's bottom lip trembled slightly. "What?"

"It happened on a boat in one of the harbors—not far from here. I was fifteen. It was late at night and I was supposed to be there cleaning the boats. My dad was there, too. He's the one who got me the job."

"What happened?"

"I heard somethin'. A noise. It was coming from one of the bigger boats. It belonged to Francine's father. I climbed on the boat and…"

"And what?"

"He was doing stuff to her. He was raping her. His own daughter."

"I hope you kicked his ass."

"No, man. I did somethin' worse," Albert said. "I killed the son of a bitch. Hit him over the head with a beer bottle. The next thing I know my old man's on the boat with us. He's pulling Sergio up and yelling at me to do something to help. I just froze. Then the boat moved. It rocked like there was a hand underneath it pushing us up. Dad slipped."

"On the boat?"

"Yeah, but he fell back. He fell overboard. I went in after him but it was too late. There was blood in the water." Albert stopped and looked in the direction of the lake. "He hit his head."

Joey stepped closer. Albert fought the impulse to reach out and touch him. He decided not to, out of fear that someone would see the gesture and try to hurt them. "I'm so sorry that happened to you, Albert."

Albert blinked away tears. He hadn't really cried since he hid in the laundry room. He swallowed his grief like a shot of liquor. He knew if he started to cry, he might not ever stop. "My dad was a good man," he said. "He didn't deserve it. If it's true, what you say about how accidents never happen, then why did that shit have to happen to my dad?"

Joey touched Albert's arm, hung on his sleeve for a moment. "He was in the wrong place at the wrong time."

Albert turned and surprised them both by taking Joey's hand in his. "It's different from us, though. Right? How we met yesterday. We were supposed to be there, on that street, you and me."

Joey nodded, pushing his long bangs out of his eyes. "I believe that more than anything," he said. "There's a reason why you and I met, Albert."

"Maybe so I could finally leave my wife."

Joey shivered a little as a cold breeze lifted off of the lake and found them. The sky darkened, as if the rain might return. "Are you thinking about doing that?" he asked. "Did you see her when you went home this morning?"

"She wasn't there. I'm kinda glad, too. I might have told her to fuck off," Albert said. He tightened his grip on Joey's hand. "Especially since I have you now."

Joey lifted his eyes. They were the color of green glass. He held Albert's stare. "You do," he said.

Albert's hand went up to his goatee. He touched, nervous. "Even after what I told you about my dad," he said. "About what I did to Francine's old man?"

Joey crossed his heart with two fingers. "I'll take it to my grave."

"Yeah," Albert said. "I'm good at keepin' secrets, too."

The expression on Joey's face brightened. "We're here to see the garden, right?"

"That's right," Albert said with a matched smile.

"And I noticed you shaved and wore some nice pants."

"They're my Dickies. You like 'em?"

"Dickies?"

Albert laughed. "It's nothing dirty," he said. "That's the name of the label, ya know."

"You smell good."

"I ain't had a reason to wear some cologne in a while. I kinda like it. I wanna look good for you, Joey. As best I can. I know I'm just an old guy who delivers flowers and thinks he's a boxer and shit like that, but I want you to think I look good."

Joey breathed in deep and spoke as he exhaled. "I think you're beautiful."

Albert smiled. "You gotta stop saying shit like that to me. You're gonna make me all dumb inside."

They started to walk.

"Some of these plants are taller than us," Joey said with a soft laugh.

"That wall is called the Shoulder Hedge," Albert said. "It protects the perennials."

"The what?"

Albert grinned, ignited by the look of wonder in Joey's pale eyes. "Some of the more *precious* flowers," he said.

Joey's eyes rose up higher. "It looks strong."

"It has to be."

They started to walk deeper into the garden. Joey stopped, caught by the sight of dark pink flowers that slightly resembled poppies. "What are those?"

"Japanese anemone," Albert answered without pause.

"And those?"

"The Latin name is *Aster divaricatus*. But in English we call 'em white wood aster."

Joey walked a few feet ahead. He pointed to a small field of knee-high grass. "Any idea what that's called?"

Albert nodded. "Northern sea oats."

They moved to a footbridge that crossed over the garden and a diagonal stream of water. "That section we were in was called the dark plate. Now we're moving over to the light plate."

"It feels like we're in another world," Joey said.

Albert agreed. "Sometimes I like to pretend that I am."

They reached the other side of the bridge. Joey went to a section of flowers. "Those are Tennessee coneflowers," Albert said. "People say they're an endangered species. In the world of flowers, ya know."

Joey moved again, intrigued by another sight of beauty. "Oh, wow," he said.

"This is my favorite," said Albert. "It's called purple love grass. You see how it soaks up the light of the sunset."

Joey moved closer to Albert, to feel the warmth that generated from his body. "The flowers seem like they're floating," he said.

Albert put an arm around Joey's shoulder and said, "Maybe that's why they make people think of love."

Joey nodded. He felt safe with Albert's arm around him. "Maybe so," he said.

"Come on," said Albert. "I want to show you the cherry trees."

❖

For the next three days, they drove around the city. The van was the only place they could be alone. Joey's roommate had an unpredictable work schedule at the restaurant. He could show up at the dorm room unexpectedly again. Albert feared coming face-to-face with the guy, as he didn't know if he could handle being labeled Joey's boyfriend just yet. He didn't know if that's what he was, but he knew that's what he wanted to be. He felt he needed to protect Joey, to keep an eye on him.

And to prevent the kid from self-destructing.

As the rage thrashing inside of Albert's heart quickly melted to bliss, he felt himself surrender toward the allure of the unknown. It caused the tip of his cock to quiver whenever he thought of Joey. He wanted the mixed-up kid in the worst way. He imagined touching his body, soft and tender. He wanted to kiss him and taste him. After they had watched the sun set at Millennium Park, Albert felt his thoughts turn primal. He longed for roughness. He wanted to feel his hips slamming against Joey's body. He wanted to dominate him, frighten him, devour him. He wanted Joey to love him.

JOEY

As Albert drove them through the city, Joey stole lusty glances at him. He studied his hands and knuckles; the smooth brown skin tinged with ribbons of red. He watched Albert's mouth as he spoke, how his full lips curled into a velvet smile. He felt the thin dark hairs on Albert's right arm tease and tickle his skin when their upper bodies occasionally touched during the sharp, quick turns the delivery van made. Sometimes Joey found himself leaning into the curves, hoping he and Albert would make contact. Whenever they touched, it triggered a rush—a thrill that shot through the nerves in his body and left him with a heart-scraping pang of hunger.

They spent each night sleeping side by side in the back of the van, parked near a row of warehouses not far from the lake. Before they crawled out of their seats and onto a navy blue blanket Joey had stolen from the laundry room in his dorm, Joey would look at Albert in the dark and his face would be illuminated by the green digital glow of the dashboard clock.

"I just want you to know how much you mean to me, Albert," he would say—or some variation of the words. "No one in this world means more to me than you do."

"Even though we hardly know each other?" Albert asked the first night in the van.

Joey reached across the darkness and touched the side of Albert's face, the diminishing black eye. "I think we know each other," he said. "Better than anyone."

Joey took Albert's hand, urging him away from the driver's seat and into the back of the vehicle. They sat together for a moment, silent and apprehensive. They were surrounded by varieties and arrangements of flowers. Deliveries that hadn't made it to their destination on time, and deliveries scheduled for the early morning. They lay down face-to-face, staring into each other's eyes as if the answers to all of their questions were staring back at them.

Joey closed his eyes, overwhelmed by Albert's nearness. Driven by impulse, Albert moved closer so their bodies touched only lightly. Joey welcomed the shared warmth radiating through their clothes. As they drifted into sleep, Joey wrapped his thin arms around Albert, holding him tightly and kissing his forehead. Albert's lips occasionally brushed against the smooth skin on Joey's neck. The two men breathed deep and in unison, drunken by the sweet, tantalizing perfumes of the yellow roses, blue carnations, ruby spice summer sweets, and white magnolias that surrounded them like answered prayers.

ALBERT

You're too goddamned *old*," Bonnie had told him as she shoveled spoonfuls of soggy cereal into her mouth on a morning eleven months ago. Albert remembered every detail of the moment, for it was precisely when he began hating his wife. He loathed her. He blamed Bonnie for every downfall he'd endured in the nineteen years of their marriage. From the moment he had met her in line at a grocery store, when she asked to borrow fifty-five cents and swore to pay him back, she'd done nothing more than suck the inspiration right out of him. It was like she'd slid a straw inside his soul, hydrating herself with every dream of his she crushed.

They lived in a one-bedroom bungalow on a quiet street that wasn't far from the spot where Joey and Albert had met. Bonnie wasn't much of a housekeeper, so the place was always cluttered and smelled like bird shit from the two mourning doves she kept in a black cage in the living room.

She worked at a coffee shop—a place where she'd been a waitress for the two decades Albert had known her—and spent most of her time living in her uniform. It was a tacky ensemble; a short brown and orange checkered polyester skirt, an oversized black peasant blouse, and a grease-stained white scarf stuck to the layers of Aqua Net in her frosted hair. She chain-smoked Marlboros, burped after every beer she consumed, and much preferred watching *Law & Order* marathons rather than conversing with her husband. She'd put on close to fifty pounds in the last five years. She blamed it on everyone else, especially her "bitch of a mother and sorry excuse for a father." Albert hardly recognized his wife anymore. Lately, she seemed unusually paranoid and constantly accused him of cheating on her. She'd become prone to violent outbursts, during which she threatened to burn the house down to the ground—with him inside.

"Who the fuck do you think you *are*?" she said with a snide laugh when Albert told her he'd decided to start training. "You think you're Rocky now? For fuck's sake, you're almost forty."

"It's something I've always wanted to do," he said. "I promised my dad—"

"If I have to hear one more sob story about your dead father, I'll puke."

Albert felt his body tense up. "I'm boxing. I've made up my mind."

"And how much is this little midlife crisis gonna cost me?"

"Not a dime. Shelley said she can give me some hours on the weekends at the book store."

Bonnie pushed her bowl of cereal away and reached for her pack of smokes. "There's things we can use that money for, Albert."

"I'm using it for boxing."

"The guys will be half your age. They'll knock you out with one punch. And you're already ugly."

Before Albert met Joey, he had visions of leaving Bonnie. He imagined instances when he'd tell her what he truly thought about her: how she'd trapped him into marrying her with her soap opera false pregnancy. How he should have married Francine instead. He wanted Bonnie to know that every time he looked at her, he was reminded of the better choices he should have made.

His only regret in life—other than the death of his father—was walking into that grocery store when he was nineteen. She was in front of him in line at the cash register. She had rummaged in a glittery coin purse for a few seconds before turning around and asking, in a polite voice she hadn't used since, if he could help her out. She explained, with a slightly flirtatious smile, that she'd just started a new job at a coffee shop around the corner and the tips had been lousy. Albert felt sorry for her. He thought she had a cute smile, a nice figure. He gave her the fifty-five cents.

He should have just walked away.

FRANCINE

"You know why I'm here," Bonnie said heatedly, both hands on the hips of her uniform.

Francine stood behind the wood-paneled counter, a pair of scissors in one hand and a rose stem in the other. She wore gardening gloves to protect her skin and fingertips from the thorns. The gloves had been a birthday present from Albert two years ago. He never forgot about her on special days, not even after all these years.

It was Friday evening. There wasn't a customer in sight. "I'm closing in a few, so make it quick," Francine said to a wild-eyed Bonnie.

The flower shop was claustrophobic and cold. If it weren't for the quaint window display, pedestrians would stroll right by and never know the place existed. But Francine's customers were loyal. Some of them had known her father. Some of them had even liked him.

Francine ran the shop by herself since she'd spotted the empty retail space from the window of the "L" train she took home one day. By the end of the week, she had applied for her business license and paid cash for the little store, thanks to the generous amount of money her father left her.

Twenty-two years had gone by since, and each one of them had taken their toll on Francine's face and body. Her spirit seemed wounded, too, as if she were waiting to discover something new to hope for in the second half of her life.

Francine seemed transformed, a different person. There wasn't a shred left of the flirtatious girl who could get whatever she wanted with one blink of her eyes. Her hair was cut short in a wash-and-wear shag. She wore little makeup, and found jewelry to be a nuisance when working with flowers. She usually wore jeans, an oversized sweatshirt, and a green apron hanging loosely around her neck.

The flower shop had a temperamental personality similar to Francine's. There were creaks in the wooden floor that couldn't be fixed. The front door hung slightly crooked. The back room was always freezing because the radiator never seemed to work the way it was supposed to. The toilet in the closet-sized bathroom ran constantly, even though at least five plumbers had tried to fix the thing over the last two decades.

But despite the flaws, the place was hers. It had become her family, and her life. Francine spent six days a week there because she really had no place else to go.

Francine sighed, and blinked at the sorry excuse for a woman who stood near the door. She pushed up the sleeves of her festive Halloween sweatshirt and continued to strip the rose stems of their thorns.

"Where is he?" Bonnie asked, peering over the counter and craning her neck so she could see into the room behind the counter.

Francine shifted and stood directly in Bonnie's line of vision, just to annoy her. "If you're looking for Albert, he's not here."

Bonnie paced from one side of the store to the other, a movement only requiring half a dozen steps. She was a caged animal in scuffed heels. "You sure about that?"

"Search the place for all I care," Francine said. "Your husband isn't here. He's out doing his job."

Bonnie's left cheek twitched. Francine knew it was a nervous tic she couldn't control. It happened when she was angry. Her words rose in volume with each syllable, like a singer who working her way up the scale. "He hasn't been home in two nights, Francine!"

"Not my problem," Francine said, and reached for another rose. "Although I'm not surprised."

Bonnie stopped in her tracks. She stood in the middle of the store, surrounded by green and white buckets of flowers, mostly roses and carnations. "You got something to say, then say it," she said, looking Francine in the eye.

Francine put down the scissors and the flowers. She came from behind the counter and stood only inches away from Bonnie, who reeked of nicotine and cheap beer. "Can you blame the man?" she said.

Francine grabbed Bonnie by both shoulders, and turned her toward the reflective door of the refrigerated case where she kept the high-end bouquets. "I mean, look at yourself! Is that what you'd rush home to every night if you were a guy?"

The women's eyes met in the glass.

"Fuck you," said Bonnie.

"Yeah, fuck *me*, Bonnie. I'm not the one whose husband isn't coming home at night." Francine returned to her roses behind the counter.

Bonnie approached. She clung to the edges of the counter with half-eaten fingernails painted a garish shade of bright lavender. "You've never even had a man," she said.

Francine shook the scissors at her gently, a reprimand. "That's not true."

"We both know the only man you've ever loved is my husband."

"I love Albert, but he's damaged goods," Francine said. "You've ruined him for the both of us."

Bonnie leaned over the counter, smashing her purse between it and her breasts. Her voice dropped to a scratchy whisper. "You're a goddamned bitch who wants to destroy my marriage," she said.

Francine didn't budge. "You need to lay off the beer, Bonnie. It's making you delusional. Not to mention what it's done to your figure."

Bonnie tried to straighten her posture but she swayed a little. She steadied herself by reaching for the counter again. Once she was standing on her own, she wiped at her bloodshot eyes with her fingertips. "You've always thought you were better than me. Just because you and Albert grew up in the same neighborhood. Just because you two think I'm some dumb white bitch who can't stick up for herself."

Francine peeled off her gardening gloves and reached for the plastic pump handle on a bottle of hand sanitizer. "Look, he married you, not me."

"Then why isn't he coming home at night? Where the fuck is he? Who's he with, Francine? You tell me since you're the smart one."

Francine maintained the control in her voice. She refused to engage in a pointless shouting match with Bonnie. "My advice is to let him go," she said softly.

Bonnie's rage lessened. Her voice thickened with self-pity. "We've been married for nineteen years."

"And you've made him miserable for every one of 'em."

Bonnie shook her head, and one of her plastic hoop earrings flew off. She bent down and started searching for it on the floor. "That son of a bitch isn't leaving me," she said. "I won't agree to a divorce. I'll fight it."

"Why are you holding on to him? You don't even love him."

Bonnie was now on her hands and knees, crawling and searching the floor desperately. "The sight of him makes me sick. You ever take a real close look at him? He's got rat eyes. He looks like an ape. A goddamn short little ape with a hairy ass and fucked-up teeth. I hope he *is* cheating on me. Let some other girl have to lie beneath that. I should fucking thank her." Bonnie found her earring, stood up, and slid the thing back into her earlobe.

Francine opened the cash register and took out a five. She offered the money to Bonnie and said, "Why don't you go back to Clyde's and buy yourself another beer?"

Bonnie eyed the cash for a second before reaching out and grabbing it. The bill disappeared inside of her bra. "Yeah, I think I'll do that."

Francine closed the register and folded her arms across her chest. "I'll be sure to tell Albert you're looking for him."

Bonnie tucked her purse underneath her arm. "Tell him to come home. We got some shit to figure out between us."

"You don't say."

Bonnie stepped forward again. "Let me ask you something else and then I'll go."

"What do you wanna know?"

"The boxing thing," she said. "That your idea?"

"No," said Francine. "He's always wanted to be a boxer."

"So the part about him promising his father about it, is true?"

"It's true. I wondered what took Albert so long to finally go after his dreams," Francine said. "We all knew he'd make something of himself. He could be the best at whatever he puts his mind to. It makes me sad to think about all the years gone by, wasted. What he could have done." Francine took a quick, sharp breath and then continued, "If nothing would have stood in his way."

"You think I held him back?"

Francine shook her head. "No, I think you dragged him to hell with you. Now he wants out and you're running scared."

Bonnie moved toward the door. "We'll just see about that, Francine," she said. "You don't fucking know me. You don't know what I'm capable of."

"All I know is…if Albert comes in here again with a busted nose, I'm calling the cops. Domestic violence isn't a one-way street, Bonnie."

Bonnie opened the door. "He should have married you when he had the chance," she said.

Francine's mouth curled up into a half-smile. "That's one thing we agree on," she said. "I would have made him a very happy man."

Bonnie shrugged. "I don't know about that. I mean, if he's not coming home to me and he's not banging you on the side, who in the hell is he fucking?"

The door rattled shut behind Bonnie. Francine reached for her gloves and flowers, whistling.

SHELLEY

Bonnie squeezed into the red leather corner booth at Clyde's. She sat directly across from Shelley, who was surrounded by a cloud of smoke swirling from her pipe. A wooden bowl of beer nuts served as the centerpiece on the table they were sharing. The large woman was wearing a red and black silk dress that looked way too expensive for her. A huge hat dipped down across her face and shrouded one eye.

"I'm surprised to see you here," Bonnie said. "I thought you never crawled out of your cave."

"Isn't there a bar stool with your name on it somewhere?" Shelley asked. She reached for her cocktail, a lethal Long Island iced tea in a fishbowl-sized glass. She drummed her red fingernails against the sweaty glass. "I'm not in the mood for you right now, if you don't mind."

"Yeah, yeah, yeah. Any idea where my husband is?"

"No. And if I knew, I wouldn't tell you."

Bonnie lit a cigarette, took a drag. "Seriously, what are you doing out among the living? I thought you were chained up in that rat trap of a store."

"Does it bother you?" Shelley asked. "Having no common sense? Leave me the fuck alone. I'm not interested in your bullshit."

"I was just curious. Jesus. Bite my fucking head off."

"If you need to know, Bonnie, I'm going to the cemetery in the morning."

Bonnie searched around the table for an ashtray and when she didn't see one in close proximity, she flicked her ashes on the floor. "Did someone die?" she asked.

"Twenty-four years ago tomorrow, to be exact."

"Your husband?"

"No, I was never married. I had a son. His name was Mickey."

"Fuck, Shelley. You had a kid? And he *died*?"

"Things you never knew," Shelley took the last sip of her drink.

"How did he die?"

Shelley puffed on her pipe and said, "He took a step off a bridge and landed in the Chicago River."

"Jesus fucking Christ."

"That's what I said when the cops showed up at my door."

"I never wanted children," said Bonnie. "Albert did. But I didn't."

"That's probably a good thing, Bonnie."

"Why do you say that?"

"No offense, but you'd make a lousy mother."

Bonnie nodded and took a final drag on her cigarette. She stubbed it on the floor with the heel of her dirty shoe. "You're probably right. My bitch of a mother did a horrible job."

Shelley almost smiled. "Did she now?"

"How in the hell do you think I ended up here? In this lovely place called Humboldt Park? She dropped me off on the front porch of an aunt's house and I've never saw that skinny bitch again."

"Sometimes it's easier when people die," Shelley said. "Then they don't have the chance to disappoint you."

Shelley could feel Bonnie's eyes on her, watching as she repacked her pipe. A moment passed before Bonnie asked, "Do you know why he did it? Your son?"

Shelley struck a match and brought the tip of the pipe up to her mouth. "I suspect he was gay."

"That must have been rough."

Shelley blew out the flame she held between her fingers. "I think he just wanted to fit in," she said. "The only friend he had was Albert."

Bonnie's shoulders tensed. "Albert knew him?"

Shelley nodded. "They weren't close, but Albert was good to my son. Treated him like just another guy. We lived in the same apartment building back then."

"I never knew that."

"Albert's dad was killed. Then two months later, Mickey committed suicide. I think that's why Albert and I are so close. Our sadness brought us together." Shelley licked her lips and took another hit from her pipe. "Now he's like a son to me."

"Albert never told me any of this shit."

"Well, did you ever ask him? Do you know what his childhood was like?" Shelley asked.

Bonnie reached for the bowl of nuts. "We don't talk much."

"You ever think about leaving him?"

Bonnie cracked a smile. "It's funny you should say that."

"You've got divorce papers in your purse?"

"He's not leaving me."

"No?"

"No. Never. I won't let that happen." Bonnie rubbed the salt and sugar between two fingertips. She wiped her hands on her checkered polyester skirt. Shelley noticed that the material looked as if it were stretched beyond its capability.

"You have to give a man a reason to stay at home, Bonnie."

Bonnie pushed the beer nuts away. They slid across the table toward Shelley. "What's Albert told you?" she asked.

"He doesn't have to say a word. I can tell he's unhappy."

"He hasn't been home in two nights."

"Maybe it's the wake-up call you need."

Bonnie opened her purse again. She took off her earrings and tossed them inside. "Yeah, I'm about to give him a motherfucking wake-up call."

"Good for you."

Bonnie froze for a moment, then relaxed as if some master puppeteer had cut her strings. "Careful, Shelley. You almost sound like you're on my side."

"Don't fool yourself. My loyalty will always lie with Albert. It's just good to see you excited about something besides another episode of *Law and Order*."

"Albert told you I like that program?"

Shelley leaned in. "Albert tells me everything."

"Did he happen to mention who he's cheating on me with?"

"That's not for me to say."

Bonnie lit another cigarette, blowing the smoke upward. "Then I was right? There *is* somebody else."

Shelley shrugged. "Again, it's not for me to say."

Bonnie's eyes surged with a new urgency. It was desperation, bordering on frightening. Shelley wondered what extremes the woman would go to, what she was capable of doing. "Well, at least tell me what to do, then," Bonnie said, her left cheek beginning to quiver.

"I'd step aside and let the man be happy," said Shelley. "We don't need another body in the river."

Bonnie's hand shook nervously as more ashes hit the grimy floor around her feet. "You're saying Albert is happy with somebody else?"

"Is that too difficult for you to imagine?"

Bonnie pointed a finger at Shelley and said, "You sound like Francine."

"I'll take that as a compliment."

She looked Shelley in the eyes. "You don't think much of me, do you?"

"You want me to be honest?"

Bonnie sat back, pressing her spine against the sticky leather seat. "I can take it," she said.

"I think you're a sad, selfish woman who doesn't know any better."

Bonnie shot Shelley a dirty look and dropped her cigarette butt to the floor. "I'm not divorcing Albert."

"Planning to torture him for the rest of his life?"

"I've been married to him since I was nineteen. If I get a divorce now, who in the hell's gonna want me? Look at what that son of a bitch has done to me, Shelley."

"Take it from me. There's nothing wrong with being alone."

Bonnie almost leapt across the table. "Yes, there *is*," she said with a tight mouth. "It's the worst feeling in the world."

"So, what are you going to do about it?"

Bonnie grabbed her purse and slid out of the booth. "If I listen to what you and Francine are saying, I should let him go find happiness and shit like that with some other woman."

Shelley nodded. "It sounds like good advice to me."

"I don't stand a chance in hell, do I?"

Shelley smiled as Joey's face flashed in her mind. The way he looked at Albert in the bookstore had nearly melted her heart. Shelley reached out and handed Bonnie a ten dollar bill. "Here," she said. "Go buy us some drinks. Happy hour is about to start and you look like you need something to take the edge off."

Bonnie nodded and crumpled the money in her hand. "Yeah," she said. "Bourbon always does the trick."

BONNIE

The idea came to Bonnie instantly. She was down on her hands and knees puking into the toilet bowl at two in the morning when the answer came to her with such force she felt like someone had smacked her on the back of the head. But there was no one home except her and the birds, and they were sound asleep in their cage in the living room.

Bonnie reached for toilet paper, but the cardboard roll was empty. She lifted the baggy T-shirt she'd slipped on when she'd staggered drunk into the house a couple of hours ago. She used some of the ratty material to wipe her mouth with.

It was then Bonnie knew exactly what she had to do in the situation.

She leaned forward and heaved as bourbon and vomit burned her throat.

Bonnie would never be a divorced woman.

Becoming a widow was a much better option.

MOLLY

Molly never arrived somewhere empty-handed, and Friday morning was no exception. She parked in front of the pale blue ranch-style house and checked her reflection in the rearview mirror. She contemplated putting on some lipstick, but worried it was in bad taste. After all, Lily's parents had just been killed, and there was no telling whether Joey would come home from Chicago for the funeral or not.

Molly worried no one would show up for the planned funeral tomorrow afternoon. Not because Miranda and Nate's deaths had been gruesome, but because Miranda and Nate had no friends. She'd been a real estate agent. He'd been a house painter. Neither had close bonds with co-workers. They had long since stopped going to church and rarely socialized with anyone—not even their own neighbors. And Molly had spent enough time in their house to know theirs was not a happy family. Still, she'd happily agreed to help with the arrangements.

If they were left in Lily's hands, the bodies might still be at the morgue.

"No lipstick," Molly decided.

She reached over to the passenger seat for a plate of Rice Krispies treats covered snugly with heavy-duty plastic wrap. Molly climbed out of her mother's Volvo, which she had borrowed to run some errands—including buying a new black dress for the funeral. She walked across the front lawn, which was dying, weeks before winter's arrival. The entire place looked uncared for. Newspapers had piled up on the front porch.

Molly knocked on the front door and waited for someone to

answer. She shifted the plate of treats to the opposite hand and knocked again. Finally, she tried the knob. It clicked and the front door creaked open.

"Just leave the treats inside," Molly told herself. She reached down with her free hand and smoothed out invisible wrinkles in her white oxford button-up blouse. She made it a point to never leave the house without looking her best. Her deepest desire was to become the perfect wife and mother. She hoped to catch the eye of the perfect man to make her dreams come true—especially since college had been postponed out of necessity. Her mother had spent the college money put away for Molly's future on new furniture and a week-long trip to Niagara Falls, from which she returned with a completely repulsive new husband named Hank.

"Is anyone home?" she called out.

There was no screen door or foyer. The front door led directly into the living room. Molly stepped inside, onto the drab olive balding-in-patches carpet, and closed the door behind her with a gentle tap of one of her new black mule-styled shoes. "Hello?" she called. Her eyes moved around the room. In the far corner was the chair where Miranda sat, hour after hour, needlepointing every night of her life. The worn-out sofa, where Nate fell asleep whenever he could. It was the two places Molly remembered seeing them the most. She shivered a little, as if their ghosts had pinched her skin. Molly moved through the archway and into the kitchen—another empty room.

"Hello?" she called out again. The floor beneath her feet vibrated a little. The washing machine? Could Lily be down in the basement doing laundry? It seemed like an odd thing to do the day before your parents were to be buried.

She put the plate down on the kitchen table next to a pile of mostly unopened mail. There was a letter on cream-colored paper lying on top. The letter was unfolded. Molly glanced down and recognized Joey's messy penmanship.

"He's always had atrocious handwriting," Molly said out loud.

Molly contemplated reading the letter. She knew she shouldn't, it was personal and none of her business. But her curiosity always got the best of her. She picked up the letter, held the thick paper between her fingers, and read as quickly as she could, fearful she would get caught.

Lily,

By now you must have realized what's been done. What you don't know is that I played a part in it—or at least I was supposed to. I'm sure you wanted this even more than I did. We both know that she never loved us. And you hated the sight of her. What you don't know is that Dad was not supposed to be in the car. She must have insisted that he go with her, promised him she'd drop him off at the lighthouse. He loved that place.

I've been studying and planning for this for over a year now. When I came home for those two weeks last Christmas, Cooper made an excellent teacher. He's always been so good with cars. But then again Cooper is good at everything. I should know, right? Then again, you should, too.

You wouldn't believe how easy it was to do this. I was there and gone and no one even knew. I gave my roommate cash and he put the round trip plane ticket on his credit card for me. He spent two years in juvie a few years ago so I doubt he'd say anything to anyone about me sneaking off to Maine for a few hours on Tuesday. For all I know, he could have killed someone. Wouldn't that be a riot? I went off to college to share a dorm room with a murderer. Imagine if it were true, what he and I would have in common.

You're probably not laughing. You're probably thinking—

There was an angry voice behind Molly. Startled, she jumped and the letter slipped from her hands, floating down to the table. "You shouldn't read things that don't belong to you," Lily said from the doorway to the basement. She held the handle of a suitcase in her hand. It was behind her, tilting forward on its back wheels.

Molly found it hard to breathe. She felt like the kitchen walls were moving, squeezing in to crush her. "What *is* this?" she asked. Lily glared at her. Molly felt self-conscious, her face burning in a mixture of embarrassment, shame, and anger.

She didn't know what to do with her hands.

"What does it sound like?" Lily said. "It's a confession, I think."

"Is this for real? Joey killed your parents?"

"I always knew you could read," Lily said, with a twisted smile.

"This is insane."

"Oh, come on, now. You know us," said Lily. "You know my family. We're fucking nuts, right?"

"It's *murder*," Molly said.

"And he's your best friend. Ever since the two of you were in diapers. So, what does that make you? Probably a hot contender for one of Oprah's sofa cushions if you play your cards right," Lily said. "Write a book. Sell it. Make millions. Everyone's doing it these days."

Molly shook her head. "Not me."

Molly moved to leave but Lily stepped to the side, blocking her path. She glanced over Molly's shoulder at the kitchen table. "You brought Rice Krispies treats. How thoughtful," Lily said, her smile looking forced and insincere. "My mother drives off a cliff and you bring me sticky squares of marshmallow and cereal. That should make it all better."

Molly's eyes darted down to the suitcase. "Are you going somewhere?"

"As a matter of fact, I am," she said. "As soon as the laundry is done."

"But, why? I mean, do you have to go *now*? The funeral is tomorrow."

"I'm sure you'll be there, Little Miss Event Coordinator. Be sure to give my parents my best. Tell them how sorry I am that I couldn't be there to watch them sink six feet underground."

Lily had changed so much in the last year, Molly reflected. She looked nothing like that girl with blond crimped hair who used to pout her away around Portland in a black tutu, fishnets, and a tuxedo shirt.

Lily had reinvented herself. She had long hair that was a gorgeous shade of sable brown. Sometimes she curled it or wore it up in a high ponytail. She often wore simple cotton dresses consisting of tiny floral patterns, or a pair of jeans with a cute blouse and some sandals. Her nails were manicured and her makeup tasteful, her jewelry minimal. She was mistaken for a young mother frequently, a well-mannered, wholesome girl. Until a stream of profanities slipped out of her well-glossed mouth.

But the biggest change in Lily was her eye. She had undergone several treatments over the last few years to correct her amblyopia. For a period of time she wore a patch; she referred to it as "my pirate phase." The eye was much stronger now and wavered only slightly when she was emotional.

"Lily, where are you going that's so important?" Molly asked.

Lily moved farther into the kitchen, trailing the suitcase behind her. "Chicago sounds nice this time of year," she said. "Though I heard it snowed on Wednesday. I should probably take a coat."

Molly turned back to the letter. She reached down and picked it up. "You're going to confront him? You're going to turn him in?"

Lily parked the suitcase near the stove. She went to the coffee maker on the counter and started to make a fresh pot. "Who? Joey?"

Molly knew she sounded too eager, but couldn't help herself. "You want answers. Maybe revenge."

"You need to stop watching Lifetime movies," Lily said. "I'm not going to Chicago to see Joey. I could give a fuck about him. Have you had coffee this morning? Would you like a cup?"

Molly nodded and then asked, "Then why? I mean, you've never even been to Chicago."

Lily took two mugs out of the cupboard. One of them read "World's Greatest Mom" on it, a gift that Molly had given Miranda on Mother's Day years ago. "I'm going to meet him," Lily announced.

Molly sat down at the table, dizzy and weak. "Who?"

Lily gestured to the piece of paper in Molly's hands. "The boy in the letter. The roommate. The guy that Joey shares his dorm with."

Molly glanced down as if his picture had been included, as if they could somehow see this stranger's face in the words that Joey had handwritten. "You know this guy?"

Lily shook her head, reached for a coffee filter in a drawer. "No. I've never meet him before. But he sounds kinda hot, don't you think?"

Molly stared at her in disbelief. "He sounds like a criminal to me."

Lily stopped. She stood with the coffee pot in her hand near the sink. "I hate that about you, Molly. How you're always such a goody-goody."

Molly straightened her posture and tossed her highlighted hair over a shoulder. "I just believe in doing the right thing."

Lily tilted her head and looked at her guest with an odd expression. "Then why didn't you ever get a nose job?" she asked.

Molly's cheeks ignited again. "I like myself just the way God made me, thank you very much."

"Yes, I suppose you do. But there's always room for improvement. I mean, look at what I've been able to do with myself," Lily said. She pushed a button and coffee started to brew. "I saw one of my teachers from high school the other day," she continued. "She was coming out of Target when I was walking in. She didn't know it was me at first. Then after I told her who I was...she said I looked remarkable. That was the word she used. *Remarkable.*"

Molly nodded and slipped the letter into her purse when Lily wasn't watching. "Everyone says you look great," she said.

Lily turned to her. "God, who's *everyone*?"

"Everyone from school, I guess."

"You still talk to them?" Lily asked. "What do they say about me?"

Molly shrugged. "People say you've changed. They talk about how beautiful you are now."

"I always forget you were a year behind me. But then, you're so fucking smart, I'm surprised they didn't let you skip a hundred grades."

"I just like school a lot," Molly said.

Lily filled the mugs with hot coffee. "Then how in the hell did you become friends with my brother? Last I heard, he's flunking out."

Molly sighed with heavy disappointment. "He gets distracted easily."

"Milk and sugar?"

Molly reached for a bowl of sugar cubes that were in the center of the table. She pulled them toward her. "The sugar's here," she said. "But I'd like some milk, please."

"It's not soy. It's two percent. Is that okay?"

"Just a splash."

Molly met Lily's eyes when she walked over to the table and placed a mug down in front of her. Molly looked up and asked the words, "Did he really do it?"

Lily looked down at her, with a half-smile, half-smirk and said, "You read the letter. What do *you* think?"

Molly reached out and grabbed Lily's arm to stop her from walking away. "You tell me."

Lily pulled her arm away from Molly. "I think he was going for shock value," she said. "Joey hasn't spent time with me in the last year so he doesn't know I've changed. He's been away building bird houses or whatever it is he does in architect school. He thought I would get that letter and it would make me proud of him. But he was probably worried that I'd do myself in or something sick and beautiful. And you know what? The old me might have done something like that. But the *new* me...I'm ready for a road trip."

"Road trip?" Molly repeated. "You don't even have a driver's license."

Lily smiled. "No, but *you* do."

Molly shook her head adamantly. "I can't go to Chicago with you."

"Afraid you'll miss a funeral?"

Molly stood up to leave. She wrapped an arm through the straps of her purse, squishing the car keys in her hand. "My mom needs her car back in a few hours," she said. "Chicago is over a thousand miles away."

Lily's voice stopped her. "Your mother doesn't deserve you," she said.

Molly turned back. "What?"

"She ruined you, Molly. You don't owe her a goddamn thing."

"I won't do it, Lily. She's my mother."

"That didn't matter to her when she was picking out a new sofa with your college fund. Or when she was getting fucked stupid at Niagara Falls by Hank the Herpes Man."

Molly looked stunned. "It was chlamydia," she corrected Lily.

"You're trapped in Portland and you shouldn't be. You belong at an Ivy League school in some stuck-up sorority getting felt up by the Future Republicans of America. Instead, look at what your mother gave you. A fucked-up job selling shoes at fucking *Payless*."

Molly took a breath, a moment. She looked at Lily and then at the suitcase. Her eyes drifted over to the coffee pot on the counter. "Do you have a Thermos?" she asked finally.

Lily stared and blinked, confused. "I'm sure my dad had one. It has to be around here somewhere. Why?"

In the span of a second, Molly decided to take a chance, live dangerously. When she handed Lily the car keys, she was already regretting her decision. She breathed in deep, exhaled, and said, "If we split the driving, we can be there by tomorrow morning."

❖

They'd been on the road for an hour. The two women had fallen into a pit of silence. Lily was behind the wheel of the Volvo. She hummed the bass line to the song on the radio, as if she were trying to keep herself alert. Molly was lost in deep thought. She couldn't comprehend the horrible crime Joey claimed to have committed. How could someone she'd known and trusted for her entire life do something so awful? She wanted to see him, face-to-face, and hear him confess in his own voice.

Lily cleared her throat. "Let's stop soon."

"Already?" Molly asked with a raised eyebrow.

"Yeah. I'm craving nachos."

Molly made a face. "Nachos?"

Lily nodded. "You know the kind with chili and cheese? That's what I want."

Molly winced and said, "That sounds disgusting."

Lily glanced at her and rolled her eyes. "Don't tell me you're a vegetarian or something scary like that."

"No. I just don't eat much junk food."

Lily shot her a look. "Does it hurt you? To be so perfect all the time, I mean."

Molly glared back. "I'm not perfect."

"But you want to be. You're like a fucking soccer mom in training."

Molly opened the glove compartment out of curiosity. She found a small tube of raspberry-scented hand lotion. She uncapped the tube and squeezed some into her palm. "I don't think there's anything wrong with setting certain standards for yourself."

"Certain standards? Who in the hell talks like that?" Lily asked. "Give me some of that stuff. It smells good."

Molly leaned over and let a few drops of lotion fall into Lily's open hand. "Just because I don't come from much doesn't mean I need to act like white trash," she said.

Lily put a smudge of the lotion on both sides of her nose. "I suppose eating chili cheese nachos means I should live in a trailer?"

Molly shrugged. "Eat whatever you want."

The silence returned as both women slipped back into their deep thoughts. This was the most time that Lily and Molly had spent together. As each mile passed, it became increasingly clear that they had little— if anything—in common, other than Joey.

Lily broke the silence. "You got quiet on me all of a sudden."

Molly looked out the window. "Why do you think he did it?" she asked. "How can someone kill their own mother?"

"We're talking about Miranda. She was a hard-ass with a cold heart. She hated me and Joey. She told us so."

Molly slipped on a pair of sunglasses. "That's not a reason to kill someone."

"She turned her back on him, Molly. She rejected him."

"When?"

"The night of the Bible study group. Remember?"

Molly shook her head. "I only heard bits and pieces of it after. I just thought it was hearsay."

"Stop using words like that. You're twenty-one, for fuck's sake."

"Sorry. I'll do my best to sound like I have no class until we get to Chicago."

Lily grinned with delight and her eyes lit up. "Mom walked in on Joey and Cooper that night," she said. "And the entire Bible study group heard the whole thing from our living room. It was fucking classic."

Molly pushed the sunglasses farther up the bridge of her nose. "What do you mean 'walked in on'?"

Lily gave her a look of disbelief. "Joey was giving Cooper a blow job."

"Cooper's gay?"

"No, Cooper is not gay. Believe me. He was high."

Molly smiled. "Isn't Cooper *always* high?"

"Who knows? I don't talk to that fucker anymore."

Molly looked confused. "I thought you guys still hang out."

"After my brother's mouth was on him, I really couldn't touch him without puking. Just the thought of it makes me sick. Even now," Lily said. "I mean, we all knew Joey was a fag. But Cooper? Gimme a break. Joey took advantage of him when he was high."

Molly nodded in agreement. But a few seconds later, she wondered aloud, "What if it was the other way around?"

Lily's knuckles paled around the steering wheel. "No fucking way. I don't believe that for a second."

"Let's ask Joey when we see him."

"Molly, he killed his own mother. Do you really think Joey's not capable of lying, too?"

Molly turned in her seat and faced Lily. "Joey isn't a bad person," she said.

Lily let out a small laugh and then said, "Yes, he is."

"He's not. He's angry."

"He's a fucking psycho! He's a predator," Lily said. "You read the letter. He was planning that shit for a year. That means he was wishing her a Merry Christmas and a Happy Birthday and carving turkey with us and the whole time he was thinking about knocking her off. That's crazy. No wonder why he's totally avoided me."

Molly shook her head. "I'm not saying what he did was right."

"Yeah, you *think*?!"

"I'm just trying to make sense of this."

"Yeah, so am I."

"Joey's been my best friend forever," Molly said. "I never knew there were secrets between us. We tell each other everything."

Lily glanced over at Molly and they made eye contact for a second. "It just goes to show that you never really know somebody," she said. "I still think you're a goody-goody and you usually annoy me with your perfect princess shit, but I have to tell you…I'm glad you decided to come with me to Chicago."

The tinge of sadness hanging in Lily's voice took Molly by surprise. She raised her sunglasses up and put them on top of her head. "Wait," she said, "are you upset your parents are gone?"

Lily shook her head, but the tears welling up in her eyes betrayed her. "Fuck it," she said. "That's all I can say right now is *fuck it*."

"Lily…are you crying?"

Lily wiped away the tears falling down her face. "It's just…my father…he didn't ask for any of this. Miranda was a bitch and she deserved to die. But not my dad." Lily struggled to catch her breath as if the emotions she felt were too heavy to hold inside of her body. "He just painted houses and stayed out of everyone's way."

Molly nodded and said softly, "Maybe he was happy to go."

This seemed to make Lily feel better as her tears subsided. "Yeah, maybe," she sniffed.

"Hey," Molly said with a cheerful smile in her voice. "I have an idea."

Lily rolled her eyes again "You sound like a human get-well card, Molly. Is everything always so chipper in your world?"

Molly continued to smile. It was contagious, so within seconds Lily was smiling, too. "Let's get off at the next exit," Molly said. "I bet they have chili cheese nachos there."

"Yeah, all right," Lily said and then added, "I think I need a Diet Pepsi, too."

They didn't have the stamina to drive straight through to Chicago. At midnight on the outskirts of Cleveland, they pulled into the parking lot of a motel after deciding it was the least scary-looking out of their choices.

They parked near a swimming pool that had been drained for the season and staggered toward the vacancy sign in the window of the wood-paneled lobby.

Lily attempted to flirt with the bald front desk clerk, trying to get them a cheaper rate on a room. He charged them full price anyway. "I know what girls like you are after. Both of you need Jesus!"

Lily crossed herself before flipping the guy off. She dragged Molly to their room on the second floor. It faced the parking lot, the freeway, and a neon sign that sputtered and begged to be put out of its misery.

They collapsed on the twin beds and stared up at the ceiling.

"This bedspread smells," Lily said, "like piss."

"So does mine." Molly gagged, pinching her nose closed with two fingers. "I have some perfume in my purse."

"Fuck the perfume. Do you have any disinfectant?"

They both laughed and spread out their arms like they were

making snow angels on top of the orange satin quilts. Lily moaned with exhaustion. Molly began to laugh and couldn't stop for nearly two minutes.

"What's the matter with you?" Lily asked with a grin. "Did you get high in the car and forget to tell me?"

"No." Molly giggled. "I was just imagining the look on my mother's face when she checks her messages on her cell phone."

"You should have sent her a text message instead."

"Are you kidding? She'd never be able to figure out how to read it."

"Maybe Hank will have to give her a hand," said Lily. "Mr. Chlamydia."

"No," Molly said. "He's more useless than she is."

"That's hard to imagine."

Molly's laughter faded. She sat up. "Oh God, I can't believe I did this. I must be out of my mind."

"Hey, it's not every day a girl has to go to Chicago to find out why her best friend murdered his parents."

"When you put it like that—" Molly erupted into laughter again.

"It makes it more true?" Lily asked.

"God forgive me. I shouldn't be laughing at a time like this."

"I am on the inside," Lily said. "I'm fucking hysterical and no one knows it."

Molly lay back down. "I feel insane right now," she said. "I think I'm just exhausted. How many states have we driven through today?"

Lily bit one of her fingernails and said, "I have no idea how Joey pulled this off."

Molly rolled over on to her stomach and looked at Lily. "Do you think he'll get away with it?"

Lily nodded. "He already has. The insurance company called me this morning. They're cutting us checks by the end of the month."

"Wow," Molly said. "What are you going to do about the house?"

Lily kicked off her sandals. "I don't know. Do you want it?"

"God, no. I hate the décor."

"It's paid for," Lily said. "I'll probably just sell it."

"What about you?" Molly asked. "Are you going to stay in Portland?"

Lily grinned. "That depends on Joey's hot roommate."

Molly attempted to fluff up one of her pillows. "You'll probably just have sex with him."

"Yeah, I probably will."

"I wish I could do that."

Lily rolled her eyes. "Don't tell me you're a virgin."

Molly shot her a look. "You make it sound like a bad thing."

"You're like one of those sappy family dramas where everybody bakes cookies together in the kitchen. *Yuck!*"

"That doesn't sound so bad," Molly said. "I'd love to meet a man who's not afraid to bake a cookie or two for me."

Lily opened her purse and took out a metal nail file. "Yeah, good luck with that one."

"I haven't been lucky so far. That's for sure."

"Well, what kind of guys do you like?"

Molly shrugged. "I'm not sure yet."

"Well, what kind of guys are you attracted to?"

Molly sat up again and pulled her feet underneath her. "If I tell you—"

Lily sat up too as if a bolt of new energy had surged through her. "You have a secret, I can tell."

"I haven't even told Joey about this yet."

Lily's eyes widened. She pulled her hair back out of her face. "Oh God, I love it. I'm never the first person to know anything."

"You have to promise me not to—"

"Yeah, yeah, yeah. Scouts honor and all that bullshit. Now, *tell me.*"

Molly took a breath before she spoke. "I think I'm attracted to black guys."

Lily's mouth dropped open. "Oh my God," she said, "you fucking slut!"

Molly blushed. "Lily!"

"That's so hot."

Molly exhaled. "You think so?"

"I don't think I could do it with a black guy, but—oh my God, Molly, your mother will completely freak out if you marry a black man."

"I know," Molly said with a grin. "I can't wait."

Lily stood up and walked to the television. She pushed the power button but nothing happened. "Is this thing even plugged in?"

"Hey," Molly said. "Let me ask you something."

"Ask away."

"You give me such a hard time about being a goody-goody, but you've changed, too."

Lily tossed Molly a look over her shoulder. "In what way?"

"You look different," said Molly. "You dress different."

Lily caught a glimpse of herself in the cracked mirror above the bureau. "I've just mellowed," she said to Molly in the glass. "But I'm not some do-gooder bitch, if that's what you mean."

Molly smiled. "I like you better now."

"Thanks. But don't expect me to teach Sunday school with you anytime soon."

Molly reached for her purse. She was dying of thirst and needed a soda from the machine she had spotted downstairs. "I think you're way too pretty for Cooper," she said.

Lily walked to the window and pulled back the curtain. "Does it feel like the air is on to you? It's hotter than hell in here."

Molly wiped her forehead with the back of her hand and then dug out a handful of change from the bottom of her purse. "Does the window open?"

"Probably not." Lily turned to the window. The broken neon sign tossed a rainbow of shadows through the glass that strobed on Lily's skin. "Oh, shit," she said. The color in her face drained. "Molly, please tell me that you moved the car."

Molly tossed the handful of change on the bedspread and stood up. Panic tickled the back of her knees when she joined Lily at the window. "What are you talking about?" she asked.

Lily pointed to the empty space below, where they had left the Volvo only minutes before. "The fucking car is gone!"

COOPER

Cooper McGill was golden. He moved like sunshine across the front lawn. His fingertips gripped the metal handle of the red mower, revving the engine, and letting it idle. Rivulets of sweat dripped down his bare chest, leaving his always-erect nipples and washboard stomach damp. He reached into the back pocket of his baggy jean shorts for the black T-shirt shoved into it and wiped his face with it. The back of his shorts dipped down so low that the white skin below his spine and the top of his ass was exposed. He kept his dark brown hair messy and unkempt always, a subtle suggestion that Cooper McGill had just finished having sex. His body was toned, but not muscular. His eyes were the dark bluish gray of an overcast sky. And his voice was deep—deeper than most guys in the neighborhood.

Cooper was not a particularly bright man, carrying a low C average in school. He never spoke about any career plans or showed any desire to leave Portland to explore the world. His conversations usually focused on the three things that mattered most to him: marijuana, Pink Floyd, and his eight-year-old Rottweiler, Biscuit.

Cooper was fantasy material for many, inducing his admirers to hours of self-pleasure envisioning the seventeen-year-old moving rhythmically inside their hips.

Cooper didn't know that two of his most ardent watchers lived in the same house. Brother and sister simultaneously and surreptitiously viewed him from behind the furtive edges of the curtains shrouding their bedroom windows. Their hidden hands roamed their own bodies, while wishing it was Cooper touching them. How could they ever thank their mother enough for hiring him to mow their lawn every Saturday afternoon? All summer long—from the last week of May until Labor Day weekend—Lily and Joey found any excuse they needed to rush to the sanctuary of their bedrooms, where they became voyeuristic viewers to the skin show an unknowing Cooper provided for them.

Lily and Cooper were the same age and had a history of making out in dark corners of house parties. After a few plastic cups of cheap beer, Cooper searched her out in the crowd of teenaged girls. He knew her name but always seemed to forget it whenever he saw her, so he typically greeted her with a resonating, "Hey." She would look up at him with that lazy eye of hers and breathe his name like it was Jesus come down from the cross to save only her.

They would make out and grope each other for an hour or two before Cooper became bored and faded away into the sea of skateboarders and wannabes. He'd find a girl who didn't matter and nail her in the bathroom. By the time he was done and washed his dick off in a dirty sink, Lily was gone.

At school, they never spoke. If she passed him in the hall, Lily tossed him a glance reminding him that one day, he'd be able to take her in a heartbeat, but he would have to wait until she was ready. He never smiled and rarely acknowledged her. Not because he was rude—he was usually too stoned to notice.

LILY

Lily started buying pot from Cooper right after she turned fifteen and discovered the intense pleasure a top loading Maytag washing machine offered a girl with a crush on a hot boy. She smoked out a few times at parties and knew she loved the stuff. She sent word to Cooper via one of his disciples that she wanted to buy some. They made the exchange just outside of the girls' locker room, right before Lily tried out successfully for the varsity volleyball team. "Here," he had said before slipping the rolled-up sandwich bag of pot into her sweaty palm. She slid the cash into his front pocket with hopeful, ball-brushing fingers. He walked away without another word.

Lily knew that she and Cooper would eventually take things further than a hot make-out session at a low-lit get-together. The thought of sleeping with Cooper constantly haunted her. After three years of near-maddening desire for him, Lily was more ready than ever to lure Cooper to her room, where she planned to let him do whatever he wanted. She hoped he wouldn't forget about her and toss her aside, like he did with every other girl he banged.

On Saturday afternoons, her moans scaled up her pink and green wallpaper and skipped across the chiffon top of her canopy bed. If she tilted her head just right, she could watch Cooper through a slightly pulled-back curtain while she used two fingers to spell out the letters in his name against the damp heat of her body.

JOEY

Joey was two years younger than Cooper, but was already devising a plan of seduction. His lust for Cooper—for any man—was new to him. A few days after an intense dream about Cooper left him with an aching hard-on for a few hours after waking up, Joey began studying Cooper's body in the summer sun, searching for a flaw in the perfection. He imagined tasting Cooper's skin, grabbing his cock, and watching him writhe with ecstasy beneath his touch.

The first time he realized he wanted Cooper, Joey was in his bedroom, sitting at the foot of the bed. A blue raspberry Popsicle was between his lips, melting down his hand and fingers. He licked his palm of the sticky, sweet juice and reached for the box of tissues on his nightstand. The box fell and hit the hardwood floor. Joey reached down for the box. As he raised his body back up to a sitting position, he peered through a crack in the curtains to the world outside. The lawn mower sounded violent as it whirred across the front yard, slicing down blades of grass with the vengeance of a heroic swordfighter.

At the sight of Cooper, Joey lifted up his T-shirt and pushed the tip of the Popsicle against his nipple. He watched the skin around it tighten and chill. His hand went to his crotch like an afterthought at the sight of Cooper, shirtless and glistening in the lunchtime sun.

It was the first time Joey touched his cock and thought about another guy. He resisted at first, worrying that Cooper might somehow see him or know what he was thinking. Joey swallowed down the last few frozen bits of his Popsicle and welcomed the cold sting in his mouth and throat and wondered how warm Cooper's tongue would feel. Joey succumbed to the trigger of heat permeating his body before it erupted between his legs.

As summer began to slip away and an icy edge started clipping the afternoon air, Cooper killed the male flesh show by wearing a T-shirt and jeans. This brought frustration to Joey and Lily, who mutually, silently, prayed for an Indian summer. Lily sulked around the house and yelled at the television screen when contestants on game shows got obvious answers wrong. Joey continued to ignore everyone in his house, skipping dinner as often as he could. Instead, he searched the Internet on his laptop for nude photos of hot guys who resembled Cooper. This only added to the throbbing discontentment searing the remnants of the summer lust, causing Joey's shoulders to bend forward in what appeared to be a permanent droop.

It was during the first week of the new school year when Joey came up with the ultimate plan to live out a fantasy or two with Cooper McGill. It would involve some vodka, some pot, some porn. Joey waited another week before spinning his plan into action.

Joey had no doubt that Cooper loved women. He trophied them like a deer hunter and left a long line of desperate and heartbroken de-virginized victims haunting the sad halls of their high school. They waited, with tearstained and bloodshot eyes, for Cooper to come back to them with a spineless, desperate hope quivering in their suicidal smiles of shame. Joey considered what he planned to do to Cooper to serve two purposes. It would certainly satisfy his summer-long desire to explore Cooper's naked body.

But it would also serve as a form of retribution for those girls Cooper had wronged.

On Monday of the week Joey seduced Cooper McGill, he stole a bottle of store-brand vodka from the supermarket. On Tuesday, he pinched some pot from the jewelry box in his sister's room. On Wednesday, he snuck down to the basement to his father's secret stash of VHS porn tapes and picked out one he thought Cooper would enjoy. On Thursday morning, he joined Cooper as he walked from the student parking lot to his first class of the day.

All Joey had to say was, "Wanna hang out tonight? I've got some vodka and some killer pot."

"What time should I be there?" Cooper replied.

"Six thirty is cool," Joey said. "But my mom doesn't like it if a lot people come over at once."

"I can come by myself. It's cool."

"Sweet."

"Is your sister gonna be there?" Cooper asked.

"You didn't hear? She hooked up with some Mexican guy on the swim team."

"That's one lucky *amigo*. Your sister is hot."

"But her eye—"

"I know," Cooper said. "It looks like she got banged too hard."

❖

Joey rushed home from school that day. He jacked off, too amped up with anticipation. He showered and changed his clothes. Made his bed. Avoided his mother, who sat at the kitchen table bent over a checkbook, a calculator, and a stack of bills. He rolled two fat joints with the pot he stole from Lily. Put a book of matches in the front pocket of his shorts. Double-checked Lily wasn't, and wouldn't, be home. Put a bottle of water next to his bed in case he got cottonmouth while sucking off Cooper. And loaded the video into the archaic VCR machine he'd brought down from the attic and hooked up to his television last weekend.

It seemed like everything was set. There was just one thing Joey had overlooked. It was Thursday.

Miranda knocked once and entered the bedroom. She had changed her clothes in the matter of minutes since Joey passed her in the kitchen. She was wearing her Sunday best: a simple long-sleeved black dress with a high collar buttoned up to her chin as if she worried part of her soul would escape and seep out of the fabric. Joey grinned at the sight of her. It didn't look natural on her. It was like a Halloween costume six weeks too early. She looked like a witch, who just needed a hat to complete the look.

"What?" Joey asked, without making eye contact.

"Stay in your room tonight," she said, one hand on her hip and the other on the door knob.

"Why?"

She sighed and her mouth tightened. "It's Thursday."

"So?"

Miranda stared at her son in disbelief. "I host the Bible study group every Thursday night, Joseph," she said. "You live here, too. How are you oblivious to this?"

Joey reached for a school book next to his laptop. "I have a friend coming over to study with."

One of Miranda's thick penciled eyebrows shot up. "Who?" she asked.

"Cooper McGill. He'll be here any second now."

Miranda's hands moved up to her slicked hair. She ran them against the sides of her scalp as if a few strands loosened and needed smoothing back into place. She tugged on the silver barrette holding back her ponytail and seemed satisfied it was secure. "Isn't he a senior?" she said.

"Yeah. So. I'm tutoring him."

That seemed to pacify his mother because she turned away and said, as she left the room and closed his door, "Well, keep it down in here. You know how much I hate disruptions."

❖

Cooper arrived ten minutes early. He lingered in the kitchen for a moment, dropping gentle reminders to Miranda she owed him for two weeks' worth of lawn mowing. Joey stood in the archway between the living room and the kitchen, watching his mother flirt and fawn over the teenager like he was a secret lover she was planning to run away with. He wondered if she also found Cooper desirable. Did she watch him from her bedroom window with the pining of a woman whose tough exterior needed to be smashed open with passion? Maybe if Cooper had taken Miranda by the hand to her bedroom and pleasured her for a few hours, she might emerge as a woman with newfound kindness. Maybe she'd even become a good mother.

Cooper leaned up against the kitchen counter with both hands lying flat against the cool surface. He was wearing his blue and gold letterman's jacket, a T-shirt with a grease stain just below his chest, and a pair of jeans hanging loose from his hips. His hair was wild and begged to be touched with slow, caressing fingers.

Miranda moved closer to him, reaching around his body for the pink box of donuts he playfully blocked her from. The way her cheeks flushed and her eyes darted all over him made Joey realize exactly why Miranda hired Cooper to mow their lawn.

She wanted to fuck him, too.

"Here," she said, handing him some cash. He took the money from her and shoved it into a pocket. "I've included a tip for you, so be nice and let me have my donuts. My guests will be arriving any moment."

"That's too bad," Cooper said with a wink.

Miranda leaned forward, as if to whisper something in Cooper's ear.

Joey coughed to announce his presence. Miranda didn't react to the sound. To do so would suggest she was doing something wrong.

Cooper stepped aside and Miranda scooped up the bakery box with swift hands. She turned away from Cooper and passed her son. It was like Joey weren't there. Miranda moved to the centrally placed coffee table in the room and began arranging a serving platter.

"Your dad's a lucky guy," Cooper said, loud enough for Miranda to hear. And she did. Joey could tell because she smiled at a donut as she placed it on the platter. It was the first time Miranda's scowl disappeared in at least two years.

"Wanna go hang out in my room?" Joey asked.

"Yeah, sure," Cooper said with a slight nod.

Miranda's voice stopped them. "Cooper," she said. "Finish this one for me, will you? I've bitten off more than I can chew."

Miranda extended her hand out to him and in her palm was a half-eaten custard-filled donut. Cooper took the donut and devoured it in a somewhat barbaric act. Miranda responded like she'd been tickled. Cooper glanced up to Miranda's mouth. "You have a little something on your lip," he said.

Joey watched as his mother reached up to her mouth with two fingers and wiped away the smudge of leftover custard overlooked somehow. She put both fingers between her lips and licked them dry. "Isn't that custard divine?" she asked. "I wonder what they put in it to make it taste so sweet."

Joey swallowed the bitter bile creeping up his throat. He felt devastated. His mother was clearly not the woman her children and husband thought she was. She'd been underestimated. She, too, craved sex.

As he waited for Cooper to follow him out of the living room and down the narrow hallway to his bedroom, things began making sense to Joey. He understood the reason behind his mother's twelve- or fourteen-hour Saturdays she claimed to be spending showing houses to clients her family never met or heard about again. The ring of keys she kept in her purse that unlocked the front doors of empty houses seemed to have a new purpose in Joey's mind. The cell phone she never allowed anyone else to answer out of fear—as she had explained to them—they would inadvertently insult a prospective home buyer was her secret connection to men her family knew nothing about.

As his mother shooed Cooper out of the room with a giggle and a smile that promised they would see each other again, the rage Joey felt for her faded and died. It was replaced by a void. Within seconds, he felt nothing for his mother. Nothing at all.

And that scared him.

It took Joey less than a half an hour to get Cooper's clothes off.

The vodka came first. Joey snagged a plastic cup from the bathroom seconds before Cooper followed him to his bedroom. After five shots, the edges of Cooper's words started blurring.

"Howwwww commmmme meeeee and yooooou neverrrrr hhhhhung out beforrrrrre?" Cooper asked.

They were sitting shoulder to shoulder on the edge of Joey's twin bed. The night light in the wall socket near the closet door struggled to project enough light to fill the dark room.

"I dunno," Joey said. "Probably because you were too busy with my sister."

"Wherrrrre is shhhhhe tonight?"

Joey grinned. "Making tacos," he said. He reached for the first joint. "Wanna smoke?"

Cooper tried to focus on the joint but his eyes were heavy. He opened his mouth, but only nodded in response.

Joey struck a match and their faces were illuminated by the amber glow. Had Cooper been sober, he might have noticed the desire flashing in Joey's gaze. He might have been able to protect himself from the twisted guiles of a family he never meant to become involved with. He might have grabbed his letterman's jacket hanging from the back of the chair at Joey's desk and bolted from the house, never looking back. He might have escaped. But Cooper licked his lips, pinched the end of the fat joint, and instant relief crept across his face. He inhaled and the tip of the joint burned like a warning sign.

Cooper offered the joint to Joey, who politely refused. "I've already had enough," he said in a sober voice. "Before you came over."

"Alllll of thisssss isssss forrrrr meeeee?"

"I just want you to feel good, Cooper. Don't you think you deserve that?"

Cooper nodded and dropped the joint. It hit the bedspread, singeing a hole in the paisley-patterned quilt. Joey's reflexes were still intact. He picked the joint up and handed it to Cooper again. "Don't burn the house down," Joey cautioned with a small laugh.

There were distractions outside then, noises in the driveway. On the lawn. At the curb. Car doors shutting. Alarms being set. Guests arriving. Words like "Jesus," "God," "church," "Bible," and "donuts" floated from the front porch, crept in beneath the wooden windowsills and bounced against the swirling tornado cloud of pot smoke.

Joey wondered how many more years his mother would keep up this ridiculous charade. The Bible study group was a nuisance disrupting the angry flow of their everyday existence. For three hours every Thursday night, Lily and Joey were forced to comply with their mother's unspoken command to appear as her perfectly behaved offspring—but only when she allowed them to come out of their rooms for an impromptu appearance. During these brief moments, Miranda's children sucked up the adoration and pride she showered on them, despite the fact their mother didn't mean it. The entire neighborhood thought she should be canonized because of her ability to balance motherhood and a busy career. They didn't know their domestic idol was an impostor.

"Heyyyyy," Cooper said, handing the joint to Joey. He slid farther back onto the bed but remained sitting up.

"You can lie down if you want," Joey said. He extinguished the joint with two wet fingers. It sizzled and died.

Cooper hesitated for a moment. Perhaps he was battling with instinct. Maybe a voice inside his stoned head was telling him to get up and go. He gave in to the high sweeping over him and pressed his head down against Joey's pillow. He blinked a few times and tried to focus on the ceiling.

Joey waited for a few minutes before he lay down next to Cooper. "Sometimes," he said, "I can see things up on the ceiling. Like crazy patterns and shit like that."

Cooper grinned and his breathing sounded deep. "Yeahhhhh, mannnnn. I knowwwww whatcha mean."

"You know the best part about smoking pot?" Joey said.

Cooper's mouth rolled into a smile. "Yeahhhhh," he said, "it's when Jesusssss talksssss to youuuuuu onnnnn Easterrrrr and shhhhhhit like that."

"What?" said Joey. "No. I mean sex. Doesn't pot make you horny?"

Cooper nodded. "Alllll the tiiiiime."

On that cue, Joey reached for the remote control on his nightstand and pressed play.

MIRANDA

Miranda knew how important appearances were at a very young age. She'd been disgraced with a mother with no decency or class who'd spent most of her life as a cocktail waitress. She shuffled from bar to bar in town to town, in search of a man drunk enough to take care of her and her daughter. The old woman had been locked away in a nursing home in New Hampshire for nearly ten years.

It had been that long since Miranda visited her.

As Miranda sat in her recliner in the corner of the living room staring at the pathetic and curious faces surrounding her, she was reminded of her mother. The way these desperate people sat on the metal folding chairs with their fat asses hanging over the edge of their seats brought back visions of her mother, perched on a bar stool prepared to offer her body to any man who could cover his share of the rent.

Miranda loathed the Bible study group. If her guests were more perceptive, they might have noticed the hatred living just behind the tight lines around her mouth. It was there when she smiled at them or handed them a napkin or complimented them on a new dress or a new tie. But they failed to recognize her rage, buying instead her façade—the one crafted with such precision and strategy. They all believed Miranda was the perfect wife and mother.

Sure, she could have avoided them. She could have shut the curtains to the world and never allowed them a peep into her life. But this game was much more fun. Disguising the contempt she felt for most people she met, including her children and useless husband, was something Miranda took delight in. She was able to turn it on and off instantaneously. In front of teachers, the minister, a neighbor—she flashed a smile and told a heartfelt story about a time she learned the important value of family.

Miranda knew Nate would never amount to much when she married him, but she needed a husband to complete the picture of bliss she wanted to create since she was a young girl. She knew he'd never stray. He listened to her every word as if it were the gospel. He lived by Miranda's rules, and she wouldn't have it any other way. He feared her, and this pleased Miranda more than anything.

However, the same could not be said for her children. Lily was reckless and wild. Joey was defiant and clever. She was prepared for a war with those two, armed with enough ammunition to emotionally annihilate them if needed. She would never allow them to damage the persona she'd spent years perfecting. Miranda was determined to be revered as a woman of high standards, with Christian morals and decent values, a woman who was devoted to her husband and children.

Only once had Nate criticized her. It happened four years earlier and fortunately, the behavior was never repeated.

"I don't think it's right," he told his wife over meatloaf, mashed potatoes, and peas at dinner one night. "To think that you're better than everyone, Miranda."

Her hand froze midair. A few peas dropped from the tines of her fork like loaded bombs destroying a village of potatoes below. "What did you just say to me?" she asked, fighting off the impulse to lunge across the table.

"You always have such horrible things to say about people, but you never say it when you see them in person."

"It's not my place to point out their flaws," she shot back quickly. "That's the work of our Lord Jesus Christ."

Nate kept his eyes on his plate. "You shouldn't make fun of Him, either."

"How dare you insinuate that I'm a woman capable of blasphemy!"

"What? What does that even mean?"

"You want to know why I think I'm better than everyone else in this world?" she asked. "It's because *I am*. I work harder. I pray harder. I fight harder. Do we understand each other?" Her husband nodded in reply. "Excellent. Now," she said, "it looks as if you're finished with your dinner. Why don't you go take a nap on the sofa?"

For the next four years, her husband did just that: sleep. Even now, as he sat on the sofa between two women who were twice his size, he looked like he could doze off at any moment. But the next question woke him up. In fact, it brought the entire room into a new state of alertness.

"What is that awful smell?" one of the women asked. She was young, was sitting a few chairs away from Miranda, and had a lap full of powdered sugar sticking to her navy blue dress like a skin disease. Miranda had watched the woman devour three donuts since arriving only fifteen minutes ago. "Is something burning?"

"I think it's a lovely fragrance," one of the nearly senile older ones said. "It's sort of like incense."

"I'm not sure what that is," Miranda answered the curious expressions turned toward her. "Perhaps it's coming from the neighbor's house. They're hedonists, I'll have you know."

"Maybe we should start reading our scriptures," one of the timid ones suggested, staring at Miranda over the top of her bifocals.

"That's an excellent idea. Why don't the rest of you start reading the scriptures?" Miranda stood up, and smoothed the sides of her hair with two nervous hands.

"Where are you going?" one of the men asked.

"If you'll excuse me for a moment," she told the group as she moved through the room with grace and poise, "I'll just go check and see if there's something wrong with the thermostat."

Miranda left the room with a big, warm flash of her most genuine smile. She moved down the hallway, unaware of the pair of feet following her.

Miranda knew exactly what the smell was. She'd smelled it on her fingers after being introduced to the nameless men her mother brought home with her. She shook hands with them to demonstrate the excellent manners she had. Later, she'd smell her skin and it was saturated with the same specific smell now slipping out from underneath the bedroom door of her fifteen-year-old son. There were puffs of smoke, too. They were ghosts drifting around Miranda's ankles as she reached for the door. She turned her hand and the knob clicked.

Light from the hallway splashed across Joey's bed and shone on her son. Joey was between Cooper's legs, with his mouth on the older boy's cock. Cooper appeared to be on the verge of unconsciousness, but bleated out a staccato rhythm of moans.

Joey looked up into the light, searching for his mother's eyes. He said to the ominous figure standing in the doorway, "I'm not finished yet."

Behind her, Miranda heard a loud gasp. She turned and collided with a navy blue dress.

"I was just looking for the restroom," the woman explained. She glanced over Miranda's shoulder and her face paled. "Dear God," she breathed. The woman's body fell limp as she teetered on the verge of passing out. She hit the wall behind her, crashing into a family portrait hanging in the hallway. The picture shattered on the hardwood floor and the terrible sound tumbled down the hall like a vicious somersault. Clouds of powdered sugar sprang from the woman's dress and drifted down to the shards of broken glass like tiny bits of snow.

Miranda ignored the woman and the fallen picture and stepped farther into her son's room. She stood next to the bed and bent down to his ear. She spoke slowly as she wanted to make certain her words would be remembered. They felt like frostbite on Joey's skin. "I will *destroy* you," she said.

Miranda straightened her posture and walked toward the light from the hall. Joey's words stopped her in her tracks. "Go ahead and try," he challenged her.

❖

Word of what had happened at Miranda's Thursday night Bible study group exploded like Fourth of July fireworks all across the neighborhood. Within hours, half of Portland knew a variation of what occurred in the house of a woman deeply devoted to God. According to the rumor mill, Satan himself had snuck in through the back door and created havoc in the innocent life of Miranda, using her young son as a pawn in his evil game.

By noon on Friday, Miranda had made her rounds: the hair salon, the supermarket, the bank, the post office, the diner where she could rely on three waitresses to spread the word about her personal tragedy. Her last stop was the private office of her minister.

"My son has sinned against God," she told the man known to have a very loose tongue after a glass or two of his favorite pinot noir. She'd thoughtfully brought him a bottle. "What can be done to prevent this from happening again?"

The members of the study group scattered like leaves once they realized something shocking had occurred, something threatening the throne their appointed Goddess of all things good had sat on for the last decade. As Miranda predicted, they defended her and shamed her son. While she was offered comfort every place she went, she was well aware his cell phone buzzed incessantly with a thousand text messages speaking of morality and virtue and detailed directions leading him straight to Hell.

JOEY

Joey welcomed the scandal with soul-grinning happiness. Immediately, he was thrust into the center of everyone's attention. It didn't matter where he went—he was the topic of every conversation. Even the librarians whispered about him when he stopped by to check out a book or two on devil-worshipping before heading to school two hours late. He decided to do anything he could to add fuel to the homophobic fire.

At school, he was stared at with hatred by some and envy by others. Both responses to his presence left him electrified. By the end of the school day, Joey realized he had done something that would linger in the halls of his high school after he was long gone. In one night, he'd become a legend.

❖

"What exactly happened last night?" Molly asked him in the cafeteria.

Joey picked at a pile of half-cooked tater tots on his lunch tray. "You've heard?"

"Are you kidding?" Molly said. She opened a can of diet soda. "It's like someone died or something. Everyone's buzzing about it."

Joey leaned in. "Tell me the version you know."

Molly looked around to make certain no one was eavesdropping. "I heard Cooper came over and forced you to get drunk and smoke pot and you did it because he had some kind of blackmail over you but then things got weird and he made you do all sorts of crazy sex stuff with him and you didn't have a choice because he threatened to kill your family."

Joey grinned. "That's perfect."

"But is it true?"

"What do you think?"

"I don't know," said Molly. "I always thought your sister was the psycho in the family. A lot of people think you and Cooper are gay."

Joey looked her in the eyes. "I'll tell you the truth, Molly, but only because you're my best friend."

She nodded. "Go on."

"Cooper isn't gay."

"Then why did he make you…"

"It was me," Joey said. "He didn't even know what was happening."

Molly folded her fingers together and put her hands on the table. "But why would you do that, Joey? It's like you tricked him or something."

"I did it," he said, "because I wanted him."

Molly stared at her friend for a few more minutes before she stood up. "I knew you were into guys," she said. "And I really couldn't care less."

"Are you sure?"

"It's just…don't take this the wrong way…but I feel bad for Cooper. I know he can be a jerk at times, but do you really think he deserved this? I mean, half the guys in this school want to kick his ass."

Joey grinned. "What about the other half?" he asked.

LILY

L ily had a physical reaction when told what her brother had done—and with whom. That night, she came home two hours past her curfew from a victory party after a volleyball game. There was Malibu rum on her breath and a hickey on her neck. She stood in the living room, the house key still in her hand, when her mother appeared in the archway to the kitchen.

"Something's happened," Miranda said, tightening the belt around her robe. "You need to know about this because everybody else does."

Lily's eyes moved to the empty sofa. "Is it Daddy?"

Miranda sighed. "Don't be dramatic, Lily. No one is dead. It's your brother."

Lily's shoulders tensed. "What did he do?"

Miranda looked into her daughter's bloodshot eyes. "I walked in on him having sex with Cooper McGill tonight. They were in Joseph's room."

The words punched Lily in the gut. She doubled over and heaved, vomited on the carpet. Some of it splashed onto Miranda's favorite slippers. Lily wiped her mouth as tears burned her eyes. She looked to her mother for comfort, for answers.

Miranda stepped over the puddle of puke and moved toward the hallway. "Clean up this mess," she instructed Lily. "And you let me handle the rumors. Your brother has almost ruined our good name."

Miranda was already out of the room when Lily spoke. "Why?" she asked. "Why would he do that with Cooper?"

Miranda smirked and held her robe closed tight around her neck.

"Wouldn't you have done the same thing if given the chance?" she asked Lily.

And then added, "I know I would have."

As Miranda disappeared down the hallway, Lily bent over and threw up once more.

❖

It seemed like Cooper appeared out of nowhere. "You gotta help me," he said to her. "You're my only chance."

Lily raised her eyes up to meet his. "What are you doing in here?" she asked. She reached across the stove top and turned off the front burner. "Home Ec doesn't seem like your style."

He lowered his voice to a soft whisper. "I need you, Lily," he said. The desperation in his words made her feel raw, scrubbed from the inside out. "Your brother fucked shit up for me real bad."

"He's an asshole," she said.

A deep sense of sadness filled his gray eyes. "I didn't even know what was happening." His words came out choked. Lily feared he might cry. "I was really messed up."

She touched his arm and was surprised to find his skin felt cold. "Are you messed up right now?"

He nodded. "A little. I have to be to deal with this crazy shit."

She slipped an arm through his and pulled him to her side. They were shoulder to shoulder, facing the stove. "You wanna go smoke?" she asked him. "I have some in my purse."

"I want you to come over," he said into her ear.

"To your house?"

"Yeah. Sunday night. My parents will be at church for that spaghetti dinner."

"Oh yeah," Lily said as if a cloud lifted. "That fund-raiser thing for that crippled girl. My mom and dad are going, too."

"But you're not going, are you?"

"No," she said. "I'll be with you."

A faint smile dusted over his lips. "Come over around seven."

He started to walk away but she stopped him. "Is this a date?"

"Sort of," he said. "And don't get all bent out of shape. But I need you to have sex with me."

Her eyes widened and her cheeks burned. "What?"

He shrugged. "I figure you kind of owe me for what your brother's done."

She shot him a look. "It's not because you're hot for me?"

"Well, yeah. I mean, you're definitely hot, Lily. Everybody says so."

She smiled. "They do?"

"Yeah. So after we do it, you'll tell everyone, right?"

She put a hand on her hip. "To convince everyone you're not a fag?"

He stepped back toward her and whispered again. "I can't take it anymore," he said. "Everyone wants to kick my ass. Except for the queer guys. They think I'm one of them now."

She put a hand on his chest and breathed her words onto his mouth. "Well, then. Prove to me you're not."

❖

Lily was already feeling no pain by the time she arrived at Cooper's house twenty minutes after seven on Sunday night. She smoked half a joint and tossed a few shots of her father's rum into a can of soda and chugged it. She stood beneath the hazy yellow glow of the porch light that illuminated the cracked concrete of the front steps of Cooper's house. She had long since stopped crimping her hair, but it was still a harsh bottle blond color, making her skin seem sallow—like she was always under the weather.

Lily burped, licked her lips, and pushed the black door buzzer again. She shivered a little in her short skirt and tank top. She hoped Cooper hadn't smoked himself into a coma. She buzzed again.

The front door opened slowly. She searched through the mesh of the screen door for his face. She heard his voice first. "Hey," he said. He unlatched the screen and pushed it open wide enough for her to come inside.

"Why's it so dark in here?" she asked, hoping her eyes would adjust quickly to the dimness of the living room.

"That's because we're down in the basement," Cooper said. He closed the front door and bolted it. "Come on," he said and she followed.

"Cool," Lily said with a slight shrug. Cooper led the way down a narrow staircase lit by an overhead bulb. The stairs dumped them out in the middle of the finished basement. It was more like a play room for adults than a basement. The walls were lined with vintage arcade games, pinball machines, a jukebox, and a massive television screen. There was a bar in the far corner and an air hockey table in the center of the room.

Although Lily was buzzed, a surge of fear cut through the numbness and caused her heart to race. She counted them: 5...6...7...8. She and Cooper were not alone. Lily was the only girl standing in a room with eight guys. Cooper's entourage of disciples had apparently decided to join them. Most of the boys wore baseball caps or New England Patriots football jerseys. They were less attractive variations of Cooper, guys used as substitutes by girls who were less popular or less attractive, who could only dream of landing Cooper—even if for one night. They were crowded around the bar, throwing back shot after shot of whatever they could get their hands on.

"What's this?" Lily asked, careful not to let her panic show on the controlled expression on her face. "I thought it was gonna just be me and you tonight, Cooper."

He pulled her away from the crowd. "I need you to do this for me."

Her mouth went dry. "Do what?"

Cooper smiled at her, warm and sweet. "I need you to...be with me," he said, "in front of them."

Lily shook her head. "Cooper, I don't understand." She glanced over at the monkeys as they howled and hooted, slamming their glasses on the bar like rattles. "You want me to have sex with you in front of these guys?"

Cooper leaned in. He kissed her neck, brushed his fingertips across her nipples. "Please," he murmured. "Do it for me."

Lily tried to ignore the fear setting her on fire. She felt a thin line of sweat slide between her breasts and melt into the skin on her stomach. Cooper was scaring her in the worst way.

He shoved her toward the center of the room. He pressed her ass up against the hockey table.

"Wait," she said as soon as she realized the boys' attention had shifted to her, to what Cooper was about to do. They watched as his hand slid up her skirt. "I'm not sure about this." She gestured to the boys who were silent for a moment. "People talk, Cooper," Lily said. She pleaded with her eyes, but he responded by shoving two fingers deep inside of her. A gasp slipped out of her mouth and her thighs trembled a little, as her body was consumed by a flash of reality, of what was happening to her.

"Tell me about it," he said. Before Lily could resist, he lifted her up in the air and planted her on the edge of the hockey table. Her sandals dropped off, hit the floor.

"Cooper," she said. But it was too late. He ripped the tank top off of her and she sat there, exposed. The other boys began to cheer. "No."

They moved like a pack of dogs. They circled around the hockey table and created a barrier, a force field of adolescent lust and testosterone. Lily glanced around at them as Cooper pushed her onto her back. There was a wild look in their eyes, like they were starving.

Cooper pulled her skirt up. This caused the boys to stomp and shout and drum their fist against the stagnant air. Cooper unzipped his pants. "Your mother's telling everyone I'm a fag," he shouted. "Well, I say...*fuck her*!"

"I'm ready to go home now," she stammered. Did she bring her purse with her? Where was it?

The hands moved toward her like a swarm of killer bees.

Lily closed her eyes and forced herself to focus on the torch song booming from the jukebox. She hummed the words and the melody. She lost herself in the complexity of the lyrics, in the sorrow in the voice of the female singer. Lily let the song take her away. In her mind, she was dancing.

Alone.

FRANCINE

Francine was already there when Albert arrived at the Diversey Harbor. She was standing on the dock near the slip where her father's boat once tapped against the splintered edges. The early evening sun cast a golden glow on her skin. The way Albert was looking at her—was he searching for a slight reminder of the girl she'd been before the tragic night? Was there a glimmer in her eyes revealing to him she'd discovered a new sense of hope?

"Why *here*?" she asked. "Couldn't we have met for coffee somewhere warm and not so…morbid?"

Albert reached for her, put an arm around her shoulder. She fell against his chest and shivered. "We needed to be here, ya know. So we can say good-bye."

She looked up at him. "Is that what the money's for?" Francine reached into her purse for a sealed envelope. "Are you leaving me?"

Albert looked down at Francine's hands. "I knew you would come through," he said.

"Here." She handed it to him. "It's only two grand. It was the most I could get for you on such a short notice."

Albert took the envelope and folded it into the front pocket of his jeans. "What about the van?" he asked.

Francine pulled away from him. She stood on the edge of the dock, her toes pointing toward the lake. "Keep it," she told him with a dismissive wave. "It's yours. I figured you've put in more for repairs than I even paid for the thing."

"I'll get you the money back."

"Maybe," she said with a small shrug.

"Aren't ya gonna ask me what it's for?"

She moved toward him again. "If you wanted me to know, Albert, you'd tell me."

"I can't give you all the details now—"

"You've met someone," she decided.

"How did you know?"

She smiled. "I see it in your eyes." Albert looked down to the wooden planks beneath their feet. He blushed. Francine reached up and brushed her fingertips across his cheek. "You're filled with this wild energy. It's like you're fifteen again."

He breathed and smiled. "I was thinking the same thing about you when I saw you standing here."

She pressed her body against his and he wrapped both arms around her, shielding her from the brutal wind whipping through the harbor. "Stop trying to flatter an old woman."

He looked into her eyes and said, "You've been good to me all these years, Francine."

Francine fought the urge to cry. "In another life, we would have been more than friends."

Albert nodded. "I know."

"But you have Bonnie."

He shook his head. "Not anymore."

Francine couldn't help but smile at the news. "She came by the shop. She said you hadn't been home in two days. Have you told her you're leaving yet?"

"She has no idea."

"I'm sure she'll think I had something to do with it."

"That's why I'm not telling you where I'm going. The less you know, the better," said Albert.

"If she comes looking for me again, she'll be out of luck."

"What do you mean?" he asked.

Francine inhaled deeply before she spoke. "I'm selling the store."

Albert locked eyes with her. "When did this happen?"

A half-grin crept over her face. "You remember your old friend Jackson?"

"Yeah," Albert said. "Of course I do. He's a good guy."

"He came and saw me this morning."

"Is he in trouble?"

"No." She shook her head. "He made me a deal."

"Was it a good one?"

"It wasn't generous, but it was decent." Francine rubbed her palms together to generate some heat. "He wants to buy the space," she said. "Says he plans to turn it into a bakery."

"He always did like the sweet stuff."

The expression on her face shifted to a serious one. "That's what I want for *you*, Albert. I don't care who it's with. I just want you to go and be happy," she told him. "Go make a new life for yourself. Start over. Become the champion boxer you know you are."

He held both of her hands in his. "I've never been happier, Francine. Never."

"Have you told your mother you're leaving?"

"No," he said. "And I'm not sure if I will. She's got a new family now. Her husband is all right. But his kids, they're too much for me. They're too fancy."

"You want me to look after her when you're gone?"

"I hadn't thought about it, but if you would…"

Francine turned back toward the water then. "I haven't been here since that night," she said.

Albert nodded. "Me neither."

"It still looks the same." Francine stood still for a moment. The cold wind circled around her body. "And that smell," she said. "I think about that night all the time."

"I try not to," said Albert. "But I have dreams about it sometimes."

She bent down and ran her palm over the surface of the icy water. "We have to let it go," she told him.

He shoved his hands into his pockets. "I wonder what my dad would be like," he said, "if he were still alive."

Francine stood up and wiped her hand on the leg of her pants. "He would tell you to get the hell out of Chicago," she said.

On impulse, Albert put his arms around her again. He held her until she surrendered to tears. "It wasn't your fault, Francine. He was hurting you."

"You saved my life, Albert," she whispered in his ear. "I want you to know that."

They pulled apart slightly, but Albert still had a firm grip on her. "I didn't have a choice," he told her. "I was in love with you then."

She placed a hand over his heart and looked into his eyes. "Then let's hold on to that part," she said. "How you and I used to drive around the city and it felt like anything was possible, anything we wanted."

Albert glanced to the city skyline in the near distance. "I feel that way now," he said.

This made Francine smile again. "Then it must be love," she said before she kissed his cheek and walked away.

ALBERT

Albert went to the gym Saturday morning, while Joey went to the school library to quit his part-time job and collect his last paycheck. He also needed to grab the last of his belongings from his dorm room, since they'd be on the road by sunrise the next morning.

"I want you to know...if you want out of this...it's okay," Joey told him that morning while Albert drove them through the city.

"I don't want out," Albert said.

"Are you sure?"

"I don't really understand it—what me and you got—but it's what I'm supposed to do, ya know," he said.

"Still. If you change your mind, I'll understand," said Joey.

Albert hit the brakes; then leaned across the van to the passenger seat and put both hands on Joey's face. The kid's breath quickened, and Albert felt his skin heat beneath his touch. Albert drew Joey's face to his and kissed him passionately. He slid his tongue into Joey's hot mouth and silenced any lingering questions or doubt. He let Joey go and resumed driving. Joey pressed his cheek against the car window.

"We're going to Vancouver," Albert reminded him.

They planned to meet up later. They'd probably eat dinner at some hole-in-the-wall diner, curl up in the back of the van, and pray they didn't freeze to death by morning.

Sunday was only a day away, and this caused Albert a tremendous amount of anxiety. He wanted to go *now*. He couldn't understand what was keeping them in Chicago.

"I don't want to make anyone suspicious," Joey had said when they were parked outside of the university library a couple of hours ago.

"The cops said it was an accident. No one suspects nothin', Joey."

"I think it will look strange if I leave Chicago before the funeral."

"But we're leaving the day after the funeral. What's the difference?"

"I don't know. I just feel like we should stay here until Sunday."

"Fine, then," Albert said. "If that's what you want."

It was almost a week since Albert had worked out. His body felt unusually tense after seeing Francine. His knuckles flinched and his shoulders ached. He climbed into the van and drove to the fifth-floor gym on Belmont. There he could rid his body of whatever was plaguing him.

That morning, he pushed his body further than before. He forced himself to find the limits of his endurance, and cross them. He tripled his workout. Pushups. Situps. Jump rope. Weights. The heavy bag. The speed bag. The double end bag. The pedestal bag. For three hours, Albert endured his most grueling training session to date.

He stepped into the ring with his sparring partner, a Mexican guy named Guillermo, who Albert suspected hated him because he was Puerto Rican, and because Albert was a better boxer. Guillermo was a lightweight boxer, at least three inches shorter. He claimed to not speak a word of English when it was convenient for him. He was only a few years older than Joey.

"C'mon, *viejo*," the young boxer taunted Albert.

"We're only sparring, Guillermo. This ain't a real fight," Albert said.

"Tonterías."

Both men slid gum-shields into their mouths and the sparring began. Immediately, it was clear by Guillermo's aggressiveness in the ring this was more than a training session for him. He was out for blood. He had been since Albert had embarrassed him in a sparring session months earlier, resulting in two black eyes for Guillermo.

It was in the ring where Albert's grace emerged. He had an indescribable prowess. He bobbed and weaved in a spellbinding rhythm. A hush blanketed the gym as other fighters and athletes quickly took notice of the boxer. It was impossible to look away. His precise moves were impulsive and unpredictable. He was hot liquid, pouring and sliding around the ring, avoiding every hit of his opponent. The other men who watched knew Albert had the makings of a star fighter. Even if the guy was pushing forty.

Guillermo got one good hit in toward the end of the match. He punched Albert's eye hard enough for it to swell shut almost instantly. A nearby trainer intervened and insisted the two men call it quits for the day. They reluctantly obliged.

Guillermo strutted off to the locker room spewing Spanish profanities like verbal punches.

As Albert stepped out of the ring, proud and envious hands patted his back and touched his arms. Words floated into his ears like "champion," "winner," and "star." He felt the adrenaline surge through his body with such intensity he had to glance down to see if the rush of it all had blistered his skin.

Minutes later, he stripped down in the locker room and stood beneath a blast of steam and hot water. His muscles began to relax and the addictive high he always felt after boxing started to slip away. It swirled down the drain at his feet. He rubbed a bar of soap across his chest and chuckled. He could still hear Guillermo carrying on even though the guy was in a shower stall on the other side of the locker room.

Albert turned his back toward the water. Everywhere he looked was a constant parade of naked male flesh. Dicks of all lengths and shades dangled around him like flaccid reminders that he wasn't as straight as he pretended to be. Albert never lusted after any of the guys at the gym. He'd been careful not to look at their bodies, not to let his eyes fall and linger on them. But after having kissed another man and after having slept beside him, the men in the locker room seemed appealing to Albert in a new way. Their tattooed skin caused Albert to lick his lips with a hunger pang he hadn't felt before. Their firm asses beckoned to Albert like wet beacons begging to be touched.

Albert turned and faced the water and the tiled wall. His cock was starting to grow, and the head of it throbbed with an ache to be played with. He reached for the temperature control for the shower water and slid the handle over to the cold side. Otherwise, he would never make it out of the gym alive.

❖

The ground at the cemetery was still damp from the melted snow. Albert carried the beautifully arranged bouquet of wildflowers in his hand, walking across the muddied landscape. He could smell the flowers, and the heavy scent tickled the inside of his nose.

Shelley was there, as Albert knew she would be. She stood next to her son's headstone with a stoic expression on her face. She was wearing a periwinkle dress with tiny rhinestones embroidered on the collar. She had one hand braced against the trunk of a red maple, as if the tree were giving her the strength she needed to stand. She heard Albert approach. She turned and met his eyes. She didn't smile but the color in her cheeks brightened. "I knew you'd come," she said.

He bent down and placed the flowers on the grave. "This is my last delivery," he said, still kneeling.

Shelley stepped forward and put a hand on her friend's shoulder. "Still working six days a week, huh? You must be extra busy since it's Sweetest Day."

Albert reached down and brushed dirt and debris from Mickey's headstone. "I'm leavin', Shelley. For good."

The large woman breathed deep. "I figured you would."

"Oh yeah?"

Shelley searched the pockets of her coat for her pipe and matches. "It's the college boy, isn't it?"

Albert stood and said, "Joey."

Shelley looked him deep in the eyes. "It's obvious what the two of you have found in each other."

Albert leaned in and whispered as if he were worried the trees would overhear him. "I never thought of being a queer before."

Shelley gave him a strange look and said, "My son thought you were."

Albert shrugged. "We only hung out a few times."

"I guess it was enough for him. He used to tell me you were the nicest person. Everybody else liked to beat the shit out of him, but not you."

Albert grinned at her. "I wasn't a fighter then."

She reached for him and slipped her arm through his. "Oh, Albert," she said. "No matter how brilliant of a boxer you become, you'll never be able to escape your heart. You're one of the few good men left in this world. It's no wonder why my boy loved you so much." Shelley stopped for a moment to swallow her emotions, to hold back the wave of tears threatening to rip through her body. "And this Joey—I knew he would take you away."

Albert looked down at the headstone. "I'm sick of this place," he said.

"Me, too, darling. There's too many ghosts here for me."

"I gotta chance to leave with somebody who I...love. We can start over somewhere."

"This might kill Bonnie, you know," Shelley said. "I just saw her over at the coffee shop this morning. She looks like hell and she's probably hung over since she always trashes around Clyde's way past happy hour."

"Bonnie will get by without me."

Shelley nodded. "She will. But the rest of us will never hear the end of it. She didn't do that to you, did she?"

Albert's hand went up to his swollen eye. The pain had subsided a little. "No. I was at the gym earlier. Had a sparring partner who didn't like me."

"I hope you kicked his ass."

"I was hoping that you'd be here, Shelley. So I could talk to you."

Her eyes fell to the ground, to her son's engraved name. "Twenty-four years ago he jumped," she said. "If I would have been there..."

"You were a good mom to him."

"I appreciate you saying that."

"I sort of think of you as a second mom sometimes."

"I'm afraid my maternal instincts have become very dull, Albert. Once Mickey died, that part of me died, too."

"No." Albert shook his head. "You're wrong. You've always been there for me."

"It's only because you bring me such beautiful flowers."

Albert reached for her hand. "I would really like your blessing."

"My blessing?" Her mouth pulled back as she attempted to smile. "Who am I, the pope?"

"You're someone who's real important to me. And I care about what you think and say and shit like that."

"Well, nobody else does."

"I want you to tell me what I'm doin' is right. That there's nothin' wrong with me for wantin' to be with Joey."

Shelley squeezed his hand. "I say love whoever the fuck you wanna love, Albert. God knows I wish my son would've been able to. If you don't follow your heart, you might end up jumping, too. And I can't lose another man to a bridge."

Albert blinked back the cold and the tears stinging his dark eyes. "I might not ever make it back here, Shelley."

She touched his face and said, "God, I hope you don't."

Albert stood in the middle of the living room of the house he had lived in for the last nineteen years. The sofa, sunk in the center from where Bonnie had placed her ass night after night watching her crime dramas. The coffee table had become a landfill for remnants of meals and milkshakes purchased from an array of fast food restaurants. The television set was coated with an inch-thick skin of dust. The smell of bird shit hung heavy in the air. The stench was so strong it burned Albert's eyes. He blinked and coughed. The birds looked to be on the verge of death in their black cage in the corner of the room. Albert wondered if Bonnie had forgotten to feed them again. Once, five days passed before she remembered to give the poor bastards some food.

Albert turned. The kitchen table was covered with piles of unopened mail, overflowing ashtrays, and permanently stained coffee cups. The kitchen itself reeked like rotting garbage. He considered opening a window, but decided Bonnie deserved to live in the filth she'd created.

From the attic, Albert dug out a cardboard box of wedding photos that never made it to the inside of a photo album. There were little lavender silk pouches filled with bird seed, to be emptied and thrown on the bride and groom when they left the church and headed off to their honeymoon. Although Bonnie swore she'd mailed out the wedding invitations, only three people had shown up at the church: Albert's mother, the minister, and an elderly woman who played the organ. No bird seed was thrown after the ceremony. Instead, the soft bags were stashed in the box in the attic where they spent the last two decades.

Albert dumped the pictures and pouches on the carpet in the bedroom. He would leave the shit there for Bonnie to pick up. He would leave it as a reminder of the years she'd stolen from him.

He sifted through the piles of laundry covering the floor. As he slowly began to fill the box with the few items he wanted to take with him to Vancouver, an overwhelming sense of relief caused Albert to catch his breath.

He spoke the words of gratitude aloud, to the foul air licking his skin for the last time. "Thank you, Joey."

Bonnie

Bonnie met him in the alley behind the coffee shop she worked at. He washed dishes there part-time. Her waitress uniform clung to her thighs, and the peasant blouse was plastered to her breasts. She straightened the white scarf barely covering the dark roots in her hair and took a final drag on her Marlboro. She dropped the smoke to the ground and squashed it with one of her scuffed pumps.

"Can you do it?" she asked him. He was standing with his back against the cinder brick wall, surrounded by milk crates and wooden pallets. There was a Dumpster nearby, and the smell of old produce floated from it.

Once Bonnie made up her mind, she knew he was the one to ask. Rumor had it that he'd earned himself quite a record in juvenile courts when he was younger. She watched him for a while. The way he scrubbed the pots and pans and greasy plates with a hidden fury intrigued her.

His eyes convinced her he was the right person for the job. They were cold and bottomless and void of any emotion. Maybe he was the type of person who was unable to feel anything.

"Tonight," the boy replied. He was only twenty. He was short, but solid, and exuded a sense of danger Bonnie found simultaneously seductive and repulsive.

"And the gun?" she prompted.

"It'll be at the bottom of Lake Michigan," he answered, with a sneer.

Bonnie studied his features. In another lifetime, the kid could be a model. In this one, he would be her husband's killer.

She fished a white envelope out of her tan, faux-leather purse. "It's the amount I promised." She passed it to him. He took it, without counting the money.

Bonnie sighed and struggled with a wild mixture of sadness and excitement. Her hands and mouth trembled with anticipation. "It took me four years to save up that money," she told him. "It was supposed to take me on vacation," she continued. "Bora Bora."

"Never heard of it," he said. He gestured to her for a cigarette. She opened her pack and gave him one. She handed him a lighter, which he shoved into his pocket after he lit his smoke.

"You should go inside soon," he told her. "We need to get back to work."

A tiny flicker of guilt started burning in the pit of Bonnie's stomach. She felt the need to explain herself, not sure why she was concerned with what the boy thought of her. She wanted him to know she didn't want her husband murdered just for insurance money. No, she wanted him to pay for the nineteen years he'd stolen from her, for the promises he'd made that fell apart like the seams in her secondhand wedding dress, for his ridiculous dream of becoming a boxer, for hatred, pure and simple. "I think my husband is cheating on me," she offered the boy. "I think he's sleeping with a whore at a flower shop."

The boy shrugged, shoved his hands deep into the pockets of his faded jeans. "It's none of my business," he cautioned her. "The job will be done tonight."

Bonnie took a step forward. "Where'd you get that scar?" She almost touched his chin with one of her fake fingernails.

"Skateboarding accident," he told her. "When I was twelve."

He left her there, returning to the coffee shop through the crooked screen door.

It slammed shut, and Bonnie winced.

It sounded just like a gunshot.

JOEY

There was no room for error. Cooper and Joey had the plan down perfectly.

Joey finished his last class on Tuesday afternoon. He worked two hours at the library before complaining of stomach flu symptoms. As he predicted, he was sent home for the day. He went to the dorm and made sure at least half a dozen people saw him, including the always-nosy resident advisor Buddy. He went up to his room and crawled into bed. He waited until his roommate headed out for a graveyard shift at the diner.

It was almost eight thirty when Joey snuck out of the dorm through the freight elevator. On the street, he hailed a cab and headed to O'Hare Airport. Within an hour, he was on the last plane out to Portland. On the flight and in both airports, he wore a hooded sweatshirt he hid beneath whenever someone came too close.

At the Portland International Jetport, Cooper was waiting for him at the curb outside of the baggage claim, just as he'd promised. Only two months had passed since they'd seen each other when Joey had come home for a two-week visit during the summer. In just the short time, both men already looked different. The small flicker of optimism that once floated in Joey's eyes and burned beneath his smile was extinguished. Cooper's confidence had been shattered five years ago when Miranda made it her personal mission to destroy his good name. But since the summer, Joey sensed Cooper had finally given up on everything. It was evident in his appearance. His hair was too long. He needed to shave. And when Joey sat down in the passenger seat next to him in the compact car, he said, "Cooper, you need a shower."

"I'm fucking nervous, all right," he said, pulling away from the airport. "It's not every day you kill someone."

Joey turned and looked at him in the dark. "I already told you, I'm the one who's cutting the brakes."

Cooper tightened his one-handed grip on the steering wheel and said, "Yeah, but I'm the one who taught you how."

Cooper

It was three years before Cooper spoke to Joey again after that infamous Thursday night. Initially, Cooper wanted to kick Joey's ass in the worst way. He stalked him in the hallways at school. He intimidated him in the locker room. He gave him death stares every time their eyes made contact. But Cooper knew that if he destroyed Joey, there'd be a high price to pay. If something happened to Joey—like he got jumped or was found with a bullet through his head in a field somewhere—all eyes would be on Cooper. And Cooper now wanted to go to college. He wanted out of Portland in the worst way. So, he backed off Joey and ignored him. Instead, Cooper directed his rage at Miranda.

In addition to giving her son the permanent silent treatment, Miranda made destroying Cooper McGill her new favorite hobby. First, she had a private meeting with the swim team coach, who agreed Cooper should be dismissed from the team immediately. The owner of the hardware store where he worked part-time offered Miranda a tissue as she sobbed about the immoral acts Cooper had committed on her son. The principal of the high school recommended that Cooper should spend his senior year being home-schooled. His parents agreed. His schedule would be more flexible for therapy appointments. Miranda also found time to sign him up for every pamphlet and brochure she could find addressing sexual deviancy. This material spewed from the McGill mailbox constantly. Finally, she wrote an anonymous letter to the editor of the local paper from the perspective of a concerned citizen who felt the relationship between the two young men had demoralized the city of Portland. The letter was published—and while no names were specifically mentioned and Miranda's homophobic rant fueled angry responses from many members of Portland's gay community— Cooper's life had never been the same.

Although everyone knew that Cooper and Lily had a serious thing for each other and were certainly having sex, a layer of doubt still lingered about Cooper's sexuality. After Miranda put her vengeful plan into action, not a single straight guy would be caught hanging out with Cooper. He went from superstar social status to the boy no one wanted to be seen with.

Except for Lily.

She stood by him through it all, even after what he let the guys do to her in his basement. She somehow still wanted to be his girlfriend. And he was falling in love with her.

Until two years ago, when he found out she'd been messing around with two other guys, both of whom openly talked about Cooper being gay. He ended his relationship with Lily and made a vow to never associate with her family again.

❖

Three years after the night that marred Cooper's name, Joey walked into the auto garage where Cooper worked to help his uncle out.

Joey was eighteen now, and according to the rumors, he was heading off in a month to Chicago to attend a university that gave him a generous scholarship to study architecture.

Cooper was nineteen. He had taken a year off between high school and college to work hard and save up as much cash as he could. His grades had been less than stellar and he wasn't an athlete. He knew there were no scholarships in his future. Yet, he had hope. Washington College in Chestertown, Maryland, had accepted him with certain requirements. He had to maintain a B average and work on campus in a part-time position to cover the cost of the tuition he could not afford.

Cooper's bags were already packed. He made a secret vow to himself he would never return to Portland.

"When I tell you what I know, I'm sure you'll agree with me," Joey said when he found Cooper with his head under the hood of an SUV. "She needs to die."

"What do you want, Joey? I already know what Lily's been doing. It's over between us."

Joey shook his head. "This isn't about Lily," he said. "This is about my mother. This is about what she's done to you. To both of us."

Cooper's hand froze and then clenched the oily rag he held. "What is that bitch up to now?" He stood up and stepped away from the car. Joey followed him to a quiet corner in the garage.

Joey sighed and then asked, "No one's told you yet?"

"I'm always the last to know everything in this neighborhood."

Joey folded his arms across his chest and his eyes darted around the garage, avoiding Cooper's cold stare. "My mom talked to the people at that school you wanted to go to in Maryland," he said in a half-whisper.

The color drained from Cooper's cheeks and his gray eyes darkened even more. "Washington College," he said.

"You're not going to school in the fall," Joey said. "My mother made sure of that."

"You've gotta be fucking kidding me."

"I wouldn't lie to you, Cooper. Not about this."

Cooper's face flashed hot red. He turned and punched a hole through the wall next to them. His rage caused Joey to jump. "That goddamn bitch!"

"My thoughts exactly."

Cooper shook his hand trying to get rid of the pain throbbing in his spliced knuckles. He wrapped the red rag over his busted skin and asked, "What did she tell them?"

"That you were a sexual predator who destroyed the lives of her children. I'm sure you'll be getting a phone call soon."

Cooper reached into the pocket of his dull blue jumpsuit and pulled out his cell phone. "Looks like I already did."

"I'm sorry, Cooper. You didn't deserve this."

"Yeah, well you should have thought of that before you helped yourself to my dick. This whole fucking town thinks I'm a fag and I'm *not*."

"I know that."

Cooper suddenly grabbed Joey's arm. "You gotta help me fix this," he said. "You owe me."

"I know," Joey said. "That's why I'm here."

Cooper released his arm. "Talk."

"No one hates her more than you do."

"She's got it out for me because I wouldn't fuck her. You know that, don't you?"

"I figured as much. I think she's jealous because I got to you first. So is Lily."

"Let's leave Lily out of this," Cooper said. "And for that matter, let's leave me and you out of this."

"How can we?" Joey asked. "She's determined to ignore me for the rest of her life, and she won't die happy until you're destroyed."

Cooper touched the frayed edges of the hole in the wall, the damage he had done. "She picked me up from school one day," he said. "It was a couple of weeks before…well, before what happened between me and you. I didn't know what was up. She said she needed to talk to me in private. She took me to an empty house. Her name was on the for sale sign on the lawn, so it didn't surprise me that she had keys."

Joey swallowed. "Did you go inside with her?"

Cooper nodded. "Of course I did. But then she started trying to kiss me and she touched me. She grabbed my cock a few times and asked me to fuck her."

"I hope you said no."

"I did. She got angry. She said she could make things really bad for me and my family. I reminded her I was only sixteen and that I was hot for Lily. She told me Lily wasn't good enough for me. That she could please me more because she was an older woman."

Joey looked away, to a neatly stacked display of cans of oil. "What did you do?"

"I bolted. I left the house and went home," said Cooper. "I called a couple of my buddies to tell them about the situation and they all said the same thing…they'd all been with your mom, Joey. By the time Lily graduated last year, your mom had already boned down on half the swim team. Probably the coach, too. She likes to take 'em to those houses and play all sorts of twisted games with them, like she's the mom or the nanny or the babysitter and then she makes them—"

Joey held up a hand. "I've heard enough, thank you."

Cooper looked him directly in the eyes. "I'm not making this shit up, I swear."

"I believe you," Joey said. "Now it's my turn to talk."

"Say what you gotta say, then."

Joey leaned and dropped the volume in his voice. "The only way you and I will ever be rid of her is to take matters into our own hands."

Cooper's eyebrow shot up. "Are you talking about killing her?"

Joey shrugged slightly. "As a matter of fact…I am."

Cooper nodded and gnawed on his lower lip for a few seconds. "Okay. But how?" he asked.

Joey glanced over at the SUV and said, "An accident."

❖

Once the plan was set into motion, their lives were tossed into a permanent state of hyperspeed.

They met secretly as often as they could. Once the garage was closed for the day, Joey met Cooper there. Their evenings were spent with Cooper serving as an instructor and Joey as his enraptured pupil. In detail, Cooper went over every element of the brake system of a car. How to bleed the brakes. How and where to cut the brake lines. How to make it look like an accident. Wear and tear is what Cooper kept repeating.

Wear and tear.

When Joey left for school and embarked on a new life in Chicago, Cooper enrolled in a couple of classes at a local community college, determined to not let Miranda win.

Joey came home for Christmas that year. He told Cooper that Miranda boycotted his visit and kept herself locked in her bedroom while he was in the house. There was no tree. No gifts. No love. Joey turned to Molly for comfort, and the two best friends spent Christmas morning together at an all-you-can-eat buffet. Joey met with Cooper a few times during his visit, and they developed their plan further and in more detail.

"I'm anxious," Cooper told him on New Year's Eve. They were at the same house party being thrown by some girl who'd just been cast on a new reality television series. Cooper had long since been ostracized by everyone there, so he couldn't care less if anyone saw him talking to Joey. They stood outside, shivering on a wooden deck beneath a cluster of pines. The moon was almost full. Inside, the party was raging and the walls were thumping with the beat of a hot dance song. "I want to get this over with."

"We will," Joey said. "I'm waiting for the right moment."

"But you're going back to Chicago. You probably won't come home until summer."

"I still want to study more."

"It's not a fucking midterm, Joey. It's a goddamn brake line," Cooper said. "Let's do it and be done with it."

"Trust me, we will," said Joey. "The bitch hasn't said one word to me since I've been home. She keeps herself locked away like I'm contagious."

"Yeah, well, you don't have to see her almost every day like I do. She comes in to get an oil change and tells my uncle I'm a queer and I need Jesus and shit like that. Thank God he's cheating on his wife and I know about it or else I'd be unemployed. I see her at the grocery store, at the gas station, even in the fucking drive-thru at Taco Bell. She fucking haunts me, Joey. Everywhere I go."

Joey looked at Cooper and said, "Not for much longer."

"You say that, but I don't think you mean it. I want her dead. You hear me?"

Joey put a finger up to his lips, reminding Cooper to keep his voice down, even though they were alone. "Loud and clear."

Cooper took the hint and spoke in a soft whisper. "You know she's still messing with those high school boys. She's got a bunch of new ones now. I hear them talking about her at the basketball courts. A few of them are even doing her on a regular basis."

Joey cringed. "Well, I hope she enjoys it while it lasts."

Cooper shook his head and moved closer to Joey without realizing it. "It wouldn't matter even if I was a fag and you and I were fucking each other every night," he said, "we still wouldn't be as fucked up as she is."

The sliding glass door opened and Lily staggered out on to the deck. She was wearing a red dress with spaghetti straps that kept sliding off her bare shoulders. Her hair was a mess and her makeup was smeared. She was wearing a patch over her bad eye as part of some new treatment she was trying. Cooper thought she looked like a reject from clown school. Lily held a pack of cigarettes in one hand and an overflowing shot glass in the other. She swayed like one of the pine trees as the wind pressed hard against her trunk. "What is this?" she asked. "A reunion?"

"You're drunk, Lily," Cooper said.

She stumbled forward and stood between them. She leaned the front of her body up against the wooden railing. "Light me up," she told Cooper. He pulled out a Zippo and she breathed in deep to ignite her cigarette. The tip of it glowed and cast fiery shadows on their faces. "If only you were such a gentleman when I was your girlfriend."

"Joey and I were just catching up," Cooper said.

Lily turned to her brother. "I have no idea why you even bothered coming home to this shit hole for the holidays. Nobody but Molly wants you here."

"And miss seeing you like this?" Joey said. "You're a fucking mess, Lily."

"And you're a goddamn homo. Stay away from Cooper. He's mine."

Joey cleared his throat and then said, "He used to be yours."

"I don't belong to anybody," Cooper reminded them. "I'm taking off. This is the last place I want to be when the clock strikes midnight."

He turned away and went back inside to the party.

JOEY

When Cooper decided to leave her standing on the deck with her brother, Lily teetered to the sliding door. For a moment, Joey thought she might walk right through the glass. But she stopped and waved at her distorted reflection. Or maybe she thought Cooper was on the other side. She blew kisses at the door and turned back to her brother. "Did he tell you about it?"

"Tell me about what?"

"About the abortion?"

Joey shot his sister a look. "You were pregnant?"

She nodded and wiped at her face with the back of her hand, almost singing the ends of her fried hair with her cigarette. Her lipstick became a bigger smudge across her mouth. "For a couple of months I was," she said. "Until I had to borrow the money from Cooper to kill my baby."

Joey tried to hold his sister's stare, but she could barely focus on him. "How could you do that, Lily? I mean, you're grown now. You're twenty. You could have handled it. And Cooper would have been an okay father."

Lily took a drag and spat a puff of smoke out the corner of her mouth. "That's just the thing," she said. "We weren't sure if he was the father."

"Well, who else were you with?"

Lily winced as if the wind was hurting her. "All of his friends," she said. "The bastards decided to pull a train on me. Just to prove Cooper wasn't gay. One of the fuckers recorded the whole thing on his cell phone and e-mailed it to a bunch of guys."

Joey fell silent.

Lily took a breath before continuing. "I had to have an abortion because I didn't know who the baby belonged to," she said. "Besides, what would I do with a baby? By the way…I'm working now."

Joey swallowed. "Oh yeah? Where?"

"Didn't Molly tell you? We got jobs at Payless. The shoe store. But I think I might quit soon if I can get something better. Like something at the mall maybe."

"That's great."

"Yeah, I'm sure it's not as exciting as going to college, but at least it's something."

Joey glanced up at the moon. "I don't think Mom will ever talk to me again," he said.

Lily lifted the glass to her lips and tossed back the shot. "No big loss," she said and licked her lips. "Sometimes I feel like we never even had a family. Like we were orphans or foster kids and we were raised by the wicked witch from a fairy tale and her dumb assistant who does whatever she tells him to."

Joey turned to his sister. He reached for her but she pulled away. She almost lost her balance and grabbed for the railing. The shot glass slipped from her hand and tumbled into the dark below them. "You and I still have each other, Lily."

"Yeah, whatever the fuck that means," she said. "You got the guy of my dreams drunk and gave him a blow job and now he wants nothing to do with me. I hardly consider you and me close."

She turned to go back inside to the party. Her brother's words stopped her when she reached the glass door. "Remember," he said, "fairy tales are supposed to have happy endings."

JOEY

Cooper and Joey resumed their auto training when Joey came home for a two-week visit that summer. Miranda still hadn't spoken to Joey and was shunning Lily as well. Rumors about the video clip featuring her and a handful of Cooper's friends had started circulating around the neighborhood. Joey heard Miranda had sent an e-mail to the dean of the community college Cooper was struggling through. The dean did not respond kindly to Miranda's accusations and informed her she could be sued for slander if she continued a personal war against his student. She resorted to posting photocopied fliers featuring a yearbook picture of Cooper with the words "Beware of This Sexual Predator" underneath it. She made certain the fliers were on every telephone pole and streetlight in a five-mile vicinity of the community college.

The day before Joey flew back to Chicago to start his sophomore year, he met Cooper at the garage. The lights were low and the cement floor had just been swept. Cooper stood with a broom in one hand and a crumpled flier in the other.

"Your mother's a fucking psycho," he said. "Doesn't she have anything else better to do?"

"Apparently, she's bored with needlepoint," Joey said. "We're doing it on the third Tuesday in October."

"For real?"

"Yes."

"That's two months away."

Joey sighed and then grinned. "Some things are worth the wait."

"How are we going to pull this off? You'll be in Chicago then."

Joey sat down on the floor and Cooper joined him. He spilled out the plan and Cooper agreed it sounded foolproof. A mutual thrill shone in their eyes they reflected back and forth to each other. They had a secret forever bonding them. They weren't friends and never would be. Becoming lovers was certainly out of the question. Instead, they would have a shared moment only the two of them would be able to understand. They'd been driven to extreme action by the callousness and manipulation of a woman they loathed for their own reasons. Retribution would become their common ground, their common bond.

❖

"Let's go over it again," Joey insisted as they exited the freeway and were greeted by the familiar sights of the neighborhood they'd grown up in.

"We pull up across the street. You sneak in through the side door into the garage. I go to the front door and ring the bell. She comes to the door and answers it. I ask to talk to Lily. She insults me and I let her. In the garage, you take care of the brakes. I go back to the car and wait for you. You hide on the side of the house. She leaves the house. Once she's turned the corner, you come back to the car to meet me."

"Then we follow her," Joey said.

"I didn't know we we're going to do that."

"We've waited five years for this. Don't you want to see her crash?"

Cooper sped up. "More than anything," he said.

"Go on," Joey said.

"Then after she crashes, I hide you out at the garage until dawn. You take the first flight home to Chicago in the morning. You miss your first class because you're sick. But you go to your second class so no one gets too suspicious."

"And you?"

"My uncle thinks I'm working late at the garage. I didn't turn the alarm on before I left, so no one will know I took off for a while. After I drop you off at the garage, I'll swing by Taco Bell and throw a fit at the drive-thru window because they get my order wrong."

"Don't forget to ask to speak to the manager on duty."

"Yeah, I got that part. Then I head home and make enough noise coming in to wake up my mom and dad."

"That's perfect. With all of these witnesses, no one will ever suspect you."

"Hey," Cooper said, "I'm just the driver."

"Yeah, but I couldn't do this without you."

"This is the kind of thing we gotta take to our grave, Joey. No matter what. We can't tell *anybody*."

"I know," Joey said, crossing his heart with two fingers.

"By the way, I'm thinking about getting back together with Lily."

Joey shot him a look. "Why would you?"

"She's gonna be so torn up about your mom, she might need someone. A shoulder to cry on and shit like that."

"Don't fool yourself, Cooper. My sister hates my mother as much as you do. She'll probably hire a DJ and buy a piñata just to celebrate."

"Yeah," Cooper said, "but I still have feelings for her."

"Lily's a fucking mess. She's bad news. She always has been."

"No." Cooper shook his head, made a left turn. "You haven't seen her lately."

"I was home in August, remember?"

"I know, but she's changed since then. She doesn't even look the same."

"I'll believe it when I see it."

"At the funeral probably."

"Yeah…probably."

Cooper braked at a red light. "Oh fuck," he said. "It's Molly."

"What? How do you know?"

"I'm a mechanic," Cooper said. "I'd know her mother's Volvo anywhere. Get down, God damn it!"

As Molly pulled up next to Cooper, Joey unlatched his seat belt and dove head first across Cooper's lap. His face landed between the steering wheel and Cooper's crotch. Joey could feel Cooper wince a little and his body grew tense.

Cooper rolled the window down and stuck his head out into the night. Cold air rushed into the car and chilled them. Joey shivered a little and tucked his hands underneath his chin. "Hey, Molly," Cooper said.

"Cooper, what's up?" Joey smiled at the familiar sound of his best friend's voice.

"Not much. Going to get some food."

"I just got off work," she said.

"Oh yeah? Where you working these days?"

"At a shoe store. It's awful."

"I thought you were going to college," Cooper said.

"Yeah, me, too. It's a long story."

The light changed.

"See you around," Cooper said and hit the accelerator. He waited for a couple of blocks before he grabbed the back of Joey's head and lifted him away from his body. "Get off of me."

Joey sat up and reached for his seat belt. "We weren't planning on that, were we?"

"Fuck. Do you think she'll say anything?"

"To who? I'm the only person she really talks to." As if on cue, Joey's cell phone buzzed. He fished it out of the pocket of his jeans. "It's her."

"Answer it," Cooper said.

"I'm supposed to be in Chicago."

"Well, then pretend like you are."

Joey answered the phone. "Hello?"

"You'll never guess who I just talked to," Molly said.

"Who? Tell me."

"Remember Cooper McGill?"

"Of course I do. I still haven't lived down that rumor."

"He looked really bad."

"What do you mean?" Joey said.

"Like something was bothering him. Maybe he's got a lot on his mind."

"Maybe he got back together with my sister."

"God, I hope not. Lily deserves so much better than him. She's doing really well, by the way. She got a makeover or something at the mall and she looks like a completely different person. She has a new job, too."

Cooper turned on to the street Joey had grown up on. Joey felt a kick of fear against the outer ridges of his heart. His breath quickened and tiny beads of sweat emerged on his forehead. The porch light was on. The garage door was closed. Joey could see his mother's silhouette in the front window. She was putting on a coat. Now she was reaching for her purse. She was getting ready to leave.

"Molly, I have to go," Joey said. "My tutor is here."

"This late at night?"

"I'm an hour behind you, remember?"

"Yeah, but still…what time is it? It's after eleven already."

"I'll call you tomorrow."

"Okay," she said. "I hope you decide to come home for Christmas again. Or maybe I can come to Chicago."

"We'll figure it out soon. I promise. Call me tomorrow." Joey pushed a button and ended the call.

"She's still home," Cooper said. He turned off the car. They were parked across the street from the house.

"Where's she going at this time of night?"

Cooper grinned. "To meet me," he said.

Joey's face paled in the dark. "What?"

"I called her yesterday. I told her to come up with an excuse so we could meet. So I could finally give her what she'd been wanting all these years."

"Wait," Joey said. "Cooper, that wasn't part of our plan. It was supposed to be a dinner party or—"

"It's a little late for a dinner party, Joey."

"So she thinks she's meeting up with you for *sex*?"

"I can't wait to see the look on her face when she opens up the front door and sees me standing on the porch," said Cooper. "She'll be pissed as fuck when I ask if Lily's home."

Joey shook his head. "This isn't going to work. You'll fuck this up. It'll backfire on us."

"She wants it bad, believe me. Why else do you think she has a fucking vendetta against me?"

"You should have told me this, Cooper. This changes everything."

"You can't chicken out now. It's too late."

Joey shook his head. "I can't do it."

"What the fuck are you talking about?" Cooper said. "You get over there and get in that garage and get under that car. Let me take care of the rest."

"No," Joey said. "As much as I hate her...she's still my mother."

"She's a fucking monster and you're a coward."

"Cooper, no." He opened the car door. "Where are you going?"

"You think of something to distract her. I'll take care of the brakes."

"Cooper, I don't know if I can..."

"Just do it, God damn it. This fucking bitch has taken everything from me."

"I'm scared, Cooper. We might get caught."

"I'm not backing out. We're doing this, Joey. We've waited long enough. Now give me the key."

Reluctantly, Joey pulled the golden metal key out of his pocket. He reached across the car and placed it in Cooper's hand.

Cooper got out of the car and darted across the street, careful to avoid the pale white pools of streetlight falling in circles across the asphalt. Joey watched as Cooper slid between the juniper bushes and the side of the house. He unlocked the back door that opened into the garage and disappeared through it.

Joey eyes moved to the driver's seat. An object had caught his eye. It was Cooper's cell phone. He picked it up and held it in his hand. *Call her*, he thought. *Warn her. She's your mother.*

Joey contemplated making the call for a few seconds more. Finally, he dialed the number. If there was an investigation and phone records were checked, the call would be traced back to Cooper's cell phone. *He can say that he was calling the house looking for Lily.*

Miranda answered on the first ring. "Hello?" Her voice was tight, annoyed.

"Mom?"

She sighed, exasperated. "Let me get your father. You can speak to him. Nate!"

"No," Joey said. "I want to talk to you."

"I have *nothing* to say to you. You're a disgrace to me and this family," she said. "I wish you were never born."

"Listen," he said. "I know what you've been doing."

"What are you talking about?"

"The boys," Joey said. "I know everything."

"You're sick."

"Am I? I'm not the one having sex with half the swim team."

"Who told you that?" she asked.

"I almost felt sorry for you...but now...you deserve what you get."

"We'll have to finish this mother/son conversation later. I have to leave. I have somewhere to be. I'm dropping your father off at the lighthouse and then I'm visiting a friend at the hospital."

The cell phone almost slipped from Joey's hand. "What?" he heard himself say in a cracked whisper.

"I said—"

"Dad's going with you?"

"Please don't call this house again." She hung up the phone.

Cooper emerged from the garage through the same door he had entered it. He dashed across the street and returned to the panic and darkness in the car. "I did it," he breathed.

"My dad," Joey said, tears swelling up in his eyes.

"What are you talking about?"

The garage door clicked and rolled up, opening with a rattle. Joey and Cooper ducked down in their seats in unison. Miranda was in the driver's seat. Her husband was sitting next to her. She backed up and out of the driveway, into the street.

"What's he doing with her?" Cooper asked.

"I called her."

"You did what?"

"I used your phone. I had to distract her."

"I thought you had cold feet."

Joey closed his eyes for a moment and then opened them again. "I've changed my mind."

Cooper sat up behind the steering wheel and started the car. They pulled away from the curb. "Talk to me, Joey. Why is your dad with her?"

Joey sat up. "She's dropping him off at the lighthouse."

"By the cliffs?"

"She said she's going to visit a friend. At the hospital."

Cooper shook his head. "The brakes won't last that long."

They turned a corner. They were a few yards behind Miranda. "Is he going to die?" Joey asked.

Cooper nodded and then said, "I don't know what to do."

They passed the high school. "He's not supposed to be in the car, Cooper."

"If we stop them now—Joey, we can't risk it. We'll go to jail."

"But my dad…he doesn't deserve to die."

"She hasn't hit a red light yet."

"What do you mean?"

"She doesn't know about the brakes."

They were on a two-lane coastal road now, only moments from the old lighthouse that Joey's father liked to hang out in with his buddies. The bottom floor of the old building had been turned into a pub years ago. It was the only place where Joey knew his father could find peace.

"There's still time," Joey said. "We could do something." The highway twisted around the steep edges of a series of cliffs. Joey glanced out the window, trying to make out the shoreline in the dark.

"Like what?" Cooper asked. "Damn it, Joey, we both wanted this to happen."

Ahead of them, Miranda lost control of the car. It slid and ripped through the metal barricade. The car launched into midair, floating for a few seconds above the jagged cliffs. Then, as if invisible strings had been cut and a magnet was pulling it back to earth, the car plummeted straight down. The explosion rumbled up the side of the cliff and bellowed in Joey's ears. He covered them with his palms as hot tears spilled down his cheeks. The sky lit up with a flowering orange flame shooting up from the car as if the burning shards of metal were propelling its passengers directly to Heaven.

MOLLY

Lily and Molly said good-bye to their new friend Roberta when she dropped them off in the parking lot of a department store in Chicago. They watched with a mixture of sadness and relief as the philosophical truck driver drove off into the distance.

"I know this sounds strange," Lily said, "but I think I might actually miss that fucking nut job."

"She's an odd woman," Molly agreed. "But she has a good heart."

Lily buttoned up her coat. "It's freezing in fucking Chicago, even if it isn't snowing."

"It's not that cold."

"Any idea where we are?" Lily asked.

Molly shook her head. "No clue. And we're almost out of cash."

"I hope Joey can give us enough to get home with."

Molly looked away for a moment and then back at Lily. "I'm not going back to Portland," she said.

Lily shot her a look. "Oh God, don't tell me Roberta's speech about being true to yourself and you've only got one life to live crap actually worked on you."

"She gave me a lot to think about."

"She was drinking whiskey straight out of the bottle, Molly."

"She's seen a lot in her years," Molly said. "She's gathered a lot of wisdom on the road."

"Can you try not to sound like a camp counselor for once?"

"I was terrified at first. Hitchhiking."

"I told you we would be fine," Lily said. "We made it here alive, didn't we?"

Molly nodded and said, "I've made up my mind. I'm staying here."

Lily put a hand on her hip and sighed. "What are you going to do for money?"

Molly shrugged and then answered, "I'll get a job."

"Where are you going to live?"

"I'll get an apartment."

"How? We've spent almost everything we had just to get here."

"I don't have all the answers right now, I just know I can't go back there."

"What's so bad about Portland?"

"My life," Molly said.

"You hate it that much?"

"You have no idea how much. If I have to sell one more pair of shoes—"

"I think you've lost your fucking mind," said Lily. "Does your mother know about this?"

Molly grinned. "I called her."

"When?"

"At that coffee shop in Indiana."

"Where was I?"

"Trying to win something from the claw machine."

"I lost five bucks to that thing," Lily said. "I hate that game."

"I told her the car was stolen."

"Was she pissed?"

"You can say that. She practically disowned me over the phone," said Molly. "Until I reminded her she had insurance and it would cover the cost of the car. That seemed to brighten her mood."

Lily nodded and bit her thumbnail. "Money has that type of effect on people," she said.

"But she hung up on me."

"What a bitch. Why did she do that?"

Molly smiled again. "Because I suggested she send me the insurance money to make up for the fact she bought a new sofa for her fat ass with the money my grandparents left me to go to college with."

"Oh my God, Molly. I'm so proud of you. Did you actually say that to her?"

"Every word."

"Even the part about her fat ass?"

"I got that in right before she hung up."

Lily laughed. "That's fucking awesome."

"It felt good to tell her how I felt."

"I bet you can't wait to tell Joey."

Molly's smile dimmed. "I don't know what I'm going to say to him."

"You guys never stop talking whenever you're together. You're like two old ladies."

"What he did was wrong."

Lily looked away. "So," she said, "you made your mind up about staying here before we even pulled up?"

They started to walk across the parking lot. "I made my mind up back in Portland," Molly said. "If Joey was able to come here and survive, why can't I?"

"Speaking of which, I need to find that bastard brother of mine. It's going to be dark soon. This place seems dead. Especially for a Saturday night."

They left the parking lot and crossed the street. "Let's look for a train station," said Molly.

"You mean like Amtrak?"

"No. We need to find a subway station. From there, I think I can get us to Joey's university."

"Then what?" Lily asked.

"Then you can have casual sex with his roommate and I can ask my best friend face-to-face if he had anything to do with murdering his parents."

Lily nodded. "Sounds like a plan."

JOEY

"Albert, you got another black eye," Joey said with a strange smile. "Just as the old one was almost healed. And it's the same eye, too."

It was dark inside the van, except for the thin strips of silver streetlight sliding in through the windows. Joey shivered and lifted the hood of his sweatshirt, pulling it up to cover the back of his head. In his lap was an odd-shaped object inside of a tied plastic grocery bag.

Albert was sitting next to him with his flannel jacket zipped up to his chin. There was an atlas in his lap and he was outlining their trip to Vancouver with an orange highlighter. "I went to the gym today," he said. "While you were packing up your stuff. My sparring partner had it out for me."

They were parked across the university. Albert had arrived just minutes ago to pick up Joey. They hadn't seen each other for most of the day. A low-level giddiness had been injected into their veins when they saw one another. Their words were fueled with an infectious energy and their eyes were filled with teases and dares.

"I hope he looks worse than you do," Joey said.

Albert grinned. "He won't be able to eat for a week."

Joey glanced toward the back of the van. Albert's belongings were overflowing out of a cardboard box. Joey's green duffel bag sat next to it. The zipper strained to hold all Joey had shoved inside. What Joey wasn't expecting to see was the petals. There were hundreds of them of all different shades, tossed all over their makeshift bed.

"Albert," Joey said. "The flowers…the petals."

Albert slammed shut the atlas and tossed it onto the dashboard.

"Damn it, Joey," he said, "they're supposed to be a surprise. I can't get nothin' by you."

Joey smiled and said, "No wonder why you insisted on putting my stuff in the van."

Albert started the van and reached for the temperature controls. "Tonight's our last night in Chicago."

"And?" Joey asked.

"And I want it to be special."

Joey smiled and his eyes burned with an illuminated joy. "Do we have a date?"

Albert nodded. "We do."

Joey climbed out of his seat and moved over to Albert's. He climbed onto the boxer's lap, sitting sideways so that his feet could rest on the edge of the passenger seat. They were face-to-face now, eye-to-eye. Albert put an arm around Joey's waist. "What have you got planned for us?" Joey asked.

"First…" Albert stopped for a moment, welcoming the quick kiss Joey offered. "I'm taking you to Pizza Capri for dinner since you're always talking about that place."

Joey ran a hand through Albert's curly, dark hair. "It looks beautiful through the window," he said. "I've always wanted to go there."

"Yeah, well, that's where we're going."

Joey placed both palms against Albert's cheeks. "There's more," he said. "I can tell by the look on your face."

Albert looked up into Joey's eyes. "I can't keep any secrets from ya, can I?"

They kissed again and Joey said in a hot breath, "Probably not."

"I'm taking you to this place I heard about. It's a bar. For guys like us."

"A gay bar?"

"Yeah, but I don't think it's for those pretty, sissy types."

Joey almost laughed. "You mean like me?"

"Yeah, yeah…you're pretty. But this place is more my speed from what I read in this newspaper I picked up today. I might not like it there, but we can try it out, a'ight."

"You've put a lot of thought into this."

Albert slid a hand beneath Joey's sweatshirt and then his T-shirt.

His palm moved up the front of Joey's body, brushing over his smooth skin. "I'm not finished yet," he said.

Joey blinked as if the pleasure he felt from Albert's touch made it difficult for him to speak. "There's more?"

"Today is Sweetest Day."

"That's right."

"And...since you're the closest thing I have to a sweetheart...I figured you deserved the deluxe treatment." Albert playfully pinched one of Joey's nipples. Joey responded with a small gasp. He reached between Albert's legs and squeezed the head of his cock through his jeans.

"That sounds hot," Joey said.

"We're going to Navy Pier. There's a fireworks display in a few hours."

"Cotton candy, too?"

"Sure. Whatever you want."

Joey reached up and touched Albert's face again. "The only thing I want is you," he said. The two men held each other's stare for a moment.

Finally, Albert broke the silence with a laugh. "I think you're evil," he said.

Joey giggled. "You do?"

"Yeah, I think you put some kind of spell on me. Are you into Voodoo?"

Joey shook his head. "Never touched the stuff."

Albert put both arms around Joey, pulling him close to his chest. "Until four days ago, I never knew it would happen for me. Finding somebody like you."

Joey closed his eyes and listened to the rhythm of Albert's heartbeat. "Same here," he said. "Wait." He sat up. "I almost forgot."

"Forgot what?"

"I made something for you."

"Ya did what?"

Joey reached for the grocery bag on the seat next to them. He handed it to Albert. "This is for you."

Albert smiled. "For me? I'm not used to getting presents." Instead of untying the bag, Albert ripped it open. Inside was a house made of tongue depressors. Joey had covered the wood with tiny flowers made of colorful tissue paper. "Joey...man, this awesome."

"It's the perfect place for us," he said into Albert's lips. "If things ever get shitty, you can close your eyes and go inside this place." Their mouths met briefly. "You'll know that I'm there...waiting for you."

"I can't believe you made this for me."

"It's not much...but I wanted to build something for you with my own hands. I only wish it were a real house for us."

Albert pulled Joey back toward him. "I'm serious," he said. "What me and you got, not many people have, Joey. And I still don't understand it. I don't know if I'm queer or bisexual or just...maybe you're the only guy I could do this sort of thing with."

Joey grinned. "This sort of *thing*?"

"Fall in love."

Joey pulled back and looked the boxer in the eyes. "Albert..."

Albert breathed deep before he spoke. "Because it's true," he said. "I'm in love with you, kid. And I don't give a fuck what anybody says about it. You belong with me."

Joey nodded and a tear slid down his cheek. "I do."

Albert reached up and touched the tear with his fingertip. "Why are ya crying?"

Joey struggled for a moment to catch his breath, to find the right words. "My heart...I feel it in my heart, Albert," he said. He wiped his eyes with the back of his hand as more tears spilled. His emotions surprised them both. "When I look at you...my God, I can't tell you how much I feel. But I know one thing for sure...and that is...that I love you."

Silence hung in the van and they both slipped inside the center of it like an embrace.

"Wow," Albert said. "It sounds cool to hear you say that."

Joey pressed his ear against Albert's chest and whispered to him, "You'll always be my champion, Albert."

ALBERT AND JOEY

The Peacock was a smoky pool hall offering their all-male, over-forty clientele watered-down drinks and decades-old selections on the jukebox. The machine was temperamental and wouldn't play unless exact change was put into it. There was a concrete dance floor, a few club lights spiraling and twirling from where they were bolted into wooden posts. There were pool tables, both of which had seen better days. The pool sticks were on the verge of splitting in two and there wasn't a chalk cube in sight.

A row of men sat at the bar, hunched over bottles of beer and the occasional shot of Jack Daniel's. They chain smoked their way through packs of Winstons and Marlboros, rarely speaking to anyone except the bartender. He was in his thirties, straight, and looked like a dark-haired former exotic dancer. He wore a tight shirt and even tighter jeans to ensure a good night of tips. He winked at anyone suggestively who had cash in hand.

There was little response from the men at the bar when Albert and Joey walked into the place just after seven o'clock. A few of them glanced over at the door and one of them raised his beer bottle as a welcoming gesture. Albert gave a quick nod of his head in response and ushered Joey inside and away from the door, the cold outside.

"This place seems all right," Joey whispered. He reached for Albert's hand.

"Should we get a beer?" Albert asked.

Joey smiled. "I'm only twenty," he reminded Albert.

"I don't think that matters here."

Joey sat down at a round wooden table and nibbled on a bowl

of stale pretzels while Albert went to the bar. He returned with two icy bottles and handed one to Joey. Albert turned a chair around and straddled it. He draped his arm over the round wooden back of the chair. He lifted the bottle in his hand and said, "To Vancouver."

Joey raised his bottle and added, "To flower gardens." They clinked and shared a grin. Joey took a sip of the sudsy liquid and grimaced a little. "I've never had beer before."

"Jesus," Albert said, "how'd ya make it through high school?"

Joey looked away. "I barely got out of that place alive."

"Yeah, well, I'm glad you did."

Joey cleared his throat. "Albert, I have to tell you something."

"You're not married, are ya?"

"No. It's nothing like that."

The fever in Albert's eyes dimmed a little. "Whatever it is…I hope we're still going to Vancouver."

"We are. We definitely are."

"Good. 'Cause that's all I've been thinking about, you know. Just being wit' you in those gardens. Getting outta Chicago."

Joey closed his eyes and let the words slide out of his mouth. "I didn't do it," he said.

Albert licked the beer foam from his lips. "What are you talking about?"

Joey opened his eyes. "My parents," he said. "I didn't kill them."

Albert put his bottle of beer down on the table. "What the fuck… are they alive?"

"No…they died. The car went through the guardrail and everything. It happened Tuesday night. I was there…but I chickened out."

Albert stared at him, stunned. "You didn't fuck with the brakes?"

"I was supposed to."

"What happened?"

"I don't know…I felt like even though she was bad to me, she was still my mother."

"Who did it?"

"My sister's ex-boyfriend. He's a mechanic."

"But you didn't stop him?"

Joey shook his head. "I wanted it to happen, Albert. I just couldn't be the one to do it."

"And your dad?"

"When I realized he was in the car with her, I thought about stopping them. I really did."

"Why didn't ya?"

Joey's eyes swam with tears. "Because I figured he'd be happier somewhere else. Away from me and my sister. Our fucked-up family. He never did anything wrong to us. He just painted houses and snuck off to the lighthouse for a beer every chance he got. I wanted to give him peace."

Albert waited for a moment before he spoke. "I'm glad ya told me, Joey. Here I was thinkin' I was datin' a killer."

Joey leaned in closer to the table. "Does this change anything between us?"

Albert lifted his eyes to meet Joey's. "Why would it?"

"I didn't mean to lie."

"Well, now I know the truth."

"I guess I wanted to impress you," Joey said. "You seemed so tough."

"I don't anymore?"

"You do. But there's a softness to you that I love."

Albert looked away. "Don't tell nobody about it."

Joey reached across the table for Albert's hand. "It'll be our secret."

"We got lots of those, me and you."

"Doesn't everybody?"

"You gonna let this guy take the fall for it?" Albert asked.

"I don't think he'll get caught. It's over and done with. No one will ever know."

"But *you* do. Can you live with it?"

Joey shrugged and squeezed Albert's hand tighter in his. "I don't have a choice," he said. "I'm the one who came up with the idea. I saw it through. I didn't stop them from driving off the cliff. I'm ready to move on now."

Albert raised an eyebrow and Joey felt tempted to touch the moon-shaped scar above it. "To Vancouver?" he asked.

Joey took another sip of beer and said, "I'll go with you wherever you want."

"What will we do after we see the gardens, Joey?"

"I say let's wait and see where fate takes us."

Albert stood up and smiled. "I hope it takes us over to the jukebox, because this music sucks."

Joey stood up and followed Albert to where the jukebox was planted up against a wood-paneled wall. "I've got some change," he offered, digging a hand into a pocket in his jeans.

Albert moved to the empty dance floor. He stood there for a moment, looking awkward and unsure of himself. He put his hands in his pockets and took them out again. He looked around the room. Something caught his attention. There was a full-length mirror bolted into the brick back wall. Albert glanced at his reflection in the streaked glass and moved closer to his image. "They got any Pat Benatar?" he called to Joey.

Joey shook his head. "No, I don't think so."

"That figures."

"Wait…I think you're in luck."

"What song is it?"

"'In the Heat of the Night,'" Joey answered. He slid some coins into the metal slot and waited for the first chords of the song to be heard. "I don't know this one," he said. The song had a sultry, seductive beat to it. The mood of the music was sensual. Joey swayed a little as he felt the song creep inside of him. He was still holding on to the glass curves of the jukebox. He tapped two fingers against the machine, welcoming the warm glow of the neon lights shining up into his face.

Joey turned to look for Albert. He felt his breath catch in his throat. Albert stood in the back of the bar, where the end of the dance floor met a brick wall. He was facing a mirror with both fists up and ready to fight. He moved a little to a rhythm that only existed in his world. The music was an afterthought. All that mattered was the battle. Albert began to shadowbox with his reflection. Right. Left. Left. Right. He pummeled the air with a fury and passion that caused Joey's heart to race.

Joey moved slowly across the cold concrete and went to Albert. He stood behind him and their eyes met briefly in the mirror. Joey reached around Albert's body and his fingers trembled as he unzipped the flannel jacket that Albert wore. He pulled back on the material and the jacket slid off of Albert's shoulders and down his arms. The coat landed between them on the ground. Albert stood in a white tank top that clung to his chest. Joey leaned forward and closed his eyes as his lips brushed over the words *Love is a Battlefield* tattooed across Albert's bare shoulder.

Joey took a few steps back. He bent down and scooped up Albert's discarded jacket.

Albert locked into the image before him and weaved right to left and back again on the balls of his feet. He punched an imaginary opponent with enough strength to bring the round to a quick end with a knockout. He knew Joey was watching him with sweet adoration in his eyes. It was the same look that drew Albert in just days ago when they met. It made Albert feel like he could do anything.

He turned away from the mirror and looked to where Joey stood in the middle of the dance floor. Albert's breath was quick and fierce. Sweat rolled from the sides of his face and down to his chest. His fists unclenched and he slowly raised his arm and stretched out a hand, offered it to Joey.

Joey stepped forward without taking his eyes off the boxer. He reached out and pressed his palm against Albert's and their hands met midair. Their fingers slid and meshed together into a single grasp. Joey felt the air shoot out of his lungs as Albert pulled him with such an intensity, their bodies collided.

There was a hunger in the way they pressed against each other. Albert's hands went to Joey's hips while Joey draped his long, thin arms around Albert's neck as if he were a life preserver. The men moved as one, grinding with a ravage-like mutual passion. They created a palpable energy that caused the lights in the bar to flicker and the record on the jukebox to snap and pop a few times as if the room wasn't strong enough to contain the power the two lovers ignited.

Albert's hands inched up to the waistband of Joey's sweatshirt. He lifted up and pulled the sweatshirt over Joey's head and off of his body. He tossed the sweatshirt across the dance floor, where it landed only inches away from Albert's jacket. Joey shivered in his thin T-shirt, so Albert pulled him closer to keep him warm.

Their mouths met and they kissed until they needed air. Albert's lips moved to Joey's neck. Joey's head tilted back and his eyes closed in ecstasy. He clung to Albert, clawing at his chest and his shirt. Albert lifted Joey up and sat him down on the edge of one of the pool tables. Joey wrapped his legs around Albert and pulled him close enough so that their cocks throbbed against each other through their jeans.

"I want you," Albert breathed and his words fell, setting Joey's skin on fire. "I don't give a fuck about anything but you."

"I love you, Albert," Joey said over the music.

"We can do anything we want," Albert said. "*Anything*. Just like you said…the world is ours."

They kissed again and their lips glowed with lust. Joey's fingers slid through Albert's hair. He grabbed a handful of it and pulled gently. Albert let out a soft moan and pressed his angry hips against Joey's.

The men at the bar looked up from their drinks and ashes and stared with eyes full of envy and awe. The love between Joey and Albert was raw and flooded the hearts of those who watched them with the hope that something similar existed somewhere in the world for them. The men shifted on their bar stools and craned their necks to watch the dance and the display of hot affection. Each of them ached for a hand to hold, skin to touch. Instead, they wrapped their hands around their bottles and squeezed the glass with a firmness they had not felt in ages, if ever.

The bartender finally looked away long to fix himself a drink.

With extra ice.

❖

Albert parked in a patch of darkness near a loading dock behind Navy Pier. He turned off the ignition and a sudden hush filled the van. Both men were certain the other could hear him breathing. In the near distance, Lake Michigan brushed across the shores of Chicago, and the lulling sound felt hypnotic.

Albert's deep voice cut through the mute barrier between them. "We still have some time before the fireworks start."

Joey flashed a nervous smile. He turned in the passenger seat and his eyes darted to the back of the van. "What do you want to do?"

Albert ran his palm over the top curve of the steering wheel. He stared straight ahead, through the windshield and toward the water. He tilted his head as if the water was speaking to him and he finally understood what it was saying. His gaze remained fixed when he said, "I want to touch you."

Joey's face reddened. He wasn't sure what to do with his hands. He looked at Albert, at his distinctive profile, and felt the overwhelming need to be as close to him as possible.

Outside, Joey could hear the strain of music flowing from the breathtaking Ferris wheel overshadowing the pier. Lights from the ride were splashed across the van, as if they had parked in the middle of their own private light show. The colors crept in to them through the steam-covered windows, creating a stunning sense of shadow and beauty. Joey turned to his window and smiled at the moving hues. It was like being inside of a metal snow globe and the glass case was blurred by the twirl of kaleidoscopic lights.

"I like being with you, Albert," he whispered. "It's better than anything."

Albert moved then. He unlatched his seat belt and then rolled away from the steering wheel. He landed on his hands and knees in the center of the blanket. A few petals lifted up in the air and then dropped back down like tears.

Joey heard the zipper of Albert's jacket and then a rustling sound. He waited until his curiosity was terminal before he turned and looked to the back of the van.

Albert was lying in the center of the blanket. He wore only a pair of blue and white striped boxers. Joey gulped as he felt the tip of his cock twitch with desire at his first sight of a half-naked Albert. His eyes drifted over Albert's Latin brown skin. The patches of dark hair that covered the boxer's chest and stomach. The sculpted flesh of his firm biceps offering protection and power. The thick thighs and lean calves. Those incredible lips frozen in a permanent pout pleading to be kissed away. Joey's eyes came to rest on the bulge straining against the thin cotton boxers. Albert was rock hard and he was waiting.

Albert's eyes were focused on the ceiling of the van. "I like being with you, too," he said in a soft voice Joey had not heard before.

Joey's hand trembled as he undid his seat belt. He took a breath and climbed to the back of the van. The wild mixture of the rose petals filled the air around them with a sweet smell that made Joey think of summertime. Joey lay down next to Albert, curling up beside him. He kissed Albert's cheek and placed a gentle hand in the middle of his stomach.

"Are you as scared as I am?" he asked.

Albert swallowed and a single tear slid from the corner of his eye, fell to the blanket beneath them. "I'm terrified," he said.

Albert rolled over on his side so they were face-to-face. They stared into each other's eyes, allowing the drift of the music from the Ferris wheel to calm their tender nerves. Finally, Albert leaned in toward Joey and their mouths met and they breathed hot air against each other's lips.

"Don't be scared," Albert offered, "and I won't be either."

Joey moved then. He sat up and moved his body over Albert's, forcing him onto his back. Joey straddled him and pressed his ass against Albert's rigid cock. He started to grind slowly, teasing Albert with the intense pleasure that was still to come. Albert's desire became almost animalistic. He bucked his hips quick and fierce against Joey, ramming his jeans with near violence. Soon, their bodies were thrashing together as their hard cocks slammed and rubbed against each other. Joey scooped up handfuls of flower petals and released them. They rained down on Albert's skin like soft drops of seduction.

Joey lifted his sweatshirt over his head. Before he could take his T-shirt off, Albert reached for the collar and ripped the material in two. The soft, worn shirt slid off of Joey's pale, smooth skin. Albert reached for Joey's nipples, which hardened from his touch. He pinched them until Joey moaned.

Joey's hands moved down to the button on his jeans. Albert pushed his hands away and yanked the jeans open with a single tug. He shoved a fast hand between Joey's skin and the waistband of his underwear. Joey's eyes closed and he moaned again as he felt Albert's hand wrap around the head of his cock.

Joey scrambled down to Albert's crotch. His tongue slipped through the open slit of Albert's boxers and he licked the shaft of Albert's cock. Albert grabbed a handful of Joey's hair. "Suck it."

Joey pulled Albert's boxers down to his knees. Albert reached for his own dick and pulled back the foreskin to reveal the shiny head that quickly disappeared inside of Joey's warm mouth. Joey looked up at Albert and his light eyes were filled with hot lust when he took Albert's cock as deep into his mouth and throat as he could. He moved down to Albert's balls and licked them with quick flicks of his wet tongue. "Fuck yeah."

Seconds later, Albert sat up and wrapped both arms around Joey's thin body. He turned the kid around and laid him down on the blanket. He hovered over Joey and looked deep into his eyes. Joey reached down and pushed his jeans and underwear toward his knees. He kicked them off with a few quick movements of his legs. Albert's hand landed on his cock and he started to stroke Joey. Joey's breath quickened, and his body shuddered with pleasure.

Albert lifted Joey's legs and placed them over his shoulders. Joey's socks brushed against Albert's earlobes as the boxer positioned himself close to Joey's ass. Albert brought his hand up to his mouth and spat into his palm. He reached down and spread the natural lube over the tip of his cock.

Joey raised his ass with eager anticipation and cautioned, "Go slow." His back arched slightly as he felt the head of Albert's dick pressing against his ass. He felt it slide inside of him and he exhaled as ecstasy throttled his soul until he teetered on the point of consciousness.

"God, I love you," Albert declared as drops of sweat fell from his Latin skin, burning the tips of Joey's reaching fingers. Albert began to move, and the sensation of his cock slowly diving in and out of Joey's ass almost made him come immediately.

Albert searched for Joey's eyes in the occasional flashes of red and white lights. The kid looked up at Albert and begged, "Fuck me."

Albert's body was seared with a hot intensity. He moved faster and started to thrust deeper. Soon, the pleasure became too much. Images flashed in his mind. Mickey in the laundry room. The feel of his dick brushing against Albert's young ass. The guys in the locker room at the gym with their oversized cocks and low-hanging balls. The cashier at the convenience store with his why-don't-you-fuck-me eyes. Then, there was Joey. The only person who loved him in the entire world. The person he was inside of and finally felt like he was one with. The person he knew he could trust no matter what. The man he wanted to spend the rest of his life with.

"I'm gonna come," he panted. He pulled out of Joey and pumped his dick a few times and shot hot splashes that landed in thick streams across Joey's soft skin. Joey's back arched as he jerked his own cock into a frenzied orgasm that caused him to pass out for a few seconds.

Albert collapsed on top of Joey. His breath was strained and sharp. Joey's hands shook as he reached up and wrapped his arms around Albert's neck.

"Don't ever leave me," Joey said into Albert's skin.

"Never," Albert exhaled.

They knew the moment was monumental. They had crossed a line that could never be retraced. The depth of what they felt for one another expanded to immeasurable limits within those seconds as they held on. They were now lovers. And they knew, now more than ever, loving someone else in this lifetime was impossible.

❖

It was Albert's idea to watch the fireworks show from the roof of the van. He climbed up first and then reached down for Joey's hand. He pulled and Joey was lifted into the air. They shifted to the center of the metal roof.

"I should have brought the blanket," Joey said. He had slipped on Albert's brown and blue flannel jacket and his jeans before climbing out of the van. Albert had put on a pair of black sweats and his white tank top. The temperature outside had dropped, and it felt cold enough for snow.

"That's what you got me for. To keep you warm," Albert said.

"Among other things," said Joey with a grin. "Aren't you freezing?"

"No, man, I'm Puerto Rican. We're warm-blooded."

"Seriously, it's cold up here."

"I need to cool off," Albert said with a wink.

They sat shoulder to shoulder and glanced up at the velvety October sky. The fireworks had just begun.

Albert watched Joey carefully. The way the kid got wide-eyed at each colorful splash exploding above them tugged at the center of Albert's heart. He knew he was making Joey happy. And that was all Albert needed.

"This is incredible," Joey said.

"Here. Lay with me," Albert suggested. Joey accepted the invitation and leaned back into Albert's arms. Their fingers found each other and locked.

"Have you ever seen something so beautiful?" Joey asked.

Albert caressed the side of Joey's face and said, "Yes."

With their eyes lifted up to the sky, they held each other while the world above them ignited and quaked. For a brief moment, they each felt as if their lives had somehow ended up exactly the way they'd imagined they would. That each step they'd taken up to this point had led them directly here. They could have called it destiny, if they could find a word to describe all that was running through their hearts. It wasn't specific details like the landscape or the smell of the lake that made them feel as if fate had hand-carried to them the roof of the van. It was a feeling of contentment that had somehow seeped into their bones since Wednesday. It was a rapture they did not question or fear. Instead, they silently said thanks to the stars above.

❖

After the fireworks show had ended, they crawled down off of the roof and back into the van. Albert turned the ignition and clicked on the heater. He rubbed his hands together and then cupped them and blew hot breath into the center of them.

Joey had just sat down in the passenger seat when he said, "I almost forgot."

Albert shot him a look. "Did you leave something on the roof?"

"Cotton candy," he said. "I want the blue kind."

"You want me to go get you some?" Albert asked.

"No." Joey zipped up Albert's coat he wore. He reached for a baseball cap on the floor of the van. He picked it up and looked at the front of it. The word on it read "Francine's" in the same flowery script on the side of the van. He put the cap on. "No, you stay here and warm up. I can go and get it. It'll just take a second."

Albert reached for his wallet on the dashboard. He opened it and took out a few bills and handed them to Joey. "Here," he said. "Get one for the road."

Joey took the money and then looked at Albert. "Are we leaving tonight?"

Albert nodded. "I figure we might as well. Get a head start, ya know."

"Good idea."

"The sooner we leave Chicago, the sooner we get to see the flower gardens."

"I can't wait to see the look on your face," Joey said. "I want to see you standing in those gardens with those flowers all around you."

"Yeah, it's gonna be fucking incredible." The expression on Albert's face changed. "You know, nobody woulda ever done something like this for me."

Joey's hand was on the door handle. "That's because they're scared of you."

"But you aren't."

"No." Joey opened the door and stepped out into the cold. He looked back into the van and said, "I love you."

Albert's smile glowed in the dark. "Every time you say that, it makes me feel good inside," he said. "I've never felt like that before, ya know."

Joey held Albert's stare. "Me either."

"Listen to me. I sound like an idiot. Go get your cotton candy. But hurry back. It's gonna be a long ride to Vancouver."

Joey was surprised when he felt tears rising up in his throat. "It's been a beautiful ride so far."

Albert nodded. "Yeah, it has." Joey moved as if he were going to close the passenger door. Albert's voice stopped him. "Hey."

Joey clutched the money in his hand. "What?" he asked.

Albert took a breath and his words warmed up the air between them. "I love you, too."

ALBERT

A lbert kept the engine running so the van would be warm when Joey returned from the pier. He sat in silence trying to decipher the bliss permeating his soul. Albert knew no words to describe his emotions. The gallon of hope pumping through his veins felt weightless as it floated around his heart. He glanced up and caught his own eyes staring back at him in the rearview mirror. *How'd an ugly fucker like me get so lucky?*

Albert reached behind his seat and his hand rested on an object. He pulled it up to the front of the van with him and sat it in his lap. The house Joey had built for him brought tears to his eyes. He ran his fingers over the roof, touched the soft flowers made of tissue. He lifted the house up and peered inside of it, through the front door, half expecting to find a miniature version of Joey waiting to greet him in the living room.

Maybe someday they'd live together in a house or an apartment. Maybe in Seattle or even California. Maybe they could settle down somewhere and Albert could train harder and book major fights. He could make them a lot of cash, so they'd never have to want for anything ever again. Joey could build houses along the coast for families like theirs to live in. He could make places for people to be happy in. Happy and in love.

That's exactly how you make me feel, Joey.

Albert turned toward the passenger door as it clicked and floated open, pulled with an angry hand from the outside. Cold air rushed into the van, breaking through the haven of heat. Albert clung to the house in his hands with a sudden intensity. He braced himself for what would come next. It was as if he knew.

The face flashed before him. The guy wore a black ski mask, so his features were hidden. But Albert could see his eyes. And he knew they belonged to someone who was young.

The figure didn't get into the van. He didn't reach for Albert's overstuffed wallet on the dashboard. He didn't make Albert get out so he could rummage through their belongings. He didn't say a word.

The gun was black and shiny. It caught glints of moonlight that bounced off the tip of it as if some mysterious force was trying to stop the moment from happening. The gun was raised and pointed at Albert, who only said one word when he realized: "Joey."

The gun was fired just once. At close range, there was no chance Albert would survive. The bullet entered his right temple, killing him instantly. Before his hands went limp, he managed to rip a few petals from the exterior walls of the house. The flowers drifted to the floor around his feet. He fell face forward and his forehead landed against the horn on the steering wheel, setting it off. The horn screeched, screaming as if it were in pain.

The figure disappeared into the shadows from which he had emerged.

JOEY

On the pier, the crowd fell silent for a moment, frozen and stunned by the gunshot. Then they heard the car horn and they knew something bad had happened. Pandemonium exploded across the pier as mothers and fathers rushed to gather their children, each other, their selves.

Joey stood in the center of the panic and flurry, paralyzed with fear. His fingers were wrapped around the white paper cone that served as a sticking stone for the baby blue cotton candy. He moved with resistance at first, as if his own body were begging him not to return to the van. But as he left the pier and cut through a dimly lit corridor that dumped him out in the area near the loading dock, terror ripped through him and he started to run. Strands of blue cotton were unleashed and floated like tiny clouds in the air behind him. He reached the van within seconds but his feet stopped him when he saw the passenger door open. Tears swelled up in his body and hovered behind his eyes. He moved closer.

He touched the cold metal door and the sensation stung his fingertips. He pulled the door open farther and peered inside the van.

The blood was everywhere. On the steering wheel. On the dashboard. On the windshield. On the seats. Albert sat with his eyes closed and the side of his face pressed up against the cold glass of the driver's seat. In his lap was the wooden house.

Joey didn't realize he was screaming. The sound rose up in his throat, tearing out of his mouth in angry, heaving sobs. He felt the urge to collapse. He felt darkness creep in, shrouding the edges of his vision.

The last few clumps of cotton candy pushed off of the white paper cone and drifted into the van. A few pieces clung to the sides of Albert's face and lips and absorbed his blood as if they were trying to heal him. As if they were magic.

Joey heard the sirens approaching. They jolted him, injecting a sense of reality into him and somehow subduing his hysteria. His instincts kicked into overdrive and his mind shouted at him: *go.* He climbed inside of the van and reached for Albert. He touched his skin. He kissed the side of his face and he tasted spun sugar and blood against his lips. He whispered Albert's name and told the beautiful boxer he loved him and that they would meet again.

Joey moved fast. He grabbed his green duffel bag from the back of the van and swiped Albert's wallet from the dashboard, pocketing it as he tore out of the van with a rage he didn't think he'd survive the wrath of.

Don't stop running.

Joey glanced back—just once—as he felt hope disintegrate somewhere deep inside of his soul. He could still see Albert from where he stood, his broken profile. His hands that would never touch Joey again. Or win the battle. His unruly dark hair that already Joey longed to feel against his fingers.

Keep moving.

Joey wiped his mouth with the back of his hand as he ran away from the van. He entered the same ghostly corridor that connected him back to the pier, to a place where the people were. A place where he could figure out what to do next, where to go. A place where he could fade back into the crowd and return to a life of being unnoticed.

As the police arrived on the scene and surrounded the van, Joey stood beneath the Ferris wheel. He glanced up at the lights and the massive structure of the metal beast. Tears streamed down his cold face and his teeth began to chatter as his adrenaline weakened. He knew without Albert by his side, he would never aspire to build something so grand. He also realized the place he needed to be was the train station.

Joey moved through the sea of strangers until he was off of the pier and hailing a cab. He would make the journey alone. But he was more determined than ever to reach his final destination.

As Joey slid into the backseat of the cab and pulled away from Navy Pier, the lights faded away in the distance.

Vancouver and the flower gardens awaited him. Joey hoped he might catch a glimpse of Albert there, dancing in a field of purple love grass.

Bonnie

He sent word to Bonnie the deed was done. He stopped by the coffee shop after he left Navy Pier. She was behind the counter, cleaning the pie case. He slipped her a piece of paper, shoving it against her palm. She watched him walk out the double glass doors and across the street to the "L" train stop. She wondered if he was in a hurry to meet a girl he was hot for.

Bonnie uncurled her fist and opened the edges of the folded piece of paper. In black ink the words "Knock Out" were written in block letters. For a moment, Bonnie felt an intense wave of nausea grab hold of her. She could feel it all the way down to her toes. But she took a few deep breaths and the sick feeling disappeared. She turned back to the pie case and continued to clean.

An hour later, she ended her double shift at the coffee shop and said good night to the cook and busboy. She counted out her tips and slipped them into a section of her tan purse. Instead of taking a cab—because the hour was so late and the night air was bone chilling—she zipped up her pink parka and slipped on her black mittens and decided to walk home. The seven blocks would give her a little bit of time to process what happened.

Bonnie had no fear of being alone. She relished it. She'd craved it for the last five years. Even the sound of his footsteps in the house had started to irritate her. She had prayed once or twice he'd have a heart attack or that cancer would take him away. No such luck. Instead, the bastard started to work out at the gym, and within a few months he was in the best shape he'd been in since they were married.

Being a widow was going to suit Bonnie just fine. She knew the ladies in her neighborhood would feel sorry for her, offer her comfort and plates of home-cooked meals. The men—even the husbands—would want to protect her, assure her they would take care of her. Money wouldn't be an issue since Albert had insisted he purchase a life insurance policy years ago. The house was already paid for, so Bonnie knew she would have enough cash to live on for years to come.

Bonnie would not leave her job, though. The diner had been good to her. It had given her a place to come to six days a week for the last twenty years. It had become a part of her life. The smell of the place had seeped into her pores and could never be washed away. Besides, if she quit, people like Francine and Shelley would be suspicious. Those goddamned good-for-nothing bitches were always in her business. They ratted her out to Albert about everything she did or said.

But not anymore. There was no one to tell.

Bonnie was now a single woman and she was determined to stay that way. If she needed a fix of male flesh every now and then, it wouldn't be hard to come by. Half of the lonely fuckers who came into the diner would kill for a piece of her, even with the weight she had gained.

As Bonnie slid the house key into the front door, she felt rather superior, even smug. It had been worth it. Every dime of the money she had saved. Bora Bora was still a possibility, but what a marvelous vacation it would be without that fucking orangutan bastard breathing down her neck about his boxing and her bad habits.

There was a new arrogance in the way Bonnie entered her home. It belonged to her now, only her. All of it. Never again would she be forced to share anything.

She reached for the remote control, buried under a pile of unopened bills on the coffee table. She pushed a button and the television clicked on. The eleven o'clock news had just started. *How boring.*

Bonnie went to the kitchen and reached inside of the refrigerator for a beer bottle in the back. She grabbed a bottle opener and flicked off the metal cap. It flew across the kitchen and landed on the grimy linoleum. She dug inside of her purse for her pack of cigarettes. She lit one, took a few drags, and flicked the ashes in the kitchen sink. Albert had always hated it when she did that.

She slid the cigarette between her cracked lips and made her way back to the living room. The black metal bird cage caught her attention for some reason. She moved closer to it and cursed herself for forgetting to feed her beloved mourning doves. The poor birds probably hated her.

"I always knew I'd be a rotten mother," she said to them. Albert had loathed the birds. Said they made the house smell like shit. Every once in a while, just to piss him off, she would leave the cage open and let them fly around the living room while he tried to nap on the sofa. He would cuss her out and threaten to get a cat. But the birds always went back to their cage. They were well behaved like that.

Bonnie reached for the handle of the cage and lifted up until the small door unlatched and swung open. The birds barely even moved. Were they dead? *Oh shit. Maybe I killed 'em.* Bonnie rattled the cage and their eyes blinked open as they were jolted out of a deep sleep.

"Let me change my clothes and then I'll feed you fuckers," she told them.

Bonnie pried the cigarette from between her lips and stubbed it out in the overcrowded orange class ashtray on the coffee table. She left the front of the house and walked into her bedroom. She stood in the doorway and stared down at the mess on the floor Albert had left behind. For a second, Bonnie was angry he was dead because now she wouldn't get the chance to yell at him for leaving these pictures and stupid wedding favors all over the floor.

Bonnie kneeled down to the gouged hardwood and picked up a photograph. It was one of her and Albert, taken at a barbecue one of their neighbors invited them to years ago. They were cheek to cheek and had fake smiles plastered across their faces. She wondered if he had been cheating on her then. She ached to know who his mistress was. Did she know that Albert was dead? Bonnie assumed her identity would be revealed in the weeks to come. Of course, Bonnie would use Albert's infidelity to her benefit, to reap more pity from the neighborhood.

She scooped up a handful of the party favors. Some of the bird seed seeped through the satin openings of the palm-sized pouches and sprinkled all over the floor. Bonnie stood up to search for a broom. Maybe she would clean the entire house. She could stay up all night and scrub until the fucking thing sparkled. Just to spite him.

Bonnie stepped into the living room. Immediately, her eyes went to the television screen. A blond reporter with really white teeth was at Navy Pier at the scene of the crime. Into the microphone she held in her hand, she said words like "shocked," "tragedy," and "brutal."

Bonnie grinned. *They think it was a robbery. A fucking carjacking gone wrong. Beautiful.*

Bonnie's eyes moved to the empty bird cage in the corner. A tiny trickle of fear pinched the back of her neck. *Where did those fuckers fly off to?* She heard them then, the whistling that their wings made when they were in flight. She looked up and saw they were circling above her. Their heads and beaks and wings were just inches below the white ceiling. But then they changed direction. In unison, the birds dove down toward Bonnie. They ripped some of the pouches from her hands. Within seconds, a shower of bird seed rained over Bonnie as the doves shredded the bags apart with their angry beaks. They circled above her again and let out a shrill warning.

Bonnie turned to move, not sure if she should go back to the bedroom or to the kitchen or even outside. Something was seriously wrong with those birds.

They attacked her from behind. They swooped down and landed on her head. They sank their beaks into her scalp and ripped patches of her hair out with ferocity. Then they flew around to her face and aimed for her eyes. Bonnie raised her hands up to try to shield them off, to protect herself from the assault. The birds lunged toward her and tore at her skin.

Within seconds, Bonnie tasted the hot iron burn of blood as it poured down her face and into her mouth, down her throat. She began to cough and choke and she found it was getting harder and harder to breathe. She stumbled around, disoriented and only able to see out of one eye. She collided with the coffee table and it overturned. The ashtray flipped over and hit the carpet. The smoldering cigarette butt— scarred on the end by Bonnie's vibrant shade of lipstick—torched the worn fabric. The fire spread fast, and within seconds, the entire room was engulfed in flames.

Later, the local news stations would re-edit their original story about the amateur boxer whose life was taken too soon by a single gunshot. They would add new footage from the site of the house fire, of the gutted bungalow as tendrils of smoke lifted up from the black ash and debris and circled up to the starlit sky.

Most viewers would agree how sad it was Bonnie was unable to live without her Albert. And some would even consider her suicide to be romantic.

LILY

Lily felt harassed. "Buddy, why do you have to be such a jerk?" she asked. "I need to see my brother."

The round-faced resident advisor pushed his black-framed glasses up to the bridge of his nose with his middle finger and said, "Rules are rules."

There was a chest-high maple counter separating them. Lily stood close to the double doors leading in and out of the lobby of the dormitory. Every time the door opened and a student came in to the building, she'd hold her dress down to keep it from blowing up in the quick blasts of cold air. Buddy was standing in front of a wall of glass squares. They were frosted so whatever was on the other side of them appeared only as big shapes and shadows. Lily thought they were creepy.

"My parents just *died*. This is a family emergency," she said.

"I'm sorry for your loss. Really I am. But I can't let you go up there unattended."

"Then why can't you just take me up there yourself?"

"And leave the counter? I could get fired," said Buddy.

"That's exactly what somebody should do to you."

"There's no reason for bad manners," he said.

"Do you even have a girlfriend?" Lily asked. "I mean, seriously, Buddy. Have you ever had sex? Is that what I'm dealing with here?"

Buddy shook his head. He was only an inch or two taller than Lily. He had a helmet of bushy brown hair, a white man's afro. His eyes were murky blue and his skin looked unhealthy and gray. The tip of his nose was playing host to a huge pimple. "Insulting me is not going to get you upstairs," he said.

"My God, you must be gay," Lily said and rolled her eyes. "Are you messing around with my brother, by any chance?"

Buddy fought hard not to laugh. "Joseph's personal life is none of my business."

"Can you call him again?"

He nodded. "That I can do."

Lily turned as another shot of cold air exploded against the back of her legs. She smiled at the guy who walked in, secretly admiring his skater-boy style. "Do you know my brother? He's gay. His name is Joey."

"Yeah, I know him. We're roommates."

Lily's cheeks fused with a hot fever. Her eyes lit up and her smile widened. "I've heard a lot about you."

"I hope it was good."

Lily moved closer and dropped her voice to a soft whisper. "Listen," she said, "this fucking Neanderthal won't let me upstairs to see my brother. My friend and me have driven all night and our car got stolen so we had to hitchhike with this crazy bitch named Roberta just to get here. Can you help a girl out?"

He leaned in and she thought he might kiss her. Instead, he said, "Say no more." He moved past her and went to the counter. He picked up a pen chained to the wood and signed his name on a line in the guest log. He turned to her. "Your name's Lily, right?"

"Like the flower," she said. She smiled at her hero until he turned back to the counter. She then shot a death stare at Buddy.

"Looks like you got lucky this time," he said to her with a scowl.

Lily tossed Buddy another evil expression as she followed Joey's roommate toward a bank of elevators. "It's a shame I can't say the same for you, Buddy."

The double doors whipped open then and Molly stood in the entrance of the dormitory. Her hair was wind-blown and her face looked frozen and pale. "Lily, where are you going?" she demanded. "I've been waiting out here for fifteen minutes."

From his position of power, Buddy looked up and gazed over Molly with lust. "Hello," he offered with a grin that revealed a slight overbite.

"I'm going upstairs," Lily explained.

Molly's mouth dropped open. "With who?" she asked.

Lily gestured to Joey's roommate. "With him."

"That's not Joey."

"No," the stranger said. "I'm Jeremy."

The elevator doors slid open. Lily and Jeremy stepped inside.

"Wait," Molly said. "Can I go with you?"

Buddy put up an arm as if he could stop her from behind the counter. "Sorry," he said. "The rule is only one guest per room."

Molly looked at Lily and pleaded with her silently. "What am I supposed to do?"

Lily grinned and shrugged. "Buddy will keep you company."

Molly turned and looked at the resident advisor and smiled at him politely. "Do you like backgammon?" he asked with an eager movement that looked like a lame attempt at a hop.

Lily followed Jeremy inside the dorm room. She stood close to the door. She glanced across to the stripped mattress surrounded by a dozen little wooden houses. "Where's my brother?" she asked.

Jeremy shrugged. "I have no clue. I've been gone all day."

"Well, did he leave?"

"It looks like it. Most of his shit's gone."

"That makes no sense. Where in the fuck would he go?"

"Maybe he went home."

Lily shook her head. "No. He wouldn't do that." She leaned in closer to Jeremy and allowed her breasts to brush against his chest. "Our parents died."

"Yeah. He said something about a funeral."

"They had it today. I didn't go. None of us did."

"Wow. You missed your parents' funeral? That's crazy."

"I could tell you shit that would make your head spin," Lily said. She reached up and touched his chin. "Nice scar. What happened?"

Jeremy pushed her hand away. "Skateboarding accident," he said. "Happened when I was twelve."

Lily giggled. "Well, I hope you skate better now." She fell forward and placed both hands on his ass.

He looked down at her and didn't smile. "What are you doing?"

Lily's fingers met up with a soft fabric, some sort of knit. She pulled it out of his back pocket and moved her hand. The ski mask entered the space between them. Lily looked at it in her hand and then up at Jeremy. Her eyes darted over to his nightstand where he'd put his keys on top of a white envelope. A few hundred dollar bills stuck out of the unsealed envelope like a warning. "What'd you do, rob a store?" she asked.

Jeremy snatched the mask from her and shoved it back into his pocket. "Yeah, something like that." There was a layer of ice in his voice and it sent chills down Lily's spine. She backed away, glancing curiously at the posters and calendar on his wall.

"Sorry," she said, trying not to sound nervous. "I shouldn't be here. Maybe I should go. My friend…I should check on her. I can wait downstairs."

"Suit yourself. I'm taking off in a few."

"Oh yeah? Got somewhere to go?"

Jeremy nodded. "It's the weekend. I think I might head home for a day or two. Take care of some stuff."

"Where you from?" she asked.

"Portland," he said.

Lily felt the color drain from her cheeks. A cold sweat broke out on her skin, just below her shoulder blades. "Maine?" she said.

He shook his head. "Oregon."

Lily breathed again and moved toward the bare mattress in the opposite corner of the room. She sat down on the edge of the bed carefully, as if she were scared it might bite her. She watched Jeremy with cautious eyes.

He peeled off the black sweatshirt he was wearing and reached for a green hoodie. He pulled it down over his head and then grabbed his keys and the envelope from the nightstand. Both items disappeared into his front pocket. He ran his hands through his wild hair a few times and offered Lily a salute.

"See ya," he said. He moved toward the door of the room.

"Let me ask you something before you go," she said. He looked at her and it was evident the limits of his patience and kindness were being tested. "Did you have any intentions of sleeping with me when you brought me up here?"

He shook his head. "No," he said. "You're not my type."

Lily leaned back and crossed her legs. "Oh really?" she said. "What exactly is your type?"

Jeremy pointed to the Pamela Anderson calendar on the wall. "She is," he said and opened the door. He entered the corridor outside of the room.

"Well, good luck with that," Lily said loudly as he left. The door clicked shut behind him. "Fucker."

Lily didn't move from the bed. She sat there, allowing the silence to untie the tangles of nerves gnawing at her from the inside out. Her eyes moved to the wooden houses. It was a hobby of Joey's she never understood. Maybe it was his silent cry for a doll house. She leaned forward and reached for the house nearest to her. It was on the window sill. It looked like a log cabin. She touched the wood with her fingertips and then wrapped half of her hand around the chimney. The thing broke off in her hand. "Oops," she said. She tossed the chimney on the floor and lay down on the bed.

Lily blinked a few times, staring up at the ceiling. She wondered if anyone had bothered to show up for the funeral. It wouldn't surprise her if no one came to pay Miranda their last respects. After the whole Bible study group fiasco, the church practically threw her out the door. None of those Bible-thumpers would speak to her because she had a gay son.

As Lily closed her eyes, she thought of Cooper, as she often did. She knew she would always be in love with him. She knew in the morning she'd make her way back to Portland. She would find him at the auto garage and casually suggest they start seeing each other again. She was almost certain he was still in love with her. And God knows, she loved him. Even after the incident with Joey, she could never blame him for that. He was high, drunk. And Joey was a cold-blooded killer.

Or was he?

Lily doubted her brother had the balls to pull it off. He simply wasn't tough enough to do it. He wasn't heartless. Sure, he hid it well: all the torture Miranda put him through. He put on a good front, but Lily knew better. She suspected Cooper had something to do with it. Hell, maybe he was the one who cut the brakes. If it was true, Lily knew this would only make her love him more. If that were possible.

Lily rolled over on to her side and looked at the posters of skinny skateboarders that stared back at her. And then there was Pamela. Every man's fantasy.

Lily tried to imagine what thoughts ran through Joey's mind when he was about to fall asleep in the bed she was in. Did he think about men? Cooper? His hot roommate who had no taste in women? Or did he strategize how he was going to kill their mother? Did he plot and plan while slipping off to dreamland? Did he watch the city skyline light up each night from this window? And most importantly, did he ever think of his sister?

Lily surrendered to sleep as she allowed her body to relax for the first time in years. Her eyes closed and images danced across the movie screen in her mind. The police at her front door with their shiny badges and gun holsters and the way they wouldn't look her in the eyes when they told her that her parents were dead. The faces of the boys who had surrounded her naked body while she was on that hockey table in Cooper's basement. The mean eyes of her mother and the ridiculously tight ponytail she wore every fucking day of her miserable life. Her brother, around eleven or twelve, sitting in the grass in their backyard eating a blue raspberry Popsicle. Lily made a goofy face at him. And he laughed. It filled Lily with a heavy nostalgic sadness as she realized she hadn't heard him laugh since.

The darkness flooding Lily's brain slowly lifted as she slept and dreamt of summer.

MOLLY

After enduring three rounds of backgammon with Buddy—which she allowed herself to lose gracefully—Molly was ready to go. She didn't notice Jeremy come downstairs and walk out the door and into the night. From where she sat on the plaid sofa in the overheated game room, the front door was out of her view. How could she have known that while she was fighting off Buddy's blatant sexual advances, Lily was sound asleep upstairs, cradled by the warmth of the crackling radiator?

"Just one kiss," Buddy begged over the low roar of the television on the opposite wall. "C'mon." He came at her with that ginormous zit on his nose, and it made Molly think of Rudolph the Red-Nosed Reindeer. Then she thought of Christmas and how the one coming up would be her first in Chicago, on her own.

She longed to tell Joey of her plans. She hoped he would be happy she'd decided to stay. But then she remembered about his confession. She glanced at her purse and thought about the letter inside of it. The one in Joey's messy handwriting in which he claimed to have had something to do with killing his mother and father. A phrase he had written came back to her then: *What you don't know is that I played a part in it—or at least I was supposed to.*

Molly smiled then. *He didn't do it. He couldn't have. He chickened out.*

"Are you even listening to me?" Buddy asked. "You're just playing hard to get, aren't you?"

"Yes," Molly said. "That's it."

"You want to play another round?"

"No," Molly answered fast. "I'm tired. What time is it?"

Buddy checked his Scooby-Doo watch. "It's after midnight."

Molly raised an eyebrow. "Isn't your shift over soon?"

Buddy grinned and his teeth looked too large for his mouth. "I was off the clock at eleven."

Molly patted his knee and said, "Don't let me keep you."

He moved closer to her and she blinked because her eyes burned from the layer of garlic on his breath. "I figured maybe we could play another game." He winked at her and it seemed like a nervous twitch. "Up in my room."

Molly leaned back against the sofa. "I'm afraid to ask, but what did you have in mind?"

He tickled her ribs and said, "Strip poker?"

Molly shoved his hands away from her body. "I'm no good at cards."

He smiled again and Molly felt the temptation to punch him in the mouth. "Excellent."

She shook her head and wrapped her arms around her body, partly out of disgust but also because she felt the need to protect herself from being violated by the Zit Creature. "I can't do this, Buddy."

He whispered in her ear. "But I'm a man. You're a woman. We both have needs."

She leaned away from him. Her body was sideways like she was stuck on the steep turn of a roller coaster. "And I need you to stop breathing on me. Really. I've heard that Chicago pizza is the best in the world, and it's apparent you had some of it for dinner."

Buddy looked wounded. "You want me to stop breathing?"

"You know what I mean."

"That's not very nice, Molly."

She sighed, put her purse in her lap. "I'm not a very nice person."

Buddy nodded. "Yeah. I can see that."

"In fact," she said as a last resort, "I have chlamydia."

Buddy's eyes nearly popped out of his skull. "What?"

"I inherited it from my mother."

He gave her a look. "Is that possible?"

"It was a gene mutation thing. It's not pretty."

"You're sick?"

"Is that a question or an opinion?"

Buddy stood up and was extra careful not touch Molly. "I think I need to go now," he said.

She offered him a quick wave good-bye. "You do that, Buddy."

"It was...nice to meet you."

"Likewise." She offered him her hand to shake but he ignored the gesture and walked away.

Molly waited until Buddy was on his way up to his room in the elevator before she let out a huge sigh of relief. She kicked off her shoes and lay down on the sofa in the game room. She looked up at the small television screen that was mounted into the brick wall with a black brace and bolts. An old episode of *Roseanne* was on. She tried to focus on the screen, on the words the actors were saying, but she kept thinking about the letter in her purse.

If it was true and Joey really did know something about who murdered Miranda and Nate, shouldn't she do something about it? Wasn't her responsibility to tell someone what she knew? Someone like the police?

❖

Molly sat up on the sofa, half-asleep and dazed. There were a dozen college students standing around her and staring as if she were a science project. She grabbed her purse and held it in front of her, shielding herself from their eyes. "Can I help you?" she asked.

"Who are you?" an Asian girl wanted to know.

"I'm just visiting."

"Are you Buddy's new girlfriend?" another voice pressed.

Molly stood up and tried to smooth out the wrinkles in her shirt and pants. "I'd rather die," she answered. "Now, if you'll excuse me...I could really use some coffee."

"There's a machine around the corner," someone in the game room said.

"No...I think I need some air." Molly moved toward the entrance of the room. She turned back to the curious faces. "If my friend Lily is looking for me, tell her I'll be back for her in a while."

The Asian girl stepped forward. "I'm glad you're not with Buddy."

Molly managed a smile. "That makes two of us."

"You're way too hot for him."

"Thank you," Molly said. She made her way through the lobby of the dormitory and walked outside through the double doors. The temperature had warmed up and Molly welcomed the blast of sunshine on her skin. She slipped on a pair of sunglasses and tried to get the tangles out of her hair with her fingers.

She had no idea what direction to move in, so she chose by instinct and headed toward the lake. The city immediately made her feel alive. Although it was Sunday, the streets still vibrated with the electric hum of activity. She smiled at the strangers passing by with their baby strollers, shopping bags, and high-fashion jogging suits.

This is where I belong.

Molly opened her purse and reached inside of it for the letter she had swiped from the table in Lily's kitchen. She wasn't watching where she was walking and neither was he. It was a ring of shiny keys he had dropped on the sidewalk. He had bent down to pick them up when they collided.

Molly nearly stumbled over him and he reached for her with both hands, breaking her fall.

"I am so sorry," she said looking up into his warm brown eyes. "I wasn't looking where I was…"

"Hey," he said and his voice was like velvet. "It was my fault."

Molly covered her mouth with her hand. "I feel so bad. Are you hurt?"

He flipped up the collar of his polo and said with playful exaggeration, "A tough guy like me? No, I can take it."

He was taller than her and had thick dimples carved into his cocoa brown cheeks. His eyes went to her mouth and then up to her eyes.

"You look tough," she said, "but I bet you're really a nice guy."

He grinned and she felt the urge to kiss him. "This must be my lucky day, then."

"Why's that?" she asked.

"I just bought a bakery this morning."

Molly's smile lit up the space between them. "A bakery? That's adorable."

He returned her smile and said, "When it opens, you should come by."

She nodded and lifted her glasses up and placed them on top of her head. "I'd like that."

"Me, too."

"But wait…how will I know where it is?"

He shrugged and tucked his hands into the pockets of his jeans. "I could show you," he offered.

On impulse, she slid her arm through his and said, "What the hell."

"Only on one condition, though. You have to let me buy you a cup of coffee."

"After the night I've had, that would be divine," she said.

They reached a corner and crossed the street. "Do you live around here?" he asked.

"No…I mean…I just moved here."

"Oh really? For work?"

"No," Molly said. "I think I'll be going to college."

"I can tell you're a smart girl."

"Yeah, I actually am."

"What's your favorite subject?"

"I'm really good at math," she said.

"Well, I could really use a new accountant."

Molly let out a small laugh. "And I could really use a job."

They stopped outside of the coffee shop. "Sounds like it's a lucky day for both of us."

"Yeah," Molly said and then blurted out, "You're beautiful."

He grinned and blushed a little. "Thanks."

"No…I meant…oh my God…I'm *so* embarrassed."

He touched her arm and his fingers were warm. "Don't be," he told her.

"Okay."

He lowered his voice a little and the words crawled inside of her heart. "I was thinking the same thing about you."

She nodded, giddy. "Okay."

He opened the door for her, but she remained on the sidewalk. She kept looking at the letter in her hand. "By the way, what's your name?" he asked.

"Molly," she said without looking up.

"I like that name."

Molly turned away for a moment and faced the street. She ripped the letter into tiny shreds and let them fall like a paper cascade into the gutter. Joey's words floated away and disappeared down a storm drain.

Molly took a deep breath and told herself she'd done the right thing. If Joey had killed his parents, there had to be a reason for it. Some sort of justification. But in her heart, Molly knew he wasn't capable of such a crime. The only thing he seemed to be able to do was to love.

Molly turned back to the beautiful man who held the door open for her and asked, "What's *your* name?"

He reached for her and placed his hand on the small of her back as she walked inside. "Call me Jackson."

SHELLEY

Shelley was not surprised when Francine walked into the bookstore that morning. In a strange way, Shelley was expecting her. In fact, she'd brewed a fresh pot of oolong tea. She poured them each a cup when Francine approached the counter.

"Shelley?" she said. It was apparent Francine had not slept in a while. It was difficult for her to speak without crying.

"I already know, Francine," she said. She reached for the flower pinned to her dress and adjusted it.

Francine wiped her eyes. "Everything? You know *everything*?"

"He's gone," Shelley said and handed Francine a cup.

Francine took the cup and saucer and they rattled in her weak grasp. "But do you know what he did?"

The cup froze just inches from Shelley's mouth. "Tell me," she said, bracing herself inside for another storm.

Francine took a breath before she spoke. "I was at my lawyer's this morning."

Shelley reached for her pipe and bag of tobacco. "Not the best way to start off a Sunday, in my opinion."

"I had papers to sign."

"You really sold the place?"

Francine's mood brightened a little. "I did," she said. "It's a done deal."

Shelley gave her a thumbs up. "Good for you."

Francine glanced around at the shelves of books. "I'm thinking about moving to Madison."

"A change of scenery might do you some good, Francine."

She leaned against the counter then. "When I was in my lawyer's office, I got a phone call."

"From Joey?"

"Who's Joey?"

Shelley waved the subject away with her hand. "No one. Never mind."

Francine took a few sips of her tea before she spoke again. "Did you know that Albert had a life insurance policy?"

Shelley shook her head. "No. We never talked about that sort of thing."

"Well, he did," Francine said. She started to weep again. "Shelley… he left us everything. Me and you."

Shelley's hand went to the flower on her dress again. Her fingertips pressed down on the soft petals. "He did what?"

"Fifty-fifty."

Tears warmed the corners of Shelley's eyes. "That son of a bitch is still looking out for us…even when he's gone."

Francine nodded and then asked. "What are you going to do now?"

Shelley struck a match, lit her pipe, and blew out the flame. She looked at Francine and said, "I'm going to have another cup of tea."

JOEY

Joey had no idea where he was or what time it was when he woke. But he knew he was crying. The sobs were almost violent and they yanked him out of a sad dream. He sat up on the row of seats he'd slept on and glanced out the train window to a sea of darkness and stars.

I'm on the train. I'm going to Vancouver. Albert is dead.

"Albert?" Joey said aloud. The shadows from the window were playing tricks on his mind again. It looked like a figure was standing in the doorway to the compartment he was in. A person. A man. With a hand reaching out toward him. But Joey knew better. It couldn't be Albert. It would never be Albert.

The train entered a tunnel and the shadow disappeared.

Joey didn't know how long he'd slept or even how far away he was from Vancouver. He didn't care. Instead, he concentrated on the memories flickering in his mind. He played and replayed every conversation, every moment he'd shared with Albert. And as the boxer's beautiful face flashed behind Joey's closed eyes, his tears continued to spill.

Joey could think of nothing else but Albert and getting to Vancouver. He could almost smell the flowers.

❖

Joey stood in the center of beauty. In every direction he turned, he was surrounded by the most exquisite splendor he'd ever encountered.

The vibrant colors of the flowers made him dizzy, and the smell of them massaged the center of his lungs.

Except for a few tourists, he was alone in the garden. The sleek skyline of Vancouver stood behind him, offering a sense of comfort Joey had needed since leaving Chicago on a midnight train almost three days ago.

Joey hadn't showered or eaten. He could still smell Albert on his sweatshirt. He brought the edges of the sleeves up to his nose and inhaled. Tears sprang to his eyes and he struggled to maintain his composure.

For a moment, he saw Albert there. It was only his imagination allowing him the vision, but he needed it. He was thankful for it.

Albert was in his jeans and white tank top. His eyes danced with a light that was pure. He smiled at Joey and the kid couldn't help but smile back. He reached for Joey with an extended hand and pulled him toward him. Their bodies touched and their mouths trembled with love.

They were reunited beneath a cherry tree. Pink and white blossoms floated down from heavy branches, brushing against them before tumbling to the soft grass. Joey folded into Albert's arms and welcomed the strength of them wrapped around his body.

The two men began to sway. As the sun dipped down into the ocean, and day became night, they danced together to the rhythm of a bittersweet song.

It was sung just for them.

About the Author

David-Matthew Barnes is the author of the young adult novels *Mesmerized* and the forthcoming *Swimming to Chicago*, and the literary suspense novel *Accidents Never Happen*, all published by Bold Strokes Books. He wrote and directed the coming-of-age film *Frozen Stars*, which received worldwide distribution. He is the author of over forty stage plays that have been performed in three languages in eight countries. His literary work has appeared in over one hundred publications including *The Best Stage Scenes*, *The Best Men's Stage Monologues*, *The Best Women's Stage Monologues*, *The Comstock Review*, *Review Americana*, and *The Southeast Review*. David-Matthew is the national recipient of the 2011 Hart Crane Memorial Poetry Award. In addition, he's received the Carrie McCray Literary Award and the Slam Boston Award for Best Play, and has earned double awards for poetry and playwriting in the World AIDS Day Writing Contest. David-Matthew earned a Master of Fine Arts in creative writing at Queens University of Charlotte in North Carolina. He is a faculty member at Southern Crescent Technical College in Griffin, Georgia, where he teaches courses in English, humanities, and speech.

Books Available From Bold Strokes Books

Firestorm by Radclyffe. Firefighter paramedic Mallory "Ice" James isn't happy when the undisciplined Jac Russo joins her command, but lust isn't something either can control—and they soon discover ice burns as fiercely as flame. (978-1-60282-232-0)

The Best Defense by Carsen Taite. When socialite Aimee Howard hires former homicide detective Skye Keaton to find her missing niece, she vows not to mix business with pleasure, but she soon finds Skye hard to resist. (978-1-60282-233-7)

After the Fall by Robin Summers. When the plague destroys most of humanity, Taylor Stone thinks there's nothing left to live for, until she meets Kate, a woman who makes her realize love is still alive and makes her dream of a future she thought was no longer possible. (978-1-60282-234-4)

Accidents Never Happen by David-Matthew Barnes. From the moment Albert and Joey meet by chance beneath a train track on a street in Chicago, a domino effect is triggered, setting off a chain reaction of murder and tragedy. (978-1-60282-235-1)

In Plain View by Shane Allison. Best-selling gay erotica authors create the stories of sex and desire modern readers crave. (978-1-60282-236-8)

Wild by Meghan O'Brien. Shapeshifter Selene Rhodes dreads the full moon and the loss of control it brings, but when she rescues forensic pathologist Eve Thomas from a vicious attack by a masked man, she discovers she isn't the scariest monster in San Francisco. (978-1-60282-227-6)

Reluctant Hope by Erin Dutton. Cancer survivor Addison Hunt knows she can't offer any guarantees, in love or in life, and after experiencing a loss of her own, Brooke Donahue isn't willing to risk her heart. (978-1-60282-228-3)

Conquest by Ronica Black. When Mary Brunelle stumbles into the arms of Jude Jaeger, a gorgeous dominatrix at a private nightclub, she is smitten, but she soon finds out Jude is her professor, and Professor Jaeger doesn't date her students…or her conquests. (978-1-60282-229-0)

The Affair of the Porcelain Dog by Jess Faraday. What darkness stalks the London streets at night? Ira Adler, present plaything of crime lord Cain Goddard, will soon find out. (978-1-60282-230-6)

365 Days by K.E. Payne. Life sucks when you're seventeen years old and confused about your sexuality, and the girl of your dreams doesn't even know you exist. Then in walks sexy new emo girl, Hannah Harrison. Clemmie Atkins has exactly 365 days to discover herself, and she's going to have a blast doing it! (978-1-60282-540-6)

Darkness Embraced by Winter Pennington. Surrounded by harsh vampire politics and secret ambitions, Epiphany learns that an old enemy is plotting treason against the woman she once loved, and to save all she holds dear, she must embrace and form an alliance with the dark. (978-1-60282-221-4)

78 Keys by Kristin Marra. When the cosmic powers choose Devorah Rosten to be their next gladiator, she must use her unique skills to try to save her lover, herself, and even humankind. (978-1-60282-222-1)

Playing Passion's Game by Lesley Davis. Trent Williams's only passion in life is gaming—until Juliet Sullivan makes her realize that love can be a whole different game to play. (978-1-60282-223-8)

Retirement Plan by Martha Miller. A modern morality tale of justice, retribution, and women who refuse to be politely invisible. (978-1-60282-224-5)

Who Dat Whodunnit by Greg Herren. Popular New Orleans detective Scotty Bradley investigates the murder of a dethroned beauty queen to clear the name of his pro football–playing cousin. (978-1-60282-225-2)

The Company He Keeps by Dale Chase. A riotously erotic collection of stories set in the sexually repressed and therefore sexually rampant Victorian era. (978-1-60282-226-9)

Cursebusters! by Julie Smith. Budding-psychic Reeno is the most accomplished teenage burglar in California, but one tiny screw-up and poof!—she's sentenced to Bad Girl School. And that isn't even her worst problem. Her sister Haley's dying of an illness no one can diagnose, and now she can't even help. (978-1-60282-559-8)

True Confessions by PJ Trebelhorn. Lynn Patrick finally has a chance with the only woman she's ever loved, her lifelong friend Jessica Greenfield, but Jessie is still tormented by an abusive past. (978-1-60282-216-0)

Ghosts of Winter by Rebecca S. Buck. Can Ros Wynne, who has lost everything she thought defined her, find her true life—and her true love—surrounded by the lingering history of the once-grand Winter Manor? (978-1-60282-219-1)

Blood Hunt by L.L. Raand. In the second Midnight Hunters Novel, Detective Jody Gates, heir to a powerful Vampire clan, forges an uneasy alliance with Sylvan, the Wolf Were Alpha, to battle a shadow army of humans and rogue Weres, while fighting her growing hunger for human reporter Becca Land. (978-1-60282-209-2)

http://www.boldstrokesbooks.com
Bold Strokes
BOOKS
victory
EDITIONS
Drama
LIBERTY
EDITION
AEROS
BOOKS
e-Books
Mystery
CRIME
Sci-fi
SPEC FIC
HE
erotica
Erotica
BSB
SOLILOQUY
Young
Adult
MATINEE BOOKS
Romance
BOLD
STROKES
BOOKS
WEBSTORE
PRINT AND EBOOKS